The Story of Zahra
Women of Sand and Myrrh
Beirut Blues
I Sweep the Sun Off Rooftops
Only in London
The Locust and the Bird

One Thousand and One Nights

One Thousand and One Nights

A Retelling by

Hanan al-Shaykh

FOREWORD BY MARY GAITSKILL

PANTHEON BOOKS, NEW YORK

Copyright © 2011 by Hanan al-Shaykh
Illustrations copyright © 2011 by Holly Macdonald
Introduction copyright © 2013 by Mary Gaitskill

All rights reserved. Published in the United States by Pantheon Books,
a division of Random House, Inc., New York, and in Canada by
Random House of Canada Limited, Toronto. Originally published,
in slightly different form, in the United Kingdom by
Bloomsbury Publishing, London, in 2011.

Pantheon Books and colophon are registered trademarks of
Random House, Inc.

Library of Congress Cataloging-in-Publication Data
Shaykh, Hanan.
One thousand and one nights : a sparkling retelling of the beloved classic /
Hanan al-Shaykh ; with an introduction by Mary Gaitskill.
    pages cm
ISBN 978-0-307-95886-0
I. Arabian nights. II. Title.
PR6119.H398O54 2013   823'.92—dc23   2012039272

www.pantheon+books.com

Jacket design by Gray318

Printed in the United States of America
First American Edition

2 4 6 8 9 7 5 3 1

For Shahrazad and her daughters

Contents

Foreword

BY MARY GAITSKILL

One Thousand and One Nights is about worlds underground, where jewels are embedded in darkness and a beautiful woman may love a devil; it's about powerful slaves and foolish demons, secret spirits hidden in jars; it's about truth living in the treacherous heart like an abiding and holy law waiting to be revealed in the words of a story told by a porter, a tailor, a concubine or lady— all through the lips of the lady Shahrazad to an enraged, cuckolded king on a revenge mission against woman-kind. If she stops telling stories, he will kill her like every other woman he sleeps with.

Shahrazad isn't a character in the usual sense, as her voice disappears in the stories that seem to exist without a narrator; she appears only at the very beginning and very end of *One Thousand and One Nights*. Yet she is an icon of feminine force, both submissive and powerful, invisible and generative. Traditionally *One Thousand and One Nights* ends when Shahrazad presents the king with three children and, because she has proven herself, he decides to marry her rather than kill her. Perhaps the most refreshing thing about Hanan al-Shaykh's delightful retelling is that it does not end with Shahrazad's transformation from storyteller to wife and mom; instead, al-Shaykh chooses to keep her in the realm of invisibility and magic.

Shahrazad's stories are on every theme and subject, from con-artistry to justice to love; they are surreal and grimy-real, and they express powerful oppositions: male/female, union/disunion, love/hate, nature/society. The theme of betrayal and/or trickery runs through many of them: A brokenhearted woman helps her gullible fiancé to win the love of a murderous beauty while protecting him with talismanic poems which will save his life—even as he destroys hers. A woman traps five amorous fools inside a cabinet (which she's tricked one of them into building) where they eventually, to avoid bursting their bladders, pee on each others' heads. An impoverished elderly widow disguised as a holy woman and concerned mother goes on a rampage of fraud and theft, tricking one of her victims into yanking out another's teeth—and is rewarded for her crimes with a government position. A husband chops his beloved wife to pieces because, at market, a slave who in truth has never met her brags that he's the wife's lover, as he flaunts a rare fruit the husband gave her. Two sisters who betray another sister because they are jealous that she has found love are turned into dogs, and must be savagely beaten every day by the sister they wronged for the rest of their lives—even though she has long ago forgiven them and sobs as she strikes them.

The action of the stories in *One Thousand and One Nights* is dark and full of cruelty—especially toward women, who are constantly being accused of adultery and then murdered or beat up. But the animating spirit here is light and full of play, *especially* on the part of the female characters, who are consistently resourceful and witty. The supposedly enslaved mistress of a demon taunts and commands two cuckolded kings to "make love" to her; they obey and then dance and cheer, "How great is the cunning of women!" Both cunning queens are murdered, but the demon's mistress lives on to triumphantly declare: "I have slept with one hundred men under the very horns of this filthy demon as he snored happily, assuming that I am his alone . . . he is a fool, for he does not know that no one can prevent a woman from fulfilling her desires, even if she is hidden under the roaring sea, jealously guarded by a demon" (p. 217).

This apparent fear of and admiration for triumphant female lust keeps popping out against the theme of vengeance against said lust, and it is *not* al-Shaykh's invention; it is intrinsic to the complex soul of the original. But how to refer to the "original"? The stories in *One Thousand and One Nights* were told orally for centuries, coming out of India and Persia in the sixth century, and carried by traders and travelers all over the world; they were first written in Arabic in 1450. Through subsequent translations, disparate versions became folded into each other, as minor characters become major players and events are transformed, revealing the original themes differently, yet faithfully. For if the characters telling the stories within the stories are, like Shahrazad, pleading for their lives, they are also pleading for an aspect of truth to be revealed, and this desire for revelation is profoundly heartfelt. Shahrazad is not just out to save her skin, she wants to heal; she is asking for forgiveness, not only for women's sexual infidelity but for men's violent possessiveness, for human boobishness in general. She also acknowledges that certain things cannot be tolerated. In her stories, foolishness, lust, greed, jealousy, lying, cruelty, cowardice and vanity are exposed and readily forgiven; rape and cold-blooded murder are *not* forgiven. The moral codes are honored sincerely—but then there is that lewd demon's mistress, a consistent narrative mischief, a respect for pure, life-force passion that runs through the tales, which reminds me of what William

Blake said about *Paradise Lost*: that Milton, being a poet, was of the Devil's camp whether he knew it or not.

Al-Shaykh's *Nights* has special beauty in that it emphasizes this mischievous aspect alongside the expansive, revelatory and forgiving nature of the tales. With so many versions of the *Nights* it's hard to compare, but many of the older versions I've seen have a tight, convoluted quality which, while dreamishly, brilliantly inventive, can have the random feel of Grimm's least interesting fairy tales, a sort of then-this-happened-and-then-this-happened action-based narrative style. In contrast, al-Shaykh's style foregrounds structure and character. She pays little attention to the famous voyages of Sindbad, and Ali Baba (who was apparently invented by the first Western translator, Antoine Galland) doesn't even get a mention. Instead the narrative pivots around a grand party at the sumptuous home of three beautiful and independent sisters who are hosting several men—dervishes, merchants and a porter, all of whom are unexpected guests. They eat, drink and sing, but mostly they talk and tell stories that take them around the world and beyond it. The classic *Nights* features these ladies and their guests in passing, but al-Shaykh returns to them again and again, rooting her stories in the mysterious underground of male-female relations.

Many of the classic stories have long, literally underground, sequences where major action takes place: one story starts with a prince agreeing to entomb his cousin and his cousin's beautiful sister in a fabulous crypt where they will consummate their love and be burnt to cinders doing so. Another prince follows a beautiful young man down into the gorgeous underground chamber, in which the boy's father has hidden him and discovers his fate—that he must kill the boy—while doing everything possible to avoid it.

Al-Shaykh features some of these stories, but she stresses the secret underworld we experience every day, in which emotional truth is expressed in strange actions that have somehow become normal. The story of the two sisters turned into bitches, who are compulsorily whipped by their unwilling sister in the middle of a civil gathering, is a story of cruelty that is secret and mechanical even as it happens in plain sight. It is a physical metaphor for the invisible violence that goes on between people everywhere (especially in families), while civil words are being spoken and daily life goes forward.

When we first see the dogs being beaten, we don't know who they really are or why this is happening. The sisters demand that their guests ask no questions, and when one of them breaks the rule, the truths underlying the beautiful party are revealed. The very slave who caused an innocent woman to be hacked to death with his trivial marketplace bragging is exposed and pardoned by a suddenly revealed king; much later the slave reveals himself as a powerful healer with magic strong enough to lift the curse and return the dogs to their human form. Whipped dogs are also dignified women, a stupid slave is also a wise healer; the truth of this night is ugly, then beautiful then finally mysterious because of the way these qualities are linked.

But *how* such truth is revealed is as important as *what* is revealed: delicacy and attention to propriety is present in the stories, even if sometimes comically so. The first guest of the three glamorous ladies, the besotted porter, is allowed to stay, feast and bathe with them because he shows himself discreet by quoting poetry: "Guard your secrets closely / When they're told they fly / If unable to keep treasures in our own heart / Who then can forbid another, yours to impart?" (p. 29). As the night goes on, they each cuddle up in his lap and ask him what they've got between the legs—by which they mean, he's got to guess the exact name

they've given it or else be pummeled—and each lady has a different private name. In "The First Dervish" the woman (Aziza) helps
her cousin and fiancé (Aziz) to woo another woman who also
happens to be a killer. Aziza instructs Aziz on exactly what verses
to say to the lady every night, and asks how the lady replies:

He: Lovers, in the name of God
       Tell me how can one relieve this endless desperation?

She: He should conceal his love and hide
       Showing only his patience and humility.

He: He tried to show fair patience but could only find
       A heart that was filled with unease.

She: If he cannot counsel his patience to conceal his secrets
       Nothing will serve him better than death.

He: I have heard, obeyed and now must I die
       Salutations to she who tore us apart.   (pp. 58–60)

In the story Aziz has failed completely to conceal his love or
to be patient, but he can nonetheless woo the other woman; he
is also saved from death by reciting the lines, "Loyalty is good.
Treachery is bad." At the same time, the fiancée is speaking to her
rival through the words and, in the initial sequence, congratulat-
ing her on her victory. Ironically, it is Aziza, who *has* restrained
her love and shown infinite patience, who will die. The story (and
there is more to it than I have described) is essentially a fight
between sacred and profane love; it is bloody and no one can
really win. It doesn't make sense that reciting these lines should
save Aziz, none of it makes "sense"—and yet in a deeply satisfying
way it does, for the ritual nature of the incantatory words stands
as a dramatic counter to the raw power of sexuality and emotion,

and expresses the protective quality of propriety, discretion and order.

These stories of intense opposites are rich and flashing in combination, a skein of words that glimmers like a net of fast-darting fish which are also jewels. They make unity of chaos and take joy from suffering. Before he meets the demon's mistress, the brother of the cuckold Shahrayar, King Shahzaman (a cuckold too!), sulks about their wives doing it with slaves and kitchen boys, lamenting, "What treacherous world is this which fails to distinguish between a sovereign king and a nobody?" (p. 4). It's a question that asserts propriety, discretion and social hierarchy and, over the course of *One Thousand and One Nights,* Shahrazad, with her loving plenitude and subtlety, replies by revealing the entire world, with all its chaos and abiding order. He asks, "What kind of a world is this?" And she answers, "Why, king, a very wonderful world indeed." Finally, he believes; so do we.

Preface

I don't recall exactly whether I was eight or ten years old when I first heard the words *Alf layla wa layla*, one thousand and one nights, but I do remember listening to a radio dramatisation and being utterly smitten: the clamour, hustle and bustle of the bazaars and souks, the horses' hooves, the creaking of a dungeon door, how the radio seemed to vibrate and shake at the footsteps of a demon, and the famous crow of the lonely rooster at the start of each episode, which would be answered by all the roosters in our neighbourhood.

I heard that a girl in my class had *Alf layla wa layla*, and I hurried with her to peer at a few volumes in a glass cabinet, next to a carved tusk of an elephant. The volumes were leather-bound, their title engraved in gold. I asked my friend if I might touch one, but she said that her father always locked the cabinet and kept the key in his pocket, because he said he feared that if anyone finished the stories they would drop dead. Of course I didn't know then, and neither did my friend, that the reason her father didn't want any of the women of the house to read *Alf layla wa layla* was because of its explicit sexuality.

As the years passed, my obsession with *Alf layla wa layla* faded.

I wanted desperately to escape the world it evoked. But Shahrazad found her way to me. I decided I must discover why, while most Arabs considered the framing story of Shahrazad to be a mere cliché, academics regarded it as a work of genius and a cornerstone of Arabic literature.

I read page after page, marvelling at Shahrazad's perseverance in remaining the king's prisoner in order to reveal to him the truth of her mind. I came to see that her weapon was art at its best, her endless invention of all of those magnificent stories. The more I read, the more I came to admire the flat, simple style I had so criticised in the past. The simplicity of the language touched me, for it was the language of those who didn't reach for a dictionary but expressed their true, crude, raw and intense feelings, whether they praised, elegised or defamed. In these voices lay the foundation of magic realism, the flashback, and the use of the surreal to explain the ordinary—all the things I had mistakenly thought *Alf layla wa layla* lacked.

Reading *Alf layla wa layla* this time was personal: I felt as if I had opened the door of a carriage which took me back into the heart of my Arab heritage, and to the classical Arab language, after a great absence. I was astonished at how our forebears had shaped our societies, showing us how to live our daily lives, through these tales which were filled with insights and moral and social rules and laws, without the influence of religion, but derived from first-hand experience and deepest natural feelings towards every living thing. The effect of *Alf layla wa layla* was so strong and real that Arab societies shaped themselves around it; the names of its characters were embedded in our language, becoming proverbs, adjectives and even modes of speech. I was in awe of the complex society the stories evoked, which allowed relationships between humans and jinnis and beasts, real and imaginary, and I smiled at the codes of conduct and the carefully laid-out etiquette. But as a female Arab writer my real enchantment was the discovery that women in those forgotten ancient societies were far from passive and fearful; they showed their strong will and intelligence and wit, all the time recognising that their behaviour was the second nature of the weak and the oppressed.

When I finished adapting these nineteen stories for the stage and for this book, I thanked Shahrazad for leading me into a myriad of worlds. And, when I stepped back into our century, it dawned on me that in a sense my friend's father was right when he had said that anyone who finished *Alf layla wa layla* would die: the reader might find herself detached and lifeless when forced to withdraw from the sublime vividness of the numerous worlds of the One Thousand and One Nights. I hope you revel in the journey as much as I did.

One Thousand and One Nights

Shahrayar and Shahrazad

long, long time ago lived two Kings who were brothers. The elder, King Shahrayar, ruled India and Indochina. The younger, Shahzaman, ruled Samarkand. Shahrayar was so powerful and strong that even savage animals feared him; but at the same time, he was fair, caring and kind to his people—just as the eyelid protects the eye. And they, in turn, were loyal, obeyed him blindly, and adored him.

Shahrayar woke one morning and experienced a pang of longing for his younger brother. He realised, to his amazement, that he hadn't seen Shahzaman in ten years. So he summoned his Vizier, the father of the two girls Shahrazad and Dunyazad, and asked him to go immediately to Samarkand and fetch his brother. The Vizier travelled for days and nights, until he reached Samarkand and met King Shahzaman, who welcomed him and slaughtered beasts in his honour, and he gave him the good news. "King Shahrayar is sound and well; he needs only to see your face and so he has sent me to ask that you visit him."

Happy Shahzaman embraced the Vizier, replying that he too had missed his brother, and that he would prepare to leave at once.

In no time everything was ready: troops, horses and camels, and sheep to be slaughtered for food. Shahzaman was filled with happiness and excitement, for he was going to see his brother, so he set out at once, not wanting to delay one minute longer as he heard the beat of the tambourine and the blowing of the trumpets. He rushed to his wife's quarters to bid her goodbye, but to his horror he found her lying in the arms of one of the kitchen boys. The world blackened and spun, as though he was caught in a hurricane.

"I am the sovereign King of Samarkand and yet my wife has betrayed me, but with whom? With another king? A general in the army? No—with a kitchen boy!"

In his fury, he drew his sword and killed his wife and the kitchen boy, then dragged them by the heels and threw their bodies from the very top of the palace into the trench below. Then he left his kingdom with his brother's Vizier and entourage, his heart bleeding with sorrow and grief.

As they travelled, the change of scenery and the beauty and solitude of the ravines and mountains failed to provide distraction, but only heightened Shahzaman's sense of loss and misfortune. He reached India and embraced his brother King Shahrayar, who placed his guest palace at his disposal.

As the days passed, Shahzaman grew ever paler and lost his appetite. King Shahrayar noticed his brother's decline and assumed that he must be missing home and kingdom.

Finally, one morning King Shahrayar asked Shahzaman: "Dear brother, would you like to hunt with me? We shall track the roaming deer for ten days and return when you are due to set out for your kingdom."

But Shahzaman said, "I am unable to accompany you this time. I am too depressed and preoccupied. I have a wound on my soul."

King Shahrayar persisted. "Maybe the excitement and action of the hunt will revive you, my brother, and heal your wound."

King Shahzaman refused, saying, "No, you must leave me here, and go with God's blessing and protection."

Not wishing to pressure his brother, King Shahrayar embraced Shahzaman and with his entourage went out to hunt. Shahzaman remained alone in his quarters, moving from one chair to another as if wishing to escape himself, deeply depressed. He heard a bird cry and opened his shutters to look out, wishing this creature would lift him away into the sky, where he might forget the sorrow that had befallen him on Earth. He heard a commotion below him and to his bewilderment saw a private gate from his brother's palace opening, from which his brother's wife emerged, swaying like a dark, kohl-eyed deer. She was followed by a train of twenty slave girls, ten as white as the jasmine flower, and ten as dark as ebony, their bodies built to conquer, their lips luscious, as though stung by a hundred bees. As he observed unseen, they chatted, sang and laughed around the fountain below his window. Gradually they began to undress in a leisurely fashion, with a complete lack of inhibition, and Shahzaman nearly cried out in surprise when he realised the ten black slave girls were in fact men, who stood with their penises erect like bayonets, their firm buttocks jutting out as though a cup and saucer might balance on them. Shahzaman looked to see how his brother's wife would react; but she nonchalantly laughed and laughed, stopping only to call out lustily, "Mas'ud . . . Mas'ud!" Another black slave jumped over a wall and fell on her, like a coconut fruit falling to the ground. Again Shahzaman tried not to cry out in mortification as she spread her legs for the slave, lifting them until the soles of her feet faced the sky. At this, the ten white slave girls and the black slave men paired off and began to make love as though they had each been waiting for a signal from their Queen, while Mas'ud made love to her in the centre, and the sounds of their ecstasy and pleasure rose up to where Shahzaman stood hidden.

Shahzaman threw his hands up to his face and rushed from the window, but he couldn't stay away. He peeked again and again, watching as the couples disported themselves over and over, until midday, when everyone washed at the fountain, splashing each other with water, before putting on their clothes. The ten black men became ten black slave girls and disappeared behind the gate. Mas'ud jumped over the garden wall and disappeared.

Seeing the grounds empty, as if nothing had happened, Shahzaman cried out, "Oh brother of mine, you are the ruler of the entire world, length and width, the towering knight, the implacable, the pious; and yet your wife seems to find delight only with the slave Mas'ud between her thighs. And to add insult to injury, they were at it in your own home. If only it was just your wife, but all your concubines and slaves too . . . as if to them your status is little more than an onion skin. What treacherous world is this, which fails to distinguish between a sovereign king and a nobody?"

When Shahrayar came back from his hunting trip, Shahzaman greeted him with great joy and vigour. Shahrayar noticed that his brother had regained colour in his cheeks and life in his eyes. The brothers sat down to eat, and Shahrayar saw how Shahzaman fell upon his food with great alacrity and relish and sighed with relief. "How delighted I am to come back and find you brimming with energy, cheerful and happy. So tell me what had made you so miserable when you arrived . . . and what has brought about this speedy recovery?"

"I had a great wound to my soul and my heart was set on fire, for I caught my wife in the arms of one of the kitchen boys in her quarters before I set out to come to you. My anger took control and

I avenged myself by slaying both of them and hurling their bodies in a trench, like two dead cockroaches," Shahzaman answered.

At this Shahrayar exclaimed, "Shame, shame, I am filled with horror at this revelation of the deceit and wickedness of women. But how fortunate you were, my beloved brother, in killing your wife for betraying you; she who was the cause of your misery and malaise. She was a snake hiding in the grass, waiting to strike the hand which fed her. And how fortunate, too, that you killed this kitchen boy who dared to disrespect a king. Never have I heard of such a thing! Had I been in your place I should have lost my mind, gone insane and slaughtered with my own sword hundreds, thousands of women. Let us celebrate and praise God for saving you from this turmoil. But now you must explain to me how you have managed to rise above your calamity and sorrow."

"I beg you, my brother, in God's name, to forgive me for not answering this question," Shahzaman replied.

"But you must tell me. I am bewildered by the ease with which you overcame your grief in just ten days, as if what you had suffered was but a minor injury, when it takes centuries to recover from cuckoldry," said Shahrayar.

"My King, I fear that if I tell you, you will suffer greater devastation and desolation than my own," said Shahzaman.

Shahrayar pressed him. "How, brother, could that be? Now I must insist that I hear your explanation."

"I witnessed your misfortune with my own eyes," said Shahzaman. "The day that you set out on the hunt, I looked out upon the garden to enjoy the beauty of your estate and saw the palace gate open and your wife emerge with her twenty slave girls in train, ten white and ten black. As I watched, they disrobed, and the ten black girls were men in disguise, and as I stood hidden they fell upon one another and began to make love. Your wife called out the name 'Mas'ud' and another black slave appeared, jumping over the wall, and leaping upon your wife, in your own garden . . ."

"In my garden?"

"Yes, beneath my window. They must all have thought that I had accompanied you on the hunt. And so, as I watched your own misfortune unfold, I told myself that my brother was King of all the world, and yet this had happened, even to him. What he had suffered was far worse. I had been betrayed by my wife, but I alone knew of the indignity I had suffered, whereas my poor brother was betrayed even by his concubines, in broad daylight and in his own palace garden. And so in no time at all I began to eat and drink again and forgot my strife and sorrow."

Shahrayar was overcome by fury and there was murder in his eyes. "I will not, I cannot, believe one word of what I have heard, until I have seen it with my own eyes," he stammered.

When Shahzaman saw his brother's rage, he said, "If you cannot believe in your misfortune unless you have witnessed it for yourself, why don't you announce that you intend to go on another hunting trip tomorrow? Then you and I will sneak back to my quarters in disguise under the cover of darkness and you shall see for yourself everything that I have described."

Shahrayar agreed with his brother's plan and ordered his Vizier to arrange a hunting trip with his brother. The news of the journey spread through the palace like wildfire and with the beat of tambourines, the blowing of trumpets and great commotion, the hunting party departed. As they'd planned, the two Kings snuck back, disguised, to Shahzaman's quarters.

Shahrayar tossed and turned on his bed all night long, as if it was made of burning coals. When day broke, he lay listening to the chirrup of birds and water tumbling from the fountain, which he heard each morning, and couldn't help thinking that his brother had hallucinated and imagined it all. But then he heard the gate open, and he hurried with Shahzaman to the window.

Shahrayar's wife appeared, followed by twenty slave girls, ten white, ten black, exactly as Shahzaman had described. The entourage strolled in the garden under the trees and stopped beneath Shahzaman's window. As the two Kings watched, they undressed, revealing the ten black slave men, who immediately paired up with the girls, embracing and kissing them. Shahrayar's wife again called "Mas'ud, Mas'ud!" and a solid, heavily built black slave jumped from the tree to the ground, saying, "What do you want, you slut? Allow me to present Sa'ad al-Din Mas'ud." He pointed to his prick and Shahrayar's wife giggled and fell on her back and opened her thighs, ready for him.

As Mas'ud began to make love to her, the ten black slaves mounted the girls.

Shahrayar almost cried out, like a lion fatally wounded by an arrow to the eye. Quick as a bolt of lightning, he reached the garden with his sword in his hand, thirsty for revenge. All of a sudden the moans of pleasure and ecstasy in the garden became screams and yelps, piercing cries and wails, as Shahrayar cut off his wife's and Mas'ud's head, in one stroke. And then, like an insane gardener, he severed every other head and body, as if he was chopping every stem in the garden, leaving the heads to fall and roll into the earth.

Seeing that no head was left on its body, Shahrayar threw his sword on to the ground, took off his stained robe and walked with heavy steps until he reached a rock, sat on it and rested his head in his hands. The next day Shahrayar stood at the heart of his palace and decreed a new law. "I, Shahrayar, shall each night marry a virgin, kissed only by her mother. I shall kill her the following morning and thereby protect myself from the cunning and deceit of women, for there is not a single chaste woman on the face of this earth!"

Shahrayar sat upon his throne and ordered his Vizier (the father of Shahrazad and Dunyazad) to find him a wife among the daughters of the princes of his lands. As soon as the Vizier found him a princess, Shahrayar spent the night with her, deflowered her, and then when dawn broke ordered his Vizier to put her to death. The Vizier did as he was told. The next night he took the daughter of one of his army officers, slept with her and sent her to her death the following morning. On the third night it was the turn of the daughter of a merchant.

Soon, many girls had perished, and their families mourned their losses, amidst growing anger and stirrings of revolt, praying to the creator who hears and answers prayers to strike King Shahrayar down with a fatal disease. But the bloodbath continued, night after night. Then one day Shahrazad, the elder daughter of the Vizier, a woman of great intelligence and refinement, went to her father and said, in the presence of her younger sister Dunyazad: "Father, I want you to marry me to King Shahrayar, so that I may either succeed in saving the girls of the kingdom, or perish and die like them."

The Vizier couldn't believe his ears. She was so wise, so intelligent, so learned, versed in the great texts of philosophy, medicine, literature, poetry and history, and so delicate of bearing and graceful of manners. He said to her, "Foolish one, are you not aware that if I give you to the King he will sleep with you for one night only and then have me put you to death in the morning? And are you not aware that I shall have to carry out his wishes, since I am unable to disobey him?"

But Shahrazad was not to be deterred. "Father, you must offer me to him, even if it will result in my death."

The Vizier sought to understand her motivation, in order that he might discover how to change her mind. "What has possessed you that you wish to endanger your life in this way?"

"You must give me to him, father," Shahrazad answered.

The Vizier, unable to comprehend his daughter's foolishness, grew furious with rage and shouted, "He who misbehaves ends up in trouble and he who considers not the end of the world is not his own friend. I am afraid that you will meet the same fate as that of the bird who encountered a group of apes."

Shahrazad asked, "Father, tell me what happened to the bird and the group of apes."

And so the Vizier said, "A bunch of apes mistook a passing firefly for an ember. They threw wood on it and huffed and puffed, trying to ignite it. A bird tried to tell them it was a firefly, but the apes ignored the bird. A man, who was passing, said, 'Listen, bird, you cannot endeavour to bring into line something which has been forever wayward, or to enlighten those who cannot see, so listen to what I am telling you.' But the stubborn bird wouldn't give up, until one of the apes smote the bird to the ground, killing it."

But Shahrazad said to her father, "Your tale will not change my mind, and if you do not take me to the King, I will go to him in secret myself, and tell him that you refused to give me to one such as him, and that you would begrudge your Master one such as me."

The Vizier appealed to her one last time. "Must you really do this, my beloved daughter?"

And Shahrazad answered, "Yes, father, it is final."

The Vizier said, "Always remember that I offer advice only out of love and compassion for you."

"I know, my beloved father," she replied.

So the agonised Vizier forced himself to go before the King, who asked, "Have you brought me what I want?"

The Vizier kissed the ground before his sovereign and replied, "My daughter Shahrazad."

And the King, astonished and bewildered, said, "Vizier, but how, when you know more than anyone else what will be the fate of your daughter tomorrow morning, and that if you refuse to put her to death, I will, by God, the creator of heaven, put you to death as well!"

The Vizier replied, "I tried to explain to her, but in vain, she is determined to come and be with you tonight."

King Shahrayar, astonished but delighted, ordered his Vizier, "Then go and prepare her and bring her to me early in the evening!"

The Vizier went back to Shahrazad and asked her to ready herself. Then, leaving her, he said, "May God not deprive me of you."

Shahrazad called to her younger sister Dunyazad, saying, "Beloved sister, listen to what I am telling you very carefully. I am going as you know to King Shahrayar tonight and I plan to send for you. When the King has finished with me, I want you to plead with me, and say, 'Sister, since you're not sleepy, tell us a story, so that we may pass the waking part of this night.' Then I shall tell you a tale in the hope that it will engage the King fully, keep me alive, and cease his actions, thereby saving both my own life and those of all the girls who remain in the kingdom."

Soon afterwards, the Vizier came to collect Shahrazad, saying to her once again before he departed, "I pray to God not to deprive me of you."

Shahrazad was taken to Shahrayar's quarters, where the King led her at once to his enormous, terrible bed. He began to undo her dress, which had many tiny buttons. Shahrazad wept and the King asked her, "Why are you crying, Shahrazad?"

"I weep for my younger sister Dunyazad and so I should like to say farewell to her before daybreak."

The King sent for Shahrazad's sister. Dunyazad hurried into the chamber and the two girls embraced. Then Dunyazad climbed under the King's bed and waited while Shahrayar deflowered her older sister and satisfied himself. As the night wore on, Dunyazad cleared her throat and spoke into the silence.

"Sister, tell us one of your lovely stories before I must bid you goodbye, for I do not know what will happen to you tomorrow."

"If the King gives his permission," Shahrazad replied.

Shahrayar, lying restless, waiting for dawn to break, welcomed the idea, saying, "Yes, go ahead."

Shahrazad was overjoyed. She began. "It is said, oh wise and happy King, that a very poor fisherman . . ."

The Fisherman and the Jinni

I t is said, oh wise and happy King, that a very poor fisherman who swore by Almighty God that he would only cast his net three times each day, went down to the sea late one afternoon as usual, waited until he saw the moon shining above him, and then threw his net very carefully into the water. He sat there for a time, and then, when he pulled on his net and felt that it had grown heavy, he sang to himself:

> "Glide over to me, my magnificent fish
> And slither into my waiting net
> So that someone asleep on his soft silken bed
> Will awaken and buy you with his silver bread."

He opened his net and there, to his horror, found a dead donkey. "A donkey?" he cried out. "My wretched luck. You send me a donkey when you know that my family and I are starved out of our brains?" He managed to free it from his net with one hand while pinching his nose with the other to block out the horrible smell.

He cast his net carefully into the sea again, waited for it to sink, tugged on it and to his amazement felt that the net was even heavier than the first time. It was so heavy he had to climb back on to the shore, drive a stake into the ground, and tie the rope of the net to the stake. Then he hauled with all his might until he managed to pull the net up out of the sea.

But instead of an abundance of fish jumping and playing in the net he found a broken, rusty wooden chest filled with sand. He shouted in a loud voice, "A chest? Is this how you compensate my work? My labour? Or are you telling me that the key to my good fortune lies inside this coffin?"

He kicked the chest as hard as he could, but then managed to recover his patience, and washed out his net once again.

When dawn was about to break the fisherman prayed, raising his hands and lifting his eyes to heaven in supplication. "Oh God, I beg of you, have pity on me, I have no other trade and I have sworn that I shall only cast my net three times. This is my last attempt, because I believe that my fortune has been decided and this will be my fate."

He cast his net, put his hand on his heart and waited, murmuring to himself, "Let us hope that the third time will be lucky."

At last he hauled the net ashore and to his amazement found a large brass jar inside, long-necked and sealed with a lid.

"I'll sell it in the copper market and buy some wheat," he said to himself.

He tried to lift it but it was too heavy and so he shook it, trying to tell what was inside. He examined the lead seal of the lid, on which words were engraved, and then took his knife and slowly eased it open. He tilted the jar to one side but nothing came out, which puzzled him, since the jar was so heavy. He plunged his hand into the jar, but it was empty. Suddenly a column of smoke began to pour out, covering the ground and the sea and moving higher and higher up into the sky until it reached the clouds. The fisherman peered up into the sky as the smoke turned to a black fog and formed the shape of a huge jinni, his head reaching to the sky and his feet planted on the sand. The fisherman wanted to run away, but remained frozen to the spot, as the jinni's head became like a tomb, his eyes like two lanterns, his nostrils like two trumpets, his ears as large as an elephant's, his mouth a frightening cave with teeth like gravestones and two fangs like a pair of pincers. The fisherman shook with fear, his teeth rattled in his mouth, his knees knocked and his feet remained nailed to the ground.

But the jinni cried out, "Oh Suleiman, Suleiman, the mighty prophet of God, forgive me and pardon me. I promise that I have learned my lesson. I'll never disobey you again and I am now your trusted servant."

Hearing the jinni's plea and seeing how he trembled, the fisherman gathered his courage and asked him, "What are you saying? The prophet Suleiman died one thousand, eight hundred years ago. Eons have passed. Who are you? And why were you in that jar?"

"Be glad, be very glad," the jinni replied.

"Oh! My happy day has come at last," the fisherman said to himself, overjoyed.

"Be glad that I am going to kill you," the jinni added.

"Kill me? What have I done other than to haul you up from the bottom of the sea and release you from that jar?"

"Hurry up and make a wish," the jinni told him.

Hearing this, the fisherman's face lit up and he said, "This is what I love to hear! Just give me a second to think what I should ask of you."

But the jinni said, "Tell me how you wish to die. I promise you that I will fulfil your desire."

"Why me?" the fisherman shrieked. "What have I done to you, you ungrateful creature? Let me tell you that until this day I never believed the proverb 'Beware those you help.'"

But the jinni said to him, "Let me tell you my story. I'm sure that then you'll understand why I must put you to death."

The fisherman said, "Please be assured, jinni, that I shall never try to understand why you are going to kill me!"

Enraged, the jinni shouted, "Then you can be assured, fisherman, that I will not be so generous as to ask you how you would like to die."

"Hurry up then, and tell me your story," the fisherman said. "Be quick, for my soul has dropped to my feet in fright."

The jinni began his story. "I am one of the rebellious jinnis who disobeyed God. I was dragged before the prophet Suleiman who asked me to submit and surrender to him. When I declined he imprisoned me in that jar and sealed it with the name of the Almighty and Magnificent. Then he gave the jar to one of the obedient jinnis, who carried me and threw me in the sea. Before I had completed two hundred years inside that wretched jar I swore an oath that if someone were to release me I would make him rich. But nothing happened and I remained trapped in the jar. After another two hundred years had passed I vowed to myself in my loudest voice, in the hope that the waves would carry my pleas, that whosoever should release me from my prison would receive all the treasures of the Earth. But still no one came to my rescue and another hundred years passed and another and another and I remained, cooped up in the same position in that jar. I found myself screaming and raving and shouting and declaring to the whole world and to myself that whosoever set me free I would subject to the worst death imaginable and then you arrived, and released me from the jar. And so now I am obliged to fulfil my promise."

The fisherman nearly fainted, but he pleaded with the jinni, "Forgive me, jinni, for setting you free. I was only trying to fish, so that my wife and children will not die of hunger. Jinni, if you forgive me, then God will forgive you; if you strike me, then God will strike you down."

But the jinni interrupted the fisherman, saying, "I must kill you, it is the best reward that I can grant you for setting me free. Now hurry up and choose the manner of your death."

The fisherman thought to himself, "I am a human being; God has given me reason and made me superior to this jinni. I must use my cunning to defeat his demonic wiles and barbarism."

He turned to the jinni, saying, "Jinni, do with me what you will, kill me in any way you wish."

But just as the jinni took one giant step towards him, the fisherman said quickly, "Jinni, before I die, I should like to ask you something."

"Go ahead and ask then."

"Tell me, in the name of the Almighty, were you really inside that jar? Are you sure you weren't playing a trick on me?"

"Of course I was inside it!"

"But how? This jar is not big enough for even one of your giant feet."

"So you don't believe me?" said the jinni.

"No, to be perfectly honest, I don't," the fisherman replied. "I'll never believe it unless I see it with my own eyes."

But a rooster crowed, dawn broke and Shahrazad fell silent, sighing to herself. "Oh King!" her sister, Dunyazad, said from under the bed. "What a beautiful and amazing story!"

"If the King spares me and lets me live, then I shall tell you tomorrow night what became of the fisherman and the jinni," said Shahrazad.

"I shall let her live and hear the rest of the story tomorrow night and then I shall kill her," Shahrayar said to himself.

Shahrazad held her breath with great anguish and fear, awaiting the King's verdict, as if the sword might fall upon her neck at any moment, while Dunyazad peeked out from beneath the bed, panting and panicking.

This moment seemed to stretch out into a century, but finally Shahrayar left his bedroom, without calling for his Vizier, the father of Shahrazad and Dunyazad, to order him to have his daughter put to death. Instead he went and sat on his throne, to order and forbid, and the two sisters clung to each other, embracing and weeping, hardly able to believe that their plan had worked, even for one night. Dunyazad touched her sister's face, amazed that she was still alive. When the Vizier realised that his daughter would not be killed that day he shouted for joy and kissed the ground.

When night fell over the palace once more, Shahrayar entered his bedchamber, and climbed into his bed. Shahrazad climbed in next to him and the King caressed her and made love to her, while Dunyazad waited patiently under the bed. When the commotion above her subsided, she cleared her throat and spoke into the darkness.

"Sister, if you are not asleep, can you tell us what became of the fisherman and the jinni?"

"If the King wishes to hear it," was Shahrazad's reply.

"Go ahead," said the King.

And Shahrazad answered, "With the greatest pleasure."

I heard, oh happy King, that the fisherman answered, "I will never believe that you were inside that jar until I see it with my own two eyes."

So the jinni shook himself until he once again became smoke which rose into the air and stretched out over the sea and the ground. Then it gathered itself and entered the jar little by little and when the last drifts of smoke disappeared within, the jinni called out, "Do you believe me now, you stubborn fisherman?"

Quick as a flash the fisherman clamped the lead seal over the mouth of the jar and shouted, "Now, you wretched jinni, how do you wish to die?"

Realising that the fisherman had tricked him, the jinni struggled to get out. When he found that he was trapped, he called, "But fisherman, I was joking when I told you that I wanted to kill you!"

"You're lying," said the fisherman, and he began to roll the jar towards the water's edge.

"Stop, fisherman, stop! What are you going to do with me?"

"I am going to throw you deep into the sea, and build a hut right here on this spot, lest another fisherman comes along and hauls you out. I want you to remain imprisoned in the darkness of the jar for ever, until Doomsday."

The jinni was silent for a moment, and then he spoke in the softest of voices, "I beg you, fisherman, not to do that."

"Didn't I myself plead with you again and again, telling you to spare me so that God would spare you, or destroy me and be destroyed yourself? But you refused."

"Release me," the jinni begged him, "and I promise that I shall leave you in peace."

"Listen, jinni, I love my life and it was enough to have nearly lost it the first time I saved you."

"Open the jar and I promise to reward you beyond your wildest dreams."

"I don't believe your promises. They're all lies, because your situation and mine is like that of King Yunan and the sage Duban," said the fisherman.

"What is that story?"

And so the fisherman began.

here was once a King called Yunan, who suffered from leprosy which no one could cure, until a sage rid him of the disease without giving him one drop of medicine or applying a single trace of ointment. The King rewarded this sage, who had made his skin healthy and pure once more. He showered him with gifts and money and presented him with a special robe, studded with precious gems, of the kind worn only by the King's Vizier. When he discovered this, the Vizier feared the King would prefer the sage and appoint him as his counsellor and confidant. So the jealous Vizier advised the King to beware the sage, saying, "He might cause you such great harm that it leads to your death."

The King was sure that his Vizier was jealous, and he reminded him that the sage had cured his terrible leprosy.

But the Vizier said, "Indeed, Your Majesty, the way he cured you was exactly what raised my suspicions. I was horrified when he cured you by magic—he didn't even touch you! It came to me that we couldn't trust this man not to harm the King in this strange way."

The King was convinced and he summoned the sage and said to him, "I wish to save myself from your grasp, and so I have decided to have you put to death."

The sage was astonished. "But what have I done, Your Majesty, other than doing a good deed in curing you? I don't understand why you would reward me by cutting off my head."

"You have indeed cured my illness, sage, with nothing but magic. You might just as easily kill me with magic."

"Spare me, Your Majesty, and God shall spare you. Destroy me and God shall destroy you," the sage pleaded.

The fisherman stopped the story, saying, "Jinni, you have heard how the sage Duban pleaded with King Yunan. Do you remember how I pleaded with you to spare me?"

"Yes, I remember, fisherman, go on with your story: I can't bear being back in here."

And so the fisherman continued his story.

When the sage realised his end had come, he said to the King, "Let me go to my house before you kill me, so that I may prepare my burial. I should like also to present you with my most precious book, so that you may keep it safe with your great treasures. For this book is the secret of secrets. It is unique; it is miraculous; for if you strike off my head and then open the book at page six and read three lines from the left, my head will speak to you! Yes, it will answer all of your questions."

The King was amazed. "Wonder of wonders! Go home and fetch the book at once!"

The sage came before the King bearing an old book and pleaded for his life one last time. "For God's sake, Your Majesty, spare me and God shall spare you; destroy me and God shall destroy you."

"Spare you?" answered the excited King. "But I cannot wait to hear your head talk."

Then the King ordered the executioner to cut off the head of the sage. The severed head opened its eyes and asked the King to open the book.

The King did as he was told, but the pages of the book were stuck together, and so he moistened his finger with his tongue, opened the first page, then wetted his finger again and again until he had reached page six. When he saw that no words appeared upon the page, the King said, "Sage, I see nothing written on page six."

The head answered, "Open more pages."

The King turned page after page, wetting his finger with his tongue each time, until he began to feel dizzy, and shook and swayed, as he heard the head saying, "This is your end, you brutal, unjust, oppressive King."

And the King knew that he had been poisoned by the book, as he fell from his throne, dead.

"Jinni," the fisherman called to the jar. "Do you see that if the King had allowed the sage to live then he too would have lived? As for you, if you had answered my pleas and stopped insisting upon killing me, then I would have spared your life. Now, I seek revenge, and I shall hurl you to the bottom of the sea."

The jinni cried out, "I know that I was unjust and cruel, but forgive me, for forgiveness is a trait of the noblest men on this Earth. Revenge should never be the solution, for it leads to injustice. Remember the proverb: 'Be kind to him who wrongs you.' I beg you, my friend, do not do what Imama did to Atika."

The fisherman was curious. "Tell me this story of Imama and Atika."

"Not now," said the jinni. "I can barely breathe in this accursed jar. Fisherman, I swear that if you will set me free I will leave you in peace, but only after I have made you rich, rich beyond your wildest dreams!"

"You sound as though you've learned compassion," the fisherman replied. "But do you swear, by the Almighty, that if I let you out you will not kill me?"

"I swear by the Almighty's name that I shall not harm you and I shall leave you alone."

The fisherman opened his mouth to speak, but the jinni quickly added, "And I shall make you rich beyond your wildest dreams."

Hearing those last words, the fisherman broke open the seal, hesitated, and then put it in his pocket. The smoke poured from the jar and began to rise, until it covered the sea and the sky. It gathered into a fog and then the jinni once again formed. Realising that he was again free, the jinni gave the jar a powerful kick that sent it flying far out into the sea. Seeing this, the fisherman trembled and pissed himself, mumbling, "This is a bad omen."

He called out, "Jinni, you promised me, even swore an oath in the Almighty's name, not to betray me. Don't forget what the sage told King Yunan: 'Spare me and God shall spare you.'"

The jinni laughed. "Get your net and follow me, my friend."

They walked together and climbed a mountain, the fisherman all the while marvelling at the difference in size between him and the jinni and amused to now be walking alongside this vast creature which had been locked in a jar. They went down into a valley and stopped by a lake, which the fisherman had never seen before.

"Fisherman, why don't you cast your net and let us see what will happen?" said the jinni.

The fisherman reluctantly did what he was told. How would he become rich beyond his wildest dreams by catching fish? The net shook violently and the fisherman struggled to haul it in, but the jinni pushed him gently to one side and pulled the net in with one finger.

The net was filled with many strange, brilliantly coloured fish. Although the fisherman was captivated by the shapes and colours of these fish, he couldn't help but say to the jinni, "I have never seen fish such as these before and I am sure that the people at the fish market will be amazed by them and I shall sell them all. But pardon me, jinni, if I ask you a question. How am I going to become rich beyond my wildest dreams for the rest of my life, as you have promised?"

The jinni laughed, saying, "Well look, you have plenty of fish and of course you will sell them for double or triple the price."

Before the fisherman could open his mouth to object, he saw that the fish had ceased to breathe and become hard as stones, glittering and shining.

"Hey, fisherman," said the jinni, "your catch is the jewels of the sea after all."

The fisherman bent over the net and saw rubies and emeralds and pearls and coral and many other precious gems he had never before laid eyes upon.

"Hey, fisherman!"

The fisherman stared at the jinni, his mouth hanging open, still not believing what he saw.

"Yes?"

"I shall miss you!" The jinni kicked the ground with his foot, whereupon it opened, swallowing him.

"I shall miss you, too!" the fisherman called. "Farewell!"

Shahrazad fell silent, and Dunyazad spoke up from beneath the bed.

"What a beautiful and extraordinary story, my sister!"

"It is indeed," said Shahrazad. "But what is this tale, when compared to that of the fisherman's brother, the porter, and his ordeal with the three ladies?"

"Come on then, my sister, tell it to us, especially since it's still the middle of the night," said Dunyazad with great excitement.

"But it is a long tale, which I will never finish by dawn. As you know, His Majesty the King is allowing me to live only until first light. To start a story and not survive to finish it would be the same as taking you both in a boat out into the middle of the sea, and then leaving you there without oars. But, if the King wishes to hear the story of the fisherman's brother, the porter, and the three ladies, and is willing to postpone the hour of my death, then I am ready to tell it to you with great enthusiasm."

"Why not?" King Shahrayar thought to himself. "I will die from boredom if I must now lie here and wait for the dawn. And besides, I am eager to hear a new tale from Shahrazad, for she is a formidable storyteller. I find that I am becoming quite addicted to her stories. I shall let her live a little longer, and hear this new one."

"Come on, Shahrazad," he said, "tell us the tale of the fisherman's brother, the porter, and the three ladies."

And so, in the still of the night, Shahrazad began . . .

The Porter and the Three Ladies

 heard, oh wise and happy King, that once the fisherman became a jeweller his fame spread so that his name was on the lips of every person in Baghdad. His shop was as spacious as a garden and his jewellery and precious stones as big as flowers and fruit. And yet the fisherman remained true to his humble origins and never turned his back on his past. On the contrary, he gathered all his brothers and relatives and gave them jobs in his shop, which they accepted, all except for his younger brother the porter, who refused, saying, "Me, in a jewellery shop, where the customers are the nobles, the stuck up who can barely manage to smile? How would you expect me to live without the clamour of the souks?"

Now it happened that one morning this porter was leaning on his basket when a young lady approached him. She was wrapped in a brocade coat, her face hidden beneath a sheer muslin veil. She lifted it and told him in a sweet melodious voice, "Porter, take your basket and follow me." The porter saw her radiant face, which was as beautiful as the dawn, with deep black eyes and thick eyelashes and full smiling lips. He quickly followed the shopper, as delighted to be doing so as if he were entering Paradise, and when he noticed her comely figure and her tiny embroidered slippers, he said to himself, "Oh lucky day, oh happy day."

The lady stopped at a fruit seller's stall and chose Damascus quinces, Persian pomegranates, apples from Jabal Lubnan, tamrhenna from Egypt, figs from Baalbek, grapes from Hebron, oranges from Jaffa, and she placed everything in the porter's basket. Next she bought anemones, violets, Damascus lilies, narcissi and daffodils, pomegranate roses and stocks, choosing to carry the flowers herself.

"Porter, take your basket and follow me," she bade the porter in a voice of great charm and coquettishness, and he followed her, thanking God and murmuring, "What a lucky day; a day filled with gardenia and jasmine."

Next she stopped at another stall and bought Tunisian olives and Moroccan couscous, Nabulsi cheese, Egyptian pickles and fish roe, pistachios from Aleppo and raisins, Algerian thyme and Yemeni basil and Zanzibar hazelnuts. She placed everything in the basket and then said again to the porter, in the loveliest of voices, "Take your basket and follow me."

He followed her, murmuring, "What a day—as sweet as honey!" She stopped at a nearby grocer's shop and bought rose water, orange blossom water, candles and Omani incense, musk, saffron, cloves, turmeric and cinnamon sticks. Once more she put everything into the basket, saying, "Porter, take your basket and follow me." He walked behind her, murmuring to himself, "I'll follow this gazelle to the end of the world even for no reward." When she reached the sweet shop, she stopped and bought kunafa, katayef, Turkish delight, eat-and-thanks baklava, halava, mushabback, sesame rolls, hazelnut rolls, kunafa with cheese. She put everything in the basket and said to the porter, "Porter, take your basket and follow me." He followed, muttering, "What a lucky day!"

When she stopped at the butcher's and stroked with her lovely hennaed hands a lamb which was feeding, the porter said to her, "If you had told me, my good lady, that you were going to buy a live lamb, I would have brought with me a mule and carriage."

The lady just laughed and went into the butcher's, where she purchased the best meat and wrapped it in banana leaves and placed it in the basket. Next she went to a store with nothing on display in its window, but as she entered the man behind the counter saw her and quickly handed her a jar of wine.

The lady then continued on her way, holding the flowers, with the porter following at a respectful distance, murmuring to himself, "How I wish I was even a thorn in the flowers she is holding."

The lady stopped before a magnificent mansion, adorned with stately pillars and a huge garden filled with trees. She knocked on the door three times and another beautiful, blossoming lady opened the door. For the first time that day the porter shifted his eyes from the lady who had hired him. The doorkeeper's face was as round as the moon, her breasts like a pair of big pomegranates and beneath her clothes her tummy was as flat as a page folded in a book. At the sight of this woman the porter nearly fell down with his basket, but she thought he had collapsed under his heavy load and so she reproached the shopper, who had rushed inside to put the flowers into a vase. "What are you waiting for? Don't you see that this poor porter is barely able to shoulder his heavy burden?"

The porter followed the two women into a spacious room. He was unable to believe his eyes, for the room was decorated with beautiful wooden furniture inlaid with mother of pearl and ivory, and brightly coloured cushions, and in the centre was a fountain decorated in blue mosaic as if a piece of the blue sky had fallen into the sitting room. The two ladies began to empty the basket, when the porter heard the voice of a third woman calling, "Great, you're back, sister. Welcome!" At this the shopper stopped what she was doing and drew back a red silk curtain and the porter saw a woman reclining on a couch, as beautiful as if she was a shining sun. If she hadn't spoken and then stood up, the porter might have mistaken what he beheld for a painting. Her beauty was intoxicating: huge dark eyes like a *houri* of heaven with eyelashes so long they nearly touched her eyebrows and a mouth the colour of the rare wild strawberries he sometimes saw in the market. When she smiled she revealed her teeth, which were like a row of pearls. The porter nearly fell to the floor with his basket when this lady approached to see the goodies her sister had bought, overwhelmed as he was by her radiant beauty and her amber scent, which aroused all of his five senses. He let out a long sigh. The girls thought he was hurrying them up.

The shopper handed him one dinar, but the porter remained fixed to the spot, and so she asked him, "Why are you still here? Do you think that what I gave you isn't enough?" The third lady, who was the mistress of the house, handed him another dinar, but the porter shook his head and remained standing, reluctant to leave. Finally the mistress of the house asked him, "Tell us, porter, what's going on?"

"Please, I beg of you, ladies," the porter said, "correct me if I am mistaken but it seems to me that you live on your own without the presence of a man, is that so?"

"That is correct," the mistress of the house answered.

"How can that be, when God, being so generous with you three ladies, gave you everything—beauty, fine manners, fruit, meat, nuts and wine? Don't you believe that the happiness and good fortune of women cannot be attained without the company of men? It is certainly the case that a man cannot achieve pleasure without a woman. Remember also, 'The company of four is always better' as the proverb says, 'just as a steady table needs four legs and not three.'"

The mistress of the house answered, "Yes, you're right—we live on our own without men, we keep to ourselves, because we fear that if we entrust others with our secrets, they will not be kept and we will suffer as a result. As the poet said:

> " 'Guard your secrets closely
> When they're told they fly
> If unable to keep treasures in our own heart
> Who then can forbid another, yours to impart?'"

The porter said, "I'm just a mere porter, but I assure you ladies that I have studied literature and memorised poetry and above all I have learned the importance of revealing the good and concealing the bad. You may be certain that I am just as the poet described:

> " 'My secrets are locked
> In an impenetrable fortress
> To which the key has long vanished
> And the lock's forever tarnished.'"

The three ladies exchanged glances which suggested that they liked and appreciated what they'd heard and the porter sensed an understanding between them and felt emboldened to say, "Why don't you ladies let me stay with you, not as your companion but as your servant?"

The three women again exchanged glances and winks, and the mistress of the house said, "You know well how much we spent to get all these provisions. How can you contribute to our entertainment in return? Don't you know that 'without gain, love is not worth a grain'?"

"If you have nothing then you must leave with nothing," the doorkeeper added.

The shopper intervened, saying, "Stop teasing him, just listen to me, this porter served me today very well and he was so patient."

The porter took out the two dinars, telling them, "Please, ladies, take back your money. It is all that I have earned today, but my reward has been to spend time in your company."

"No, this is your money and you are welcome to join us," the mistress of the house told him.

At this, the shopper laid a table by the fountain, filling it with food and drink in beautiful ornamental dishes and cups. She asked everybody to come and sit down, poured herself a drink and offered one to the others. The porter bowed and drank his in one gulp, at which she said to him, "Drink it in good health."

The porter took her hand and kissed it and recited:

> "Share your cup only
> With those who are beloved and trusted,
> Those pure of heart and full of grace,
> For wine is delicious when shared with the sweet
> But acrid and foul with men of deceit."

Then the four continued to drink one cup after another. The porter, who was by now quite tipsy, stood and began to dance like a belly dancer, singing:

"Lover, raise your cup and let us frolic
The mezza is tasty and we are lusty
Forget the polo stick and the grassy meadows
I'm not yearning for the call of the sparrowhawk
Ribald revelry fills my mind
And the sound of lips sipping wine."

The three ladies giggled and laughed. They had by now lost all of their inhibitions. They danced with him. Then the shopper let her hair down, and it fell to her waist; she took off her outer garment and in her slip she stepped playfully into the water, and splashed the other three. The porter followed her into the water, and so did the two other girls, and they played together, all chasing each other. The porter hugged and kissed and flirted with the three of them, and finally the shopper got out of the water with her wet slip clinging to her breasts. The porter got out, too, and she made him sit beside her on the sofa, where she slapped him and bit his ear. The doorkeeper began to fondle his hair and pull it and the mistress of the house watched him intently with her beautiful eyes, as if she was devouring him.

Then the shopper jumped on to his lap. The porter kissed her on the mouth, bit her and pulled her towards him. Pointing between her thighs, she asked him, "What is this, my love?"

"Your cunt," said the porter.

"You have no shame, what is it?" the shopper said, pulling his ears and slapping his neck.

"Your womb, your clitoris, your hole, your well, your pussy, your slit, your egg factory."

The shopper boxed his ears playfully and then slapped him very hard and told him, "No, no, no!"

So the porter stood, crying out, "How am I to know what it is called when I have never met it before? I beg you, respected and good lady, to introduce me to it."

He gazed at her pussy and said, "I am known as the porter. What is your name?"

The women laughed until they nearly fell off their chairs and the mistress of the house laughed the hardest of all.

"Pleased to meet you, porter," the shopper answered. "My name is the basil that grows on the bridges."

Then the doorkeeper pushed the shopper from the porter's lap and sat down in her place. She pointed between her own thighs and asked, "What is this, my master, my love?"

"The basil that grows on the bridges," answered the porter.

But the doorkeeper slapped him, saying, "No, no, no!"

So the porter said to her, "All right, what then is its name?"

"The husked sesame," the doorkeeper answered.

Then the mistress of the house pushed the doorkeeper from the porter's lap and sat there herself. She pointed between her thighs and asked him, "Oh, light of my eye, what is this?"

"The basil that grows on the bridges, the husked sesame," answered the porter.

But the mistress of the house slapped and kicked him hard and pinched him on his cheeks, on his chest and on his arms, saying, "No, no, no!"

"What is it, then?" the porter cried out.

"It is the inn of Abu Masrur," the mistress of the house replied.

The porter laughed. "The inn of Abu Masrur! But, my beautiful ladies, I must tell you about my friend who is dear to my heart just as you are to me now, but he is cold and shivering and he wishes to rent a room at the inn of Abu Masrur. Have you guessed my friend's name?"

He pointed to his prick, and then he squeezed himself between the doorkeeper and the shopper and took the mistress of the house on his lap.

The three ladies were pleased that he understood their games and that his disposition seemed to match theirs so well. They showered him with names, "The stick, the thing, the pigeon, the panther, the shish kebab, the cock." The porter answered each time, "No, no, no!" pinching one woman, kissing another, nibbling at the third.

Finally, the three women said all at once, "All right then, you genius, what is his name?"

"His name is the smashing mule."

The three women exclaimed, "But we haven't heard of this name before and we bet you that no one in all of Baghdad has heard of it either. What does it mean?"

"The smashing mule is the strongest mule," the porter answered. "The savage one, who grazes on the basil that grows on the bridges, eats the husked sesame with his huge tongue and gallops inside the inn of Abu Masrur!"

The ladies stamped their feet and fell on their backs, laughing. They couldn't believe their luck at meeting this funny, flirtatious man. They fed him more food and gave him more to drink.

When night fell, the mistress of the house said to the porter, "It is time for you to leave. Go and put on your slippers and show us your beautiful back."

The porter sighed in disbelief, saying, "Leave you? Are you asking me to leave my soul behind and die? I have an idea, why don't the four of us turn night into day, and I promise that tomorrow morning we shall each depart to our own lives."

"Let him stay, sister," the shopper said to the mistress of the house. "He is so unique that even if we asked God for a man on the sacred night, when all wishes are granted, we wouldn't be sent one so fine as he."

So the mistress of the house agreed, saying to the porter, "You cannot spend the night with us unless you agree that no matter what your eyes may see, your tongue must freeze and not seek explanation, even if your curiosity should become unbearable."

The porter readily agreed, saying, "From this second I am dumb and blind."

He closed his eyes and began to fondle their breasts, saying, "What is this that I feel—I am blind."

The first two girls giggled, but the mistress of the house gestured to a door leading to another room, asking, "Have you read the inscription written there?"

He went over and read the words, "Speak not of what concerns you, lest you hear what does not please."

And so the porter said solemnly to the ladies, "I pledge that I shall speak not of my concerns."

Then the mistress of the house and the doorkeeper sat with the porter while the shopper lit candles and incense and joined them, and the four talked and drank wine and fondled one another until they heard a knocking at the door. The doorkeeper jumped up to answer it.

After a time she returned, bursting with laughter, and whispered, "Listen, there are three one-eyed dervishes at the door, with their heads shaved, and their eyebrows and beards shaved off. Each one is blind in the right eye. They claim to have arrived in Baghdad today and they're looking for somewhere to spend the night. They are prepared to sleep in our garden or the stables." She giggled, adding, "They look so funny, I bet you that they could pull a smile even from a new widow."

The three women exchanged looks and then the mistress of the house said, "Let them in, but on the same condition we made with the porter—that they become a pair of eyes and not tongues."

"You mean one eye," said the porter.

They all laughed. Then the doorkeeper hurried to fetch the three dervishes. They didn't disappoint, for they were as funny as she had described them. Everybody stood to greet them.

The dervishes bowed, saying, "We thank you, for we are indebted to you for your kindness."

They looked around them, enchanted with the beauty of the place. They sighed with admiration at the shining candles and the food on the table and pointed at the fountain in amazement. All of a sudden one of the dervishes saw the porter, who was stretched on the floor, exhausted by all the alcohol and cavorting with the girls. "He may be an Arab, but he is still a dervish like us."

Hearing this, the porter stood up. "Stop meddling, have you forgotten the condition of entering the house? Haven't you read the inscription on the door?"

The three dervishes read the inscription: "Speak not of what concerns you, lest you hear what does not please."

At this the dervishes said, "We promise, and please be assured that our heads are in your hands and we ask you to forgive us." The girls laughed and made the dervishes and the porter shake hands.

The shopper brought them food and drink and after they had eaten they thanked the ladies and asked for a tambourine, flute and Persian harp. The doorkeeper and the shopper brought out instruments and then the three dervishes tuned them and began to play and sing. The three ladies joined in with great passion until their voices rose higher than those of the dervishes and the porter.

All of a sudden they heard knocking at the door and the door-keeper rushed to see who was there. She returned, saying, "There are three merchants from the city of Mosul at the door. They claim that they arrived in Baghdad ten days ago and they're staying at the best inn. A fellow merchant invited them to dine at his home, and this merchant sent for musicians and women singers. They all got very drunk and made such a racket that the police raided the house. The three merchants fled by jumping over the wall. They ran until they heard our singing. They are terrified to go back to their inn, lest they encounter the police and be thrown in jail for being so inebriated. So they ask whether they can seek refuge here. They look very rich and dignified. One of them even kissed the ground before me."

The mistress of the house looked at the other two girls and saw the excitement on their faces. "Let them in," she said.

The doorkeeper disappeared and returned with the three merchants. Everyone in the hall stood to greet them.

"We are delighted and happy to have you and welcome you as our guests, but on one condition," the mistress of the house said.

"What is your condition, my lady?" one of the merchants asked.

The mistress of the house replied, "That you'll not enquire about anything that you see or hear in this house: speak not of what concerns you, lest you hear what does not please."

"Be assured that your condition is accepted," one of the merchants replied.

Everyone sat down, except for the shopper and the doorkeeper, who rushed to get food and drink. But the three merchants did not partake of the wine or the food brought to them. They seemed astonished to see that the dervishes had each lost their right eye, and that they had found themselves in such a magnificent home, belonging to three women of such incomparable beauty, charm, eloquence and generosity and yet living with the three dervishes.

The merchants were so entranced by all that they saw that they had not heard the snores of the porter, who was so drunk that he lay on the ground motionless. Soon, when the ladies too were very drunk, the mistress of the house said, "Come, sisters, let us do our duty."

The doorkeeper got up, lit more candles, replenished the incense and cleaned the table, while the shopper went to the porter and woke him, saying, "Get up, lazybones, and lend us a hand."

The porter got up, still unsteady on his feet, and asked, "What's up?"

He followed the shopper as she moved over to a large closet, inside which were two black bitch hounds, with chains around their necks. The shopper instructed the porter to lead them to the centre of the hall, where everyone was sitting. She rolled up her sleeves and picked up a braided whip. Then she returned to the closet and took out a bag made of yellow silk satin and adorned with tassels. She sat down facing the mistress of the house and took out an oud, which she tuned and began to play, singing along with great passion.

> "Oh window of my love
> Bring me lust upon the breeze."

The mistress of the house asked the porter to bring the two dogs to her. As soon as the dogs saw her they shook their heads as if trying to hide and began to whine, but the mistress of the house came down with the whip with heavy blows on the bitches' flanks, unmoved by the piteous howling and weeping of the animals, counting the blows of her whip.

The shopper still sang, in despair and pain:

> "Oh window of my love
> Bring me lust upon the breeze,

> If your mother asks for you
> I'll hide you in my hair,
> My warmly woven hair."

At this the doorkeeper wailed and shrieked "Oh oh oh," her wails mingling with the singing, the howling of the dogs and the mistress of the house counting the strokes as she beat the dogs. The shopper rolled her head against the oud, shaking the instrument on her chest as if desiring that it would produce melodies akin to the beating of her heart.

> "Oh window of my love
> Bring me lust upon the breeze,
> If your mother looks for you
> I'll hide you beneath my sash,
> And tie it around my waist."

The three girls continued with their singing, screaming, beating, shrieking and wailing. The hearts of the seven guests were ignited with disgust and curiosity at what they were witnessing. They tried to pretend that everything was fine, all except for one of the merchants, who couldn't restrain himself, and began to whisper to his friends. But the other merchants asked him to be quiet.

So the mistress of the house continued beating the dogs and counting the strokes, while the shopper continued to sing:

> "Oh window of my love
> Bring me lust upon the breeze,
> If your mother looks for you
> I'll hide you in my eyes
> Where pitch-black kohl resides."

As soon as she had finished singing, the doorkeeper, who was sitting facing the shopper, moaned "Oh oh oh" and then began to scream. She wrapped her hands around her neck but rather than strangle herself she tore her dress open, from the collar to the hem, threw herself to the ground and began to convulse, revealing to the mortification of all those present that her body was covered with black, blue and purple marks as though she too had been whipped, like the bitches. The shopper put the oud on the chair and hurried to her, taking rose water to revive her and covering her with her shawl. The mistress of the house stopped beating the dogs when she reached three hundred strokes and she threw the whip on to the floor, kneeled down and held the quivering dogs in an embrace, weeping herself. She produced a handkerchief from her pocket, dried the dogs' tears, pleading with them to stop crying. She kissed them on the head and then gave them to the porter so he could take them back to the closet, and hurried to the doorkeeper, embracing her, wrapping her in her coat and the three girls wept quietly.

Silence fell upon the room, but the expressions of the seven guests spoke volumes about their revulsion and disgust. The questions gnawed at them: what evil had befallen the doorkeeper's body and why had the mistress of the house beaten the two bitches until they nearly fainted and yet wept for them, kissed them, and wiped away their tears?

The mistress of the house and the shopper helped the doorkeeper to stand and took her to the closet, where they changed her dress, leaving the seven men fidgeting in their seats. The merchant who had spoken before whispered to his friend, who gestured that he should remain silent, pointing to the inscription on the door, but the merchant felt that he could no longer bear what he had witnessed. "Something must be done," he whispered to his friend in anger.

"You must remember what we have promised the three ladies," his friend replied calmly.

But the merchant turned to the dervishes and asked them, "Can you please explain to us what is going on?"

One of the dervishes replied, "By God—we came here just a short while before you, and now we wish that we had never set foot in this house and witnessed such heartrending sights but instead sought refuge anywhere else—even on the rubbish heap of this great city!"

Hearing this, the merchant winked at the porter and asked him the same question.

"You're asking me? I haven't set eyes on this house before today, although I was born in Baghdad. But I do know one thing that you do not. These ladies live alone, without a man."

"Did you say that they live without a man? Then listen to me, all of you," the merchant said. "Since we are seven men and they are three women, let us ask them for an explanation. If they refuse us then we shall take them by force."

The men all agreed, except for one of the other merchants, who protested, "Have you all forgotten that we are their guests and that we agreed and swore to adhere to their conditions? And who knows why they have chosen to keep to themselves?"

But the first merchant was determined to know the truth and he continued to try to convince the porter that he must find out what was going on.

The mistress of the house, who now, with the other girls, was behaving as if nothing had happened, became aware of the men arguing, and asked, "What is the reason for this clamour? What is the matter?"

The porter gathered all of his courage and said, "The gentlemen wish to know why you beat the two bitches until you had no strength left and yet then wept for them, kissed them, wiped away their tears. And they wish to know why the lady tore off her clothes to reveal such terrible marks on her body? Why had she too been flogged with a whip like a man?"

Hearing this, the mistress of the house turned to the men. "Is what the porter tells me true?"

"Yes," they all replied—all except for the one merchant.

The mistress of the house's face darkened with rage. "Did you not agree to ask us nothing? You have wronged us gravely, and yet we too are at fault. We were mistaken to have opened our doors to you and welcomed you."

She struck the floor three times, crying out, "Come at once."

In no time at all a secret door opened and seven black men emerged, waving their swords in their hands. Each quickly seized one of the guests, and tied him by the hands, and then the seven were bound to each other and led to the centre of the hall.

One of the executioners addressed the mistress of the house. "Our most noble and virtuous lady. Shall we behead them this instant?"

Hearing this, the porter wailed and wept, pointed at the dervishes and said, "I am innocent. I don't wish to die because of the mistakes of others. These dervishes were indeed a bad omen." He began to recite:

> "Great is the mercy of the Almighty,
> And greatest when bestowed upon the weak.
> Now upon our bond of undying friendship I implore you,
> Never cast aside an old friend when a new one you seek."

Hearing this, the three ladies nearly giggled, especially the mistress of the house. But she controlled herself and ignored him, saying, "Wait, let me question our guests before you strike off their heads."

She addressed the dervishes and the merchants.

"Were you not men of power and distinction you wouldn't have dared to offend us in this way. So tell—who are you?"

The merchant whispered to his friend, the reluctant one, "Go ahead and tell her who we are, so that we are not slain by mistake."

And his friend answered, "Be patient, I am trying to protect you from the embarrassment of having to plead our integrity."

The mistress of the house now turned to the dervishes. "Are you brothers?" she asked.

"No, our gracious lady," was their reply.

Then she asked them, "Were you each born with one eye?"

They answered her together. "By God, we were not, our gracious lady, we were each born with two eyes. But each of us suffered a great misfortune, which left us with only one."

"Are you friends?" the mistress of the house asked.

"We met only tonight."

"I want each of you to tell your story, explain to us what brought you to our home and if I am convinced by your tale, and feel sympathy, then I shall forgive you and free you," the mistress of the house told the bound men.

Then she turned to the executioner, saying, "If not, I shall order you to cut off each man's head."

The porter was the first to tell his story. "Mistress, you know all too well how I came to this house, but you are not aware that I am the brother of a fisherman, who until this very year was poor, when God Almighty made him so rich that he became a jeweller and even Queen Zubeida, the wife of the Commander of the Faithful, Haroun al-Rashid, sends her ladies-in-waiting to purchase for her the most magnificent precious stones. But I refused to work in my brother's shop, because I so loved the hustle and bustle of the market and the people who frequent it, both sellers and buyers, especially if they are women as pretty, sophisticated and respectable as your sister." He gestured to the shopper. "After she hired me, I followed her with my basket like her shadow, from the fruit and vegetables, to the incense and candles, pistachio nuts and sweets. But when she stopped at the butcher's and stroked a lamb on the head, I thought that she was buying him and so I turned to her and said, 'I wish you'd told me when you'd hired me that you were after a live lamb, so that I might have brought a mule and carriage.'"

Every one in the hall laughed, but the mistress of the house interrupted, saying, "Stroke your head with relief that you still have it, and leave."

But the porter said, "But my gracious lady, can I not stay to hear the tales of the others?"

"Yes you may," the mistress of the house told him. She turned to the three dervishes and said, "Let us hear your tales first. You three shall decide who will begin." The dervishes looked fearfully from one to the other as if the task of telling their story was almost as terrifying as facing death itself. After some time, one of them, who looked especially ravaged by fortune, quietly began.

The First Dervish

I stand here before you, my lady, to tell you my story—how I became a dervish with a plucked eye.

I was born Aziz, the son of one of the greatest merchants of Persia. I had a favourite cousin called Aziza and we played together every day, some days happily, other days we would fall out and argue. But we loved each other dearly. Our fathers agreed to marry us as soon as we had reached the age of puberty. But then death carried off both her parents, and Aziza came to live with us. We were not kept apart, indeed, we shared everything, even a bed, and when we had both reached puberty my father decided that it was time to draw up a marriage contract and preparations for a wedding began. The marble floors throughout the house were polished, new rugs laid out, the walls decorated with brocade hangings, and then fine dishes and sweetmeats were created for the banquet.

On the promised day, my mother sent me to the public hammam, where I was pummelled and massaged with amber and musk and dressed in the finest of suits and then sprinkled with perfume. I left the hammam and set out for home, but when I passed a lane in which a friend of mine lived, I decided to knock at his door and invite him to attend my wedding. His mother told me he would be home soon—would I wait for him? I strolled down the lane a little way to wait, noting that each person that I passed inhaled the pleasant fragrance which wafted out before me. I found a little bench and sat down, first carefully spreading out my handkerchief so as not to soil my beautiful suit and upset my mother.

Suddenly a white handkerchief fluttered down from above like a tiny butterfly. I caught it in my hand—it was as delicate as the breeze. I looked up to see who had dropped the handkerchief and saw a young woman at a window. She was so beautiful that she could have said to the moon, "Step down, for I am more beautiful than you." She smiled and I smiled back and then she put one finger in her mouth, and then she joined her middle finger to her index finger and hid both between her two breasts. Then she disappeared. With a throbbing heart I waited for her to reappear. Never before had I experienced such feelings! I glanced down at the handkerchief and saw that it was knotted. When I untied the knot a slip of paper fell from it, upon which were written these lines:

> "My lover asked, 'Why does your writing scarcely scratch the
>   page?'
> I answered softly, 'Because my fate as a lover is slowly withering
>   away.'"

I remained sitting on the bench, with one eye on the window and the other on the handkerchief, filled with desire and longing, desperate to be with this woman. Only after I had finally given up hope of her reappearing did I return home, distraught and sad, her face etched upon my imagination, my hand clenched around the handkerchief, the scrap of paper hidden in my pocket.

When I reached the house I found Aziza weeping.

"Where were you?" she asked. She described how everybody, including the greatest merchants and emirs, the *kadi*, the witnesses and relatives gathered and waited in vain for me for several hours, but eventually gave up when I did not appear. My father was so furious with me that he swore that he would not draw up the contract for another year.

"I was so worried about you, cousin. I thought that some terrible fate must have befallen you. But now I see that you are safe, I can thank God. Tell me, what happened?"

And so I answered, "What happened was bizarre and strange."

I told her about the young woman and showed her the handkerchief and the slip of paper. She took the handkerchief and smelled it, read the lines written on the scrap of paper, and tears ran down her cheeks. But I could think only of the mysterious gestures of the woman, and so I asked my cousin, "Aziza, can you help me to understand what she was trying to tell me?"

She wiped her tears away with her sleeve and said, "If you asked me for my eye, cousin, I would pull it out from beneath my eyelid. First of all, the handkerchief is the lover's greeting. By placing the finger in her mouth she is saying that you are the soul in her body and that she would hold on to you as firmly as the teeth sit in the mouth. The two lines of poetry are obvious—she is assuring you that her soul is bound to yours. And finally, when she put her fingers between her breasts she was telling you to come back and meet her in two days and relieve her of her distress at being parted from you."

I accepted my cousin's interpretation, for she was more mature than I, even though we were the same age, and she understood the ways of the world.

"But, cousin, I don't think that I can wait two whole days to see her."

But Aziza took my head in her hands and rested it on her lap, stroked my hair, consoled me, and entertained me until the time came for me to meet the young woman again. Aziza helped me to dress and sprinkled drops of perfume on my clothes. She told me that I must be strong and determined. "Aziz," she said, "all I want is to see you happy."

Out in the street, I felt that everything around me had disappeared, the shops, houses, passers-by. I heard nothing.

I reached her window, saw her looking down, took a deep breath and almost fainted. This time she held a red handkerchief in her hand, which she lowered and raised outside the window three times in the direction of the lane below. Then she spread out her five fingers and struck her breasts with her palm. Next she produced a mirror, which she held out of the window and then put her head out for a few moments before closing the window and disappearing. I found myself standing beneath the window for a long time after she had gone, mesmerised and yet unable to comprehend her signs. At last, at midnight, I gave up hope of seeing her again and made my way reluctantly back home, dragging my feet as I went.

When I arrived, I found Aziza weeping and singing to herself:

> "I love him; oh how I love him:
> His love has occupied my heart."

When she saw me she dried her tears, and lifted her head, as if asking me what had happened. I began to tell her the story, but I found myself fainting dead away. When I came to, my cousin was holding me and wiping the tears from my face.

I told her everything and she sighed, saying, "You should not be distressed, cousin, her signs must give you great hope. The five fingers mean return to me in five days. The red handkerchief and the mirror and her head out of the window mean sit in the dyer's studio until you hear from me."

"How right you are, cousin," I said, joyfully. "There is a Jewish dyer of wool and rugs in the lane where she lives."

But when I realised that I wouldn't see the young woman again for five days, I wept.

"Be strong, my cousin," Aziza told me. "Think of the lovers who wait month after month—even years—before they are finally united. Rely upon me and I promise that I will help and protect you, just as the dove protects its chicks beneath its wings."

She got up and prepared me some food and drink, but I could not swallow even one morsel. Aziza sought to distract me with tales of love and passion, leaving my side only when exhaustion overtook me and I slept. When I awoke, even in the dead of night, I would find her beside me, tears coursing down her cheeks.

The five days dragged, as if it was five centuries that had passed. When the time came I left my bed and found hot water waiting for me. I bathed and dressed in fresh clothes.

"God be with you," Aziza said to me. "I hope that you get what you want from your beloved."

I hurried to the Jewish dyer's shop and to my mortification found that not only was the shop closed up, but so was the young woman's window. I thought of taking my own life, such was my distress, but instead I remained like a statue on the bench beneath her window until the hour of midnight struck and I dragged myself home. I found Aziza standing, one arm clutching a peg on the wall, the other pressed to her heart, sighing and singing to herself:

"The furnace in my heart could melt copper,
My tears could drench thirty deserts.
My love can be no greater than what I cherish,
Yet my lover sees my passion as a blemish."

As soon as she saw me, Aziza wiped away her tears and smiled. "Why have you not spent the night with your beloved and finally achieved that for which you have ached?"

Realising that she was mocking me, I kicked her with all my strength, so that she fell to the ground and struck her head upon the threshold. Blood poured from her wound, but she got up without uttering a word and wiped her face.

"Nothing happened, just nothing! That is why I am in such a rage," I told her.

"You are mistaken," Aziza told me. "There is good reason for hope in the lady's actions. She wishes to know whether you truly love her and so she has hidden herself away in order to test you. You must go to her tomorrow, for if you do not, she will assume that you have no patience. Oh, cousin! I am glad that happiness is within reach!"

My cousin's words failed to soothe me, however, and I felt only more desperate. She offered me some food, but I pushed it away, shouting, "Every damned lover is but a fool who can no longer eat or sleep."

"But that is precisely what love is about," Aziza told me.

At first light the next day I ran down the lane and sat on the bench beneath the window. After a very short time the woman opened the window and when she saw me she smiled, her smile grew wider and she laughed! She disappeared for a moment and then returned carrying a lamp and a potted plant. She let her hair fall over her face and then put the lamp over the top of the plant and slammed the window shut.

It is strange how my love seemed to grow and intensify and yet at the same time I was tiring of these mysterious signals. I had yet to hear her utter a single word. Perhaps she was deaf and dumb?

I returned home, yet again perplexed and melancholy, but still deeply in love. I found my cousin with her head bandaged, weeping and singing to herself:

"Wherever you may come and go,
You are still secure in the depths of my heart."

She saw me through her tears and fell silent for a moment, then roused herself and asked me what had happened.

"At last you have reached what your soul has always desired," she told me when I described what had taken place. "When she let her hair loose around her face she was telling you to come to her at night, when darkness falls on the day, the pot means that you should meet her in her garden and the lamp tells you to seek out a light in the darkness."

And yet rather than feel joy at this, I shouted at my cousin. "Each time you promise that I will finally meet her and yet I don't. I think that perhaps your interpretations are wrong."

Aziza laughed, saying, "Just be patient, and don't forget that God is always with those who show forbearance."

I sat down and pleaded, "God, let the sun set even before it is time for night to fall."

I fidgeted away the hours, while my cousin sat nearby, sighing and weeping. Soon night fell and I was overjoyed and raced to the door, as if someone had released me from a long imprisonment.

Aziza called me back and gave me a piece of musk, saying, "Chew it when you see her and when your beloved gives you what you so desire, recite these lines:

" 'Lovers, in the name of God,
Tell me how can one relieve this endless desperation?' "

When I reached the lane I circled the house of the young woman and found my way into her garden at the back, for she had left the gate open for me. I followed a light in the distance and found a beautiful pergola inlaid with ebony and ivory, with a lamp hanging inside and furnished with comfortable seats and feather mattresses and cushions dotted about. Candles flickered and I could hear the soothing sound of a water fountain, next to which stood a table, spread with flowers and herbs and upon which stood a jug of wine and many delicacies, grilled chicken and game birds, fruit and sweetmeats. I waited there for many hours and when she did not come I realised I was famished and I fell upon the food as if it was the young woman I was finally devouring. I ate until I was full and then I stretched myself happily out among the cushions to wait some more.

I woke suddenly, hot and drenched in sweat. The sun was beating down on me, as if it was smothering me with its rays. It was morning and I jumped up as though I'd been bitten by a snake. A piece of coal and some salt had been placed upon my stomach.

The garden was empty and there was no sign of the pergola or the cushions, the candles or the beautifully laden table. Filled with rage and utter despair I returned to my cousin once more, to find her weeping and saying:

"Forgive me if I shed these black tears.
But your beloved loves you back
While the one I adore doesn't love me at all.
How compassionate and kind God is to you."

She stopped crying and came over to me and sniffed at my clothing.

"That is not the scent of one who has enjoyed his beloved," she said. "And now I fear for you, Aziz. I know full well that women may tease men, but this woman has deliberately wounded your heart—she has aimed to hurt you as much as she possibly could. The salt that she left on your stomach means you are a pallid dish which needs salt to add flavour, lest you be spat out. And as if this was not insult enough, she leaves you with a piece of charcoal, meaning that she wishes God would blacken your face, since you claim to be in love but your passion really lies in eating and drinking—you are a charlatan lover. So, my cousin, this woman is hard and cruel, it is she who is deceitful, not you. Why did she not wake you when she found you asleep? How I wish that God would release you from her clutches!"

"On the contrary," I thought to myself as I listened to Aziza. "My beloved was right—I fell asleep when it is known that true lovers are insomniacs. I was unjust to myself and to my lover when I allowed greed to overtake desire."

I thumped my chest and wept at my bad fortune, and pleaded with my cousin to help me, threatening to kill myself if she would not. Aziza said, "If you asked for my eye, cousin, I would pull it out from beneath my eyelid for you. How I wish I could come and go from this house as I please so I might bring the two of you together, for your sake rather than for hers. Listen to me, Aziz. Go back to her again, but this time you must not touch even one morsel of food, for that will be the spur to your appetite and you know that a full belly will only make you sleepy. Go to her and don't forget to recite these lines before you leave:

"'Lovers, in the name of God,
Tell me how can one relieve this endless desperation?'"

I entered the garden and saw that everything was as it had been the night before. This time, I didn't touch a morsel of food; instead, I sat and walked and waited, but slowly boredom crept upon me and I found myself at the table once more, saying that I'd have just one spoon of yoghurt to soothe my beating heart. But it was just as Aziza told me: one mouthful only aroused my appetite and I was unable to stop sampling the many dishes laid out on the table. Before I knew it I was full, but now, instead of lying down, I sat with my head in my hands. And yet, despite my efforts, I found that I fell into a deep sleep and dreamed that I was fully awake, slapping my face and sprinkling my eyes with water and rubbing my eyes so as not to doze off and to remain alert for our encounter. But in reality I missed my opportunity and once more the sun woke me, slashing me with its hot whips, and I found myself staggering for home, weeping. There I found Aziza, the tears running down her cheeks as she sang:

"My heart is shattered,
My body is bleeding.
Yet whatever pain my cousin inflicts on me
I welcome it with all my soul."

I felt furiously angry, I reproached and cursed her and threw the items my beloved had left on my stomach at her. But my cousin ignored my tantrum and my angry words and knelt before me, saying, "This large dice means that although you were waiting for her, your heart was absent. With the date stone she is telling you that were you her true lover you would have stayed awake, for your heart would've been on fire, just as the date stone ignites the coal. As for the carob seed, she means that you must prepare yourself for separation from her and endure it with the patience of Job."

When I heard the word "separation" I clutched my cousin's dress and wept and pleaded, "Help me, Aziza, and save me before I perish and die."

And my cousin, who seemed on that day distant and distracted (although I didn't care to know by what), answered me in a low voice. "I feel as though my thoughts are tossed upon a raging sea."

She fell silent for a while but then seemed to take pity on me, for she said, "Go to her tonight and reconcile with her. I cannot give you advice other than these words, 'Do not eat. Do not eat.'"

Then she prepared me a delicious meal and fed it to me herself, as if I were a lamb, so that I would not be tempted by the aroma of the delicacies that would be laid out before me in the garden that evening.

And so I returned that evening, dressed in a new suit which Aziza had sewn for me, and which she had carefully dressed me in, making me first promise to say to the girl:

"Lovers, in the name of God,
Tell me how can one relieve this endless desperation?"

I found myself once more in the garden, tense and waiting for the woman, just like a tiger ready to pounce. So attuned was I to the tiniest of sounds that I heard even the minute rustling of a nightingale preparing itself for sleep. But the silence and tranquillity, with the moon and stars hanging above me, and the intensity of my desire and passion, made me relax a little and pour myself a glass of wine, so confident was I that I would not fall asleep. I poured myself a second glass, pulling my eyes open all the while to ensure that they were not drooping, for I thought that a little more wine would help me to be lucid and eloquent when I finally met my beloved. And then, when she again failed to appear, my mood changed to one of utter irritation and impatience and so I drank glass after glass, until I lost count of how much wine I had consumed. And then I slept, just as I had on the two previous evenings. I was woken again by the fierce rays of the sun, and found that I was stretched out in the garden, with a knife and a copper coin upon my stomach.

I raced back home with the knife in my hand, and I must have looked insane, for people shrank back and even ran to avoid my path. As I reached our home, I heard the keening of my cousin:

> "I am alone in this cursed house.
> Its walls tighten around my soul
> Its windows waft towards me the foulest fumes
> Its doors clench me by the throat."

Her words moved me as if she was expressing what I myself felt so powerfully in my heart and mind. It seemed that I lost consciousness for a time and then I woke to find my face drenched in rose water.

"The coin is her right eye and the knife is for slaughter," Aziza told me.

I screamed in horror, "Oh God, is my beloved going to take out her eye?"

But my cousin said, "No, don't be alarmed, she is telling you, 'By God the Magnificent, I swear by my right eye that if you ever come back to my garden and sleep, be certain that I will slaughter you with this knife.'"

I shook and trembled, not with fright but out of love and compassion. My cousin registered the half smile on my face and guessed what I was thinking.

"I am so worried about you, cousin," she pleaded with me. "This woman is hard, calculating, crafty and her heart is filled with hatred, tarnished black."

But I pleaded with her in turn, "Help me and tell me what to do, Aziza."

"If you asked for my eye, my cousin Aziz, I would pull it out from beneath my eyelid for you. Come to bed and sleep, this is what you need now, try to sleep as though you are hibernating."

She took me by the hand and led me to my bed, where she massaged my shoulders and limbs, fanning my face until I fell asleep and didn't wake until the sun had set. When Aziza saw that I had woken, she jumped up, wiping away her tears. Then she forced me to eat a large meal, made me drink tamarind, washed my face and hands and then took me in her arms and held me tight to her, saying, "Aziz, you must listen carefully. Your beloved will not appear before the last hours of the night. So do not sit and wait, but seek to keep yourself occupied. Take a stroll in the garden, making sure to smell the flowers, especially the jasmine, for its fragrance will surely dominate your senses and overpower the aroma of the banquet."

I was careful to take Aziza's advice, and nearly all of the night had passed, and the cocks were crowing their first, when I heard a slight sound. I turned and was confronted by the sight of my beloved entering the garden, accompanied by ten women slaves, just like the moon surrounded by stars. She laughed when she saw me, saying, "I can see now that you are a true lover, for you have not been taken by sleep, so agonised were you by the fear that you would never see me."

She bade her slaves to leave us and we fell into each other's arms and kissed, I sucked her top lip and she sucked my lower one and then as she undid her drawers I found that my desire and excitement acted on their own, working on her until her limbs surrendered to me. I made her reach the seventh heaven of ecstasy and then I followed her, losing myself completely in the moment. When we both came slowly back from our trance I heard myself declaring to her that I was born as of that moment and that my soul from now on lay in her hands.

When morning came I whispered many amorous things in her ear and bit her gently on the breast so that she might remember me throughout the day. I knelt and kissed her legs and feet and in return she produced a handkerchief from her pocket and gave it to me, saying, "Here, take this to keep." It bore an embroidered picture of a gazelle.

I put it in my pocket and we agreed to meet that night and every night, for ever. I returned home in an intoxication of passion, swaying left and right.

I entered the house to find my cousin in bed, but she jumped up quickly to greet me, wiping away the tears with her sleeve as they fell down her cheeks. She knew without having to ask that I had finally achieved what I so desired and so she asked me, "Did you recite to her the lines, as I asked of you?"

I replied that I had forgotten to do so, and showed her the handkerchief with the gazelle embroidered upon it. My cousin examined it carefully and then asked if she could keep it. I readily agreed and when the time came for me to go to my beloved, Aziza reminded me that I must recite the lines to her. I had to confess that I had forgotten them, and so she repeated them to me, over and over.

I made my way to the garden, murmuring the lines to myself so as to memorise them. There she was, waiting for me. We flew into each other's arms and then she threw herself on my lap, until we groaned with pleasure, and then we ate and drank and then started to make love all over again, until the break of day.

Before I left her, I remembered to say the lines Aziza had taught me:

"Lovers, in the name of God,
Tell me how can one relieve this endless desperation?"

Hearing these lines, my beloved's eyes filled with tears, and she said back to me:

"He should conceal his love and hide
Showing only his patience and humility."

I reached home, overjoyed because I had remembered to carry out my cousin's wishes, but I found Aziza ill in bed with my mother sitting beside her, trying to console her.

"Did you say the lines to her?" Aziza asked immediately, even though she was very unwell.

I answered her happily, "Yes," and she said this back to me:

"He should conceal his love and hide
Showing only his patience and humility."

Hearing my words, my cousin writhed in her bed like a snake. My mother shouted at me, "Have you no shame, you selfish, frivolous and feckless young man! How dare you spend the whole night out of the house and then return without asking after any of us—not even Aziza, who is in such poor health!"

I could think of nothing to say, other than that every breath I took was for my beloved, and so I remained silent. When my mother finally left us, Aziza told me the answer I was to give to my beloved:

"He tried to show fair patience but could only find
A heart that was filled with unease."

I recited these lines to my beloved that night, after another reunion which words cannot describe. My beloved wept, just as she had the first time I'd recited Aziza's lines to her, and answered with these lines:

"If he cannot counsel his patience to conceal his secrets
Nothing will serve him better than death."

When I returned home, Aziza was not waiting for me, but lay in bed, while my mother tried to get her to eat and drink. I noticed how pale my cousin was, how her eyes had sunk into her face and how emaciated she was. I felt great pity overwhelm me and so I approached her bed as she whispered to me, "Aziz, dearest to my heart, did you recite the lines to her?" I nodded, assuring her that I had done as she wished, and recited the answer:

"If he cannot counsel his patience to conceal his secrets
Nothing will serve him better than death."

How I wished then that I had remained silent, because she fainted when she heard my words. My mother came in and sprinkled rose water on her face and revived her. I sat beside her, trying to comfort and soothe her. Aziza smiled at me with the utmost tenderness and made me memorise another couplet for my beloved that evening.

"I have heard, obeyed, and now must I die.
Salutations to she who tore us apart."

After we had made love later that evening, I recited these lines, and my beloved cried out loud in sorrow and said, "Oh God, the one who spoke these lines has died."

She wept and asked who this person was. "My cousin Aziza," I explained, "who lives for our union and who was waiting for me to come back from the hammam on the day our contract of marriage was to be signed, while I sat before your window, hypnotised, as still as a statue with a bird perched on its head."

I told her that Aziza had been the one who had deciphered all of the signs and messages, and that it was she we must thank, for it was only because of Aziza that I had reached the garden and consummated my desire for her.

My beloved sighed and spoke as though addressing Aziza directly, "What a pity, Aziza, that you so regretted your youth." And then she urged me, "Go and see her at once, before she dies."

I hurried back home, greatly distressed, and when I reached our home I heard great cries and wails and weeping and I was told that my cousin had died. My mother attacked me, weeping. "May God never forgive you for her loss and regard you as solely to blame for Aziza's death."

We attended her funeral and buried her, and my mother never ceased to ask me, "What have you done to cause her to die from pain and grief?"

"I have done nothing, mother," was my answer.

But my mother continued to reproach me, saying, "I don't believe you. Tell me what went on between you, because as Aziza lay dying she opened her eyes and asked me to tell you that she would never blame you and that she prayed that God would not punish you, since all that you had done was take her from this world to the eternal one. And she asked me to urge you to say to the one whom you visit each night, 'Loyalty is good; treachery is bad.' She hoped that these words would help you and as she died she said that she felt pity for you, in this life and in the next."

She wailed and moaned, and added, "My Aziza left you something, but she made me promise that I would give it to you only when I see you wailing and mourning for her."

And yet, despite my great sadness for my cousin, I found myself hurrying at the usual time to the garden, with nothing in my heart except passion and desire for my beloved and nothing in my mind but her beautiful face and lovely body. As soon as she saw me entering the garden she asked about my cousin and I told her that she had died. She pulled herself from my arms, saying, "You caused her to regret her youth and you killed her."

But I assured my lover that I was not responsible for her death and I repeated Aziza's instructions, saying, "Loyalty is good; treachery is bad."

When my beloved heard this, she wept, saying, "May God Almighty have mercy on Aziza, for she saved you from me even after death. She knew that I intended to harm you, but now be assured that I shall not."

I was surprised and shocked by her words, and so I asked her, "Hurt me? But are we not lovers, does each of us not feel only compassion and loyalty to the other?"

"You're so young," she answered, "and your heart is innocent, while we women have our wiles and tricks. You must promise not to trust any woman, young or old, except for me, especially now that your cousin is no longer here to protect you."

Then she asked me to take her to Aziza's grave and she carved these words on my cousin's headstone:

"I passed an ancient grave
On which grew seven red anemones.
'Whose tomb is this?' I asked
And the Earth replied,
'Tread carefully, a lover lies here.'"

She then distributed alms for the soul of Aziza to the needy and the poor.

A year passed, and yet my beloved waited for me each night as if on a hot griddle, while I would pounce upon her as if I was an eagle. We would cling to each other and make love with great fervour, and we rarely mentioned poor Aziza. If ever we spoke of her, my beloved would sigh and say, "How I wish that I had met her and knew her story, for then I would have been more careful."

Everything continued smoothly and with great happiness, until one day as I was heading for the garden, an old woman stopped me and asked if I would read to her a letter from her son, from whom she'd had no word since he'd departed on a voyage.

In spite of my state of great intoxication and desire, I agreed to help her. I read the letter and assured the old woman that her son was alive and well and then I set out once again, but the old woman followed me and asked if I was willing to read the letter to her daughter, because she would refuse to believe that her brother was safe. "Just read the letter out loud from the alleyway," she pleaded, "and then my daughter will hear you and believe that her brother is alive."

The old woman hurried to the door and opened it and I saw a hand stretched out holding the letter, and a melodious voice called, "Is that you, mother?" But as I drew closer the old woman pushed me into the house and locked the door and I realised that I had fallen into a trap. The girl who stood before me was both beautiful and coquettish. She asked me, in a voice which had now become quite harsh, "Tell me, Aziz, do you love life or death?"

"Life, of course," I answered.

"Great! Then marry me," was her reply.

"I would hate to marry someone like you!" I shrieked.

"If you marry me you will save yourself from the daughter of Alsawahi Aldawahi "

"But who is the daughter of Alsawahi Aldawahi?"

Hearing this, the girl called to her mother, "Come here, mother. He claims not to know the daughter of Alsawahi Aldawahi!" She cackled with laughter, and her mother joined in.

"So you don't know who she is?" the girl said, still laughing. "She's the one you've been with every night, for one year, four months, and two days, the one you meet each night in the garden and she is the one who kills her lovers, one by one. Why has she not yet killed you? This is what we wish to know."

My heart was pounding at what I had heard. "Do you know her, then?" I asked.

"I know her, just as time knows all tragedies," was the girl's reply. "But what I do not know is how you have survived."

I found myself telling the girl and her mother the whole story, about my beloved and how Aziza had helped me to be with her. And then I repeated Aziza's final message to my beloved: "Loyalty is good; treachery is bad."

"Now I understand," the girl said. "Do you know that these words saved you from the daughter of Alsawahi Aldawahi? Listen, you're still a young man, unaware of the ways of women and the treachery of older women in particular. Let us marry. I shall require nothing of you except that you live with me like a cock."

"A cock? But I don't know how a cock lives!"

The girl laughed and so did her mother and the girl laughed harder and harder, until she fell down on her bottom, saying, "What does a cock do with his life other than eat, drink and fuck?"

I was embarrassed and didn't know where to look. But the girl showed no shame, instead she ordered me, "Go on, prepare yourself to be strong, and to fuck me just as hard and often as you can!"

Then her mother appeared with the four witnesses. I looked towards the door, thinking I must escape, but the girl said, "Everything is locked tight, even an ant could not get out of here."

Her mother hurried up and lit four candles and then a notary drew up the marriage contract. The girl testified on her own behalf that she had received the full dowry payment from me, both instalments, paid the notary and then bade everyone leave. Then she disappeared and returned wearing only a see-through nightdress, threw herself on the bed and began to moan and writhe, murmuring, "I am your wife now."

She kept on moaning and writhing until I could wait no longer. I thrust into her and we reached our climax together, screaming with joy and ecstasy until our voices reached the street. But when I woke the next morning I was gripped by fear and panic at what I had done, and I trembled to think that I had stayed away from my beloved that evening. I hurried to dress, thinking all the time of some diabolical excuse for my absence, which would convince her of my innocence.

But the girl rose from the bed and stood with her hands on her hips, saying, "Where do you think you're going? Do you believe that entering a bath is the same as leaving it? Do you think that I am like the daughter of Alsawahi Aldawahi—that you can spend the night with me and leave in the morning? Well, I have something to tell you about this house. It is locked up all year round, except for one day."

I was mortified to hear this and I looked around to find a way to flee. "If I were you, I wouldn't waste my time trying to escape, for the house is sealed, the gates, the doors and the windows. But don't worry, we have enough provisions to last us a whole year. I promise that you shall eat only the choicest delicacies and that the months will pass by in the blink of an eye, if one lives happily, like a cock."

She laughed and I laughed with her, and she spread herself out on the bed, moaning, and in this way I was imprisoned for an entire year, which ended with her bearing me a son.

At the beginning of the new year, the huge gates swung open and the doors and windows were flung wide and men hurried in bearing provisions. I rose quickly to my feet, thinking that I would leave, but my wife made me wait until the evening, saying, "You must leave at exactly the time you arrived."

I was terrified that she would imprison me for another year but she fulfilled her promise and let me out, on condition that I would return before the gate was closed. She made me swear an oath on the holy Qur'an, the sword, and the promise of divorce, that I would not be late. I hurried immediately to the garden and found the gate open and my beloved sitting with her head on her knees. She seemed frail and sick but she was happy to see me. "Praise be God that you are safe!"

"How did you know that I would come to you tonight?" I asked her.

"I have been waiting for you every evening for twelve months," she answered.

I rushed to her and took her in my arms and she seemed to come alive again.

"Now tell me what happened to you," she said, in a voice filled with longing and curiosity.

I told her everything and she seemed calm and understanding of my situation. And so, lulled into a feeling of peace and security, I told her, "I must return to my wife at daybreak."

She fell into a rage and screamed and scolded. "I could have destroyed you at the outset but your cousin Aziza protected you from me."

She looked at me with eyes filled with all the hatred in the world, and said, "Anyhow, you're married now and you have a son and so you are of no use to me. By God I shall make that whore sorry—you won't exist for her or for me, for I shall cut your throat like a goat."

I trembled with fright and pleaded with her and begged her forgiveness but she gave a loud cry and ten slaves appeared from nowhere and pushed me to the ground and tied my wrists and ankles with ropes while she sharpened a huge knife, ignoring my pleas.

"Killing you is the least I can do, as revenge for your cousin."

I nearly fainted when I saw the knife in her hand but I went on imploring her, calling for God, but in vain, for she kept on sharpening the knife. As she came towards me God gave me the inspiration to cry out, "Loyalty is good; treachery is evil!"

When she heard my words, my beloved turned assassin cried out, "Be assured that it is your cousin who has saved you, both in her life and in death."

I took a deep breath of relief, but my beloved continued, "I will not let you go in peace, however, I must leave you with a scar that will shame you throughout your life and take revenge upon that whore."

Then she ordered the slaves to light the fire and two of them sat down upon me, pinning me still, and then she cut off my penis and I screamed the scream of death and fainted, only to come to my senses when she gave me a cup of wine to drink and said, "Now you may leave and go anywhere you desire."

She kicked me hard and I stood up with great difficulty and tottered step by step, how I got there I do not know, to my wife and child's home. I collapsed at the door, which still stood open, fainted and lost consciousness.

When I awoke I was lying in bed and my wife was calling out to her mother, "Come and witness this—Aziz is a woman now."

I fell into a deep sleep and when I woke I had been thrown out into the alleyway and the gates were securely fastened. I wept and wailed and finally managed to stand, just like an insect with a broken wing. I walked until I reached our house. I could hear my mother inside, weeping, "Where is Aziz, is he dead or alive?"

When she saw me she knelt in front of me and kissed the ground, thanking God that I was safe, but I collapsed again, unable to answer her questions, so intense was the pain.

A few days later I had recovered sufficiently to tell my mother what had happened to me at the hands of the daughter of Alsawahi Aldawahi. My mother thanked God once more that my life had been spared and that I had not been slaughtered. She cared for me and nursed me until I began to regain my strength and health. When I finally left my bed, I gazed at where my cousin Aziza had sat and wept, and recited her poems and waited for my return, all the while eaten with jealousy. My abandonment must have tormented her and yet she bore it in silence and with great patience. I began to weep, crying out, "Aziza, Aziza!"

"Son, now you deserve to see what your cousin left you," my mother told me.

She went and fetched a small box and opened it and took out a handkerchief wrapped inside a piece of cloth, together with a letter. It was the handkerchief embroidered with a gazelle, given to me by the daughter of Alsawahi Aldawahi. The letter was from Aziza, warning me not to return to my beloved if she mistreated me. "Keep this picture of the gazelle," she wrote, "for it consoled me while you were away from me. I know that you will remember me, but only when I no longer help you, and that you will think of me with love and tenderness, but only when it is too late."

When I had read Aziza's letter I fell into despair and melancholy. I sighed, and asked myself, "Where were my kindness and compassion, my heart and mind, when I saw my cousin engulfed in such grief and sadness? I was preoccupied only with myself."

I wept, and my mother wept with me, and I couldn't sleep for many nights—every time I closed my eyes I saw Aziza waiting for me on the day our marriage contract was to be drawn, I saw Aziza as I kicked her, when she poured rose water to revive me and when she explained and interpreted the gestures of my beloved, and I saw her face, showing forgiveness despite her sorrow, which had burrowed deep inside her soul like woodworm. I watched her as she withered slowly, slowly, for my sake, and her words, "If you asked for my eye, cousin, I would pull it out from beneath my eyelid for you," rang in my ears.

Days and nights passed, then weeks and months and Aziza's face never left me, nor did her echoing voice quieten, but still I heard her saying, over and over, "If you asked for my eye, cousin, I would pull it out from beneath my eyelid for you." And then one day I plucked out my own eye, calling even through the excruciating pain, "If you asked for my eye, cousin Aziza, I would pull it out from beneath my eyelid for you."

I renounced all of life's pleasures, which had once made me so careless, selfish and indifferent to others, wanting only to expiate my cruelty to my cousin Aziza. I stretched out my hand to help the tormented and, little by little, I found that my plucked eye gave me peace and serenity. I set out to roam the wide world, my blanket the sky and the stars in the heavens and my bed the ground, until I reached Baghdad. There I followed a path at random, which led me to a dervish with a plucked eye like mine. He too was searching for eternal truth. We talked together until night fell and this was when a third dervish found us and we three sought somewhere to sleep. Then fate led us to your house, and you welcomed us with kindness and generosity and now I stand before you, awaiting your verdict.

The dervish fell silent.

"Stroke your head, and go," the mistress of the house told him.

But the dervish answered, "If my lady permits me to listen to the other stories, I would be most grateful."

"Yes, you may," was her answer.

The second dervish came forward and began.

The Second Dervish

I have a unique and mystifying story to tell you, of how I came to lose my right eye. I was born to the King of Persia and raised in a palace, which was to me like a vast sea of knowledge. From an early age I showed curiosity and a great passion to study and understand the world around me. When I looked to the heavens and saw the planets and stars hanging there, I wondered out loud about their secrets; and when I saw an apple fall to the ground, I asked the adults to explain to me why the apple fell rather than flew into the air.

And so my father summoned scholars specialising in literature, religion, science and art, so that they would unravel for me the treasures and the secrets of the universe. Over the years I found myself increasingly enchanted by the art of writing, humbled by the fact that if I dipped my quill pen in the inkwell and stroked up and down I could express my feelings, each time differently, and I discovered that my handwriting would change according to the words and their meaning. I would spend hours perfecting a particular letter and I learned to form words as if I was drawing—they took the form of horses, gazelles, falcons, running rivers, long eyelashes and even lips. And whenever someone remarked upon my superb calligraphy, I would murmur modestly that I loved poetry and science too. Soon luck pointed at me and my fame spread everywhere within my country, to Bilad al-Sham, even as far as India, whose sovereign sent for me to come and discuss and exchange ideas and conventions, for he himself was a great calligrapher and miniaturist and interested in science, too. The sovereign assured my father that he would care for me as if I was his own son. So my father sent me off with many attendants and camels loaded with valuable presents. As soon as we were in the desert a sandstorm blew up, engulfing and attacking us, but soon enough we realised that the sandstorm was in fact a horde of bandits bent on robbing us. When we pleaded, explaining that we were on our way to the King of India himself, they merely shrugged.

"Why is that of any concern to us? We are not this Indian King's subjects, nor are we in his realm."

The bandits killed those who tried to defend me or protect our camels and belongings. They fell upon our treasures and I fled into the desert, as did my two surviving companions, who set off in another direction.

With great despair I reflected that only yesterday I was mighty and now I was lowly, I had been rich and was now poor, I had a family so huge that I couldn't count its members and now I was all alone. I was lost in foreign lands after having known each and every stone in my kingdom.

I walked and walked. After long days of hunger and thirst and lack of sleep and exhaustion, I arrived at a big city, blown there like a leaf. I was on the verge of collapse, but I took hold of myself and walked to the bazaar, where I came upon a tailor sitting outside his shop. I greeted him and when he returned my greetings kindly,

I found myself telling him who I was. The tailor led me inside his shop and advised me not to reveal my identity to anybody, for the King of these lands was a great enemy of my father. Then he gave me something to eat and drink and a recess in his shop next to him in which to sleep. Two days later the tailor asked me whether I had a skill which might help me to earn my living. When I told him I was interested in science and poetry and calligraphy he answered, "Such skills are not in demand here." He suggested that I become a woodcutter, because I was strong and fit. He gave me an axe and a rope and introduced me to the other woodcutters, telling me, "Gird yourself and God be with you."

The woodcutters took me with them deep into the forest. As I was about to hack into my first tree, I wondered how it could be that I, a prince who loved science, poetry and calligraphy, had become a woodcutter? But my need and desire to support myself made me strike with my axe with all my might and strength as if I was avenging my bad luck and fate. I gathered a large amount of wood, and carried my bundle on my head back to sell at the market. I spent half the money I made on food and saved the other half. This was how I lived for a year, until one day I ventured deep into the forest alone, and came upon a stand of trees as dense as the hairs on my head. I found a tree stump and when I dug around it my axe hit a brass ring attached to a plank of wood. I lifted the plank and saw beneath it a staircase, which I descended without hesitation. When I reached the bottom, I found myself in a magnificent underground palace, lit up as though it had been built in the eye of the sun and not deep beneath the earth. I stood bewitched, taking in the glittering golden columns, the seats and tables, and then, as I moved forward, I saw a young woman with a radiant face. She outshone all the gold around me. I was speechless, not because of her great beauty, but the way she stood with dignity, as if she was not all alone in that vast underground palace, but before a large company of people. She saw me, but when she didn't move, I froze, fearing that she might disappear if I took one step towards her. Then she spoke in the most mellifluous and harmonious voice. "Are you a man or a demon?"

"I am a human being, my lady," I answered.

Hearing this she sighed with relief and asked, "What brought you here?"

Then, without waiting for my answer, she said, "This is the first time I have seen a human being in twenty-five years."

"You've lived underground for twenty-five years?" I asked in astonishment.

"A demon, the grandson of Satan himself, snatched me on my wedding night and flew away with me, imprisoning me on my own in this palace. He visits and spends the night with me once every ten days, because he is married with children and doesn't want his wife to suspect anything. He has told me that if ever I need him, I am to touch the two sides of that talisman," she pointed at her bedroom door, "and he will appear at once."

"I am a son of the King of Persia, and I was on my way to the King of India, when bandits ambushed us, killing my companions and camels and looting our possessions. I ran for my life and walked until I reached this city and became a woodcutter, earning my living from gathering wood."

The young woman sighed, saying, "Be assured, my Prince, that this splendid palace I inhabit is nothing but a dark prison, which fills me with melancholy and exhaustion!"

I smiled at her and said comfortingly, "I am so pleased that my good fortune brought me here to dispel your sorrow and banish my woes."

The young woman smiled back. "The demon was here four days ago, so he will not show up for another six. Would you like to stay with me until the day he arrives?"

I was delighted at her invitation and agreed immediately, thanking her for her kindness. She took me to a magnificent bathroom; I had never seen anything like it, even at my father's palace, where hot water flows from the taps, scented with perfume and musk. When I had bathed, I found that the young woman had laid a new beautiful gown for me. I put it on and went to where she was waiting for me at a table laden with unusual and exotic food. We ate, conversed and had a wonderful time together until we were sleepy, then we each retired to a separate room. We woke the next day as soon as the artificial light flashed in our eyes, feeling great happiness at being together. We spent the day entertaining each other, laughing and joking. When we sat down to eat that evening, the young woman brought out a flask filled with delicious wine, and I drank nearly half of it alone and then pleaded with her to share a drink with me. She agreed and we surrendered to each other and felt sheer delight, cherishing and savouring the moment.

I found myself asking her if she had a quill pen and inkwell, and the girl hurried to her room to fetch them. When she returned with them in her hand, I was overwhelmed by a great sense of sorrow and at the same time tranquillity. I held the quill pen, reunited at last after a long separation caused by one nightmare after another with my most treasured art. I lifted my eyes from the paper and gazed at the girl who was now in my life and began to write the words "Thank you, God," most skilfully and carefully in the thuluthy script, a form of calligraphy in which the characters seem to lean upon one another, sway together, merge into each other, stretch out and fall asleep. When I had finished writing I saw that the phrase had taken the form of a girl: the dots above the letters were her eyes, the letter S formed her mouth, the letter R her long hair, the letter L her noble nose, the letter N her breasts. When the girl recognised herself in this beautifully drawn phrase she held the paper tight to her bosom and embraced me.

I fell deeply in love with her and she fell for me and so we made love and slept together in her big bed and so did that phrase, which slept between us and saw how we were, clinging tight, as though we were rescuing each other from drowning. But this blissful sensation left me after a few hours and I woke in the middle of the night feeling as if a heavy stone lay upon my chest. I gazed about her room and when my eye lit on the talisman on her door, I reminded myself that she was indeed the mistress of a demon, the grandson of Satan himself, and that we were together in a palace hidden in the earth beneath the forest, and that I would have to leave her in four days' time. At this final thought I woke her and whispered, "My beautiful one, let me deliver you from this prison and release you from that demon, let me find a way for us to go back to my kingdom and country, where you will become a princess and we will live happily ever after."

The girl laughed. "Don't be greedy, my love. Am I not offering you nine days with me here, with only the tenth for the demon?"

But my passion and love for her overwhelmed me. "Do you believe for a moment that you are alive while you are buried beneath the earth in this false, glaring light? I wish only to show you the brightness of a genuine day. The beautiful world, the sun, the moon and the night—from all of which you have been deprived."

But the young woman repeated her answer. "Don't you know that to be satisfied is a virtue? Nine days for you and one for the demon."

"I understand that fear makes you tolerate all the injustices bestowed upon you by this demon, but I cannot comprehend how you can tolerate being with him."

At this the girl wept. "I was inconsolable for a long time. I fainted each time I laid eyes on him, but habit and loneliness have reconciled me to his appearance and his company."

I boiled with anger, screaming, "No, I can't bear any more to think of you living in this hell. I swear by God that I will fight this demon and take revenge upon him. I will kill him."

I hurried over to the talisman, but the girl jumped up and pleaded with me. "I beg you not to touch it. If you do, it will destroy us both. I know the demon and his ways all too well."

Then she said:

"Unless you seek separation,
I beg you hold back,
Stay, jealousy destroys the very thing it loves
And such betrayal is condemned by Heaven above."

But I was oblivious to her words. I wanted to kill all demons and wipe them from the face of the Earth and I was determined to begin with him. I leaped on the talisman and broke it into pieces. The palace immediately began to shake and there were great flashes of lightning and terrible thunderclaps. At this, it was as if all the wine was sucked out of my brain, and I cried out, "What happened?"

The young woman answered, in the greatest alarm, thinking not of herself but only fearful for me, "It is the demon. Go, run for your life!"

I took to the staircase in one jump and fled, leaving my axe and rope behind. As I reached the last step I saw the enchanted palace split apart and the demon appeared in the centre, asking the girl with utmost annoyance and anger, "What's the matter? Why have you called me?"

The girl answered him hastily. "I felt unbearable pain in my belly and so I drank some wine and then when I was a little bit drunk I fell on the talisman and broke it."

The demon was enraged; his anger resembled no other anger, and when he screamed at her, the steps beneath my feet vibrated and shook.

"What about this axe and rope, you slut? You cannot tell me that they don't belong to a human being!"

"I have never before laid eyes upon them. They must have caught on to your clothes on your way here," the girl answered him innocently.

But the demon wasn't fooled. He slapped her face so hard that I felt it squeeze my heart. Then he stripped her naked and bound her feet and hands to four stakes, flogging her with my own rope in order to extract her confession. Her screams and cries filled the palace and my ears and when I could bear it no more I climbed the last step and left. Outside, my agony and despair for the girl boiled over into disgust at myself. I could not fathom how in my selfishness and arrogance I had caused this tragedy. But I replaced the wooden plank as it had been before and covered it with weeds and earth. I found the bundle of wood I had gathered just before I stumbled on the trapdoor and hurried back to the tailor. He cheered with great relief when he saw me. "I thought one of your father's enemies had discovered who you were and killed you!"

I didn't tell him what had happened to me or to my axe and rope. How I wished later that I had, rather than sitting on my own, reproaching myself over and over, thousands of times, for my terrible behaviour in leaving the young woman staked out on the ground, suffering such affliction and harrowing pain. Regret and sadness gnawed at me because I would never again see the girl with whom I had fallen in love, body and soul, and I could no longer take any joy in this life, even if I were to make my way back to my country and family. Nothing could compare to her.

All of a sudden the tailor came in to where I was sitting. "There is an old man who would like to return your axe and rope; the woodcutters recognised them and told him where to find you."

My limbs shook and trembled, I felt the colour drain from my face, and I looked for a way to escape.

"What's wrong with you, what's the matter?" the tailor asked.

Before I could answer him the floor split open and an old man appeared, holding my axe and rope. "Aren't these yours?" he said.

He didn't wait for an answer, but grabbed me by the waist and flew away with me, high among the clouds, with the wind biting my face, until I found myself back in the underground palace. I saw the young woman stretched on the floor as if she was dead, blood covering her body and her face awash with tears.

The demon threw me to the ground and cried, "Hey, slut! Look what I have brought you!" Then he dragged me by my foot until I was facing her. "Isn't this man your lover?" he asked. The girl looked at me with her dreamy eyes, without blaming me for what I had brought upon her, and said, "I don't know him. I've never set eyes on him before."

"You deny knowing him who is the cause of your punishment?" the demon screamed.

"Do you wish me to lie to you so that you may kill him without reason or pity?" the girl whispered.

"If you are telling the truth and you do not know him, then it should be easy for you to strike off his head."

He made her stand up, covered her battered body and then

handed her his sword. She took it and approached me. I looked at her, trying to signal that I wished she would forgive me for what I had done. I saw in her face and those dreamy eyes nothing but love. We must have gazed at each other longer than was safe, for the demon came closer and watched us intently. I tore my eyes away from her, while she threw the sword away, saying, "I cannot behead someone I don't know!"

"Here you are then! Your refusal is confirmation that this man is indeed your lover and that you've finally confessed to your terrible crime and deceit."

Then he turned to me. "You, human being, do you know this woman?"

I looked at the young woman, seeking to assure her that I would not betray her even if I had to sacrifice myself. "How am I supposed to know her when I find myself in this place for the first time?"

"Then it will be easy for you to strike off her head," the cunning demon replied. "Yes, go ahead and do that. I will set you free when you have satisfied me that she did not after all deceive me."

I took the sword, saying, "With pleasure."

But the girl misunderstood my answer and looked at me with reproach. "Is this how you repay me?" she asked.

I gazed back at her, terrified that the demon would see me, trying to tell her with my eyes, "I am ready to give my life for you."

Then I threw the sword on the ground and cried out, "Demon, how can you let a man kill a woman who has refused to kill him without a valid reason? How could I live with such a deed on my conscience? And why don't you leave her be? I beg you: take a look at this woman and tell me if I am mistaken that her soul will be leaving her any minute due to the torture you've inflicted on her. Why don't you leave her be?"

But my words only made the demon angrier.

"I knew it," he shouted. "You two are conniving against me. You insult my intelligence and my powers and at the same time you ignite my jealousy!"

He drew his sword and cut off the girl's arm and then hacked at the other one until it flew off like a shooting star and landed on the floor.

The young woman then bade me one final farewell before he struck at her head and she drowned in her own blood. I fainted and lost consciousness and when I came to my senses, I got to my feet, ready for the demon, crying out, "Go ahead and kill me! Release me from this agony once and for all."

But the demon said, "No, I will not kill you, human being, for I am not sure that it was with you that she deceived me. Just let me check your hands."

He grabbed my hands, tilted his head and examined them carefully. I was mortified—perhaps the demon could read the truth in the lines on my palm? But the demon muttered to himself, in a voice which shook the walls, "But these hands are rough, chapped and swollen, as if they are familiar only with ploughing, working in a smithy, building or chopping wood."

When he mentioned woodcutting I tried to control the trembling of my hands lest they give me away.

"I am sure that the axe and rope must belong to you," he muttered.

At these words I saw myself falling into the raging sea of death, but then he pulled me clear by continuing, "But how could a woodcutter be a calligrapher? Where are his long, flexible fingers?"

He dropped my hands and took from his belt the paper on which I had written that single phrase. "Go ahead, take hold of it," he said, shoving it at me.

I grasped it and held it upside down. At this his face grew dark with rage and fury. He turned the paper the right way around. "Go ahead and read what is written here, and if you can do so then your life shall be spared."

"But this is a drawing, not writing," I answered.

He sighed, long and loud, revealing his frustration and confusion. I saw my chance and pleaded with him.

"Let me go! Please be assured, demon, that I have never set eyes on your mistress before today."

"I'm not sure that it was with you that she deceived me, but at the same time I find myself unable to let you go without inflicting some harm."

He threw the piece of paper on the ground and stamped upon it, watching me carefully lest I betray my sadness and regret. I realised that he knew that whoever had written that phrase must have felt great desire and passion for his mistress. So I pretended to be confused and puzzled by his actions, although I felt as though he was stamping upon my heart.

Suddenly the demon stopped and said, "Perhaps you are a woodcutter who loves calligraphy? I wonder if I should put out your eye or cut off your hand?"

I pleaded once more, telling him, "But my work is really washing the dead."

But the demon brought the quill pen and a knife and pushed his face close to mine, saying, "I'll put out your eye so you can no longer write. I could choose to end your life while making you watch your own, slow death, but with your plucked eye you will frighten away children and be a curse upon adults."

"You must believe me, please," I cried out.

"Maybe your eye didn't guide your hand as it crafted that calligraphy, but it did see my mistress!" was his reply.

He came towards me with the quill pen and I screamed out in terror, but he poked out my eye. The blood of my heart and my brain poured out and drained from my eye along with my tears and I screamed again and again, as if my screams might lift me in the air and throw me back into the forest.

I screamed and stretched my arms wide. "Oh my life! For what reason was I separated from my father, mother and my homeland, attacked by bandits who killed my companions and my camels and looted everything, and then made a woodcutter who became the cause of the death of the only woman I have ever loved? And as if all of this was not enough a demon has taken out my eye!"

I walked and walked aimlessly until I discovered that I had lost not only my eye, but my ears and my tongue; all my senses had died.

I shaved my hair and my eyebrows and wore a black woollen cloak and set out to roam the world, seeking to forget that I had caused the death of a young woman who was the light of the sun and the moonlight. She had died in great suffering because of my greed and selfishness, and because I carried not even a tiny speck of compassion or wisdom in my heart, not even when the girl had pleaded with me not to touch the talisman. She had warned me that if I touched it I would destroy us both, and I hadn't even seen the damage I would do when she uttered those words to me:

> "Unless you seek separation,
> I beg you hold back,
> Stay, jealousy destroys the very thing it loves
> And such betrayal is condemned by Heaven above."

I heard more than once on my travels that Haroun al-Rashid, the Commander of the Faithful, was always ready with great compassion to listen to those who had suffered misfortune. So I decided to visit Baghdad and find a way to be in his presence and tell him my life story.

And so I reached Baghdad only today, where I met a dervish with one eye who told me that he too was a visitor to the city, and after we had talked for a while we met a third dervish, also with one eye. Then the three of us walked together, seeking a place to spend the night, and the fate of God brought us to your beautiful house.

The mistress of the house said to him, "Stroke your head and go."

But the dervish said, "Would my gracious lady permit me to remain and hear the tales of the others?"

"Yes, you may," said the mistress of the house.

The third dervish hurried to the middle of the room, bowed to the mistress of the house, paused to reflect for a moment before sighing, wiping tears from his eyes, and beginning in a trembling voice.

The Third Dervish

h how I wish my story was similar to those of the two dervishes who have gone before me. But I have learned, as the days have passed, that there is nothing to be gained from regret; it changes nothing, leaves us melancholy and in pain for ever.

I was born, ladies and gentlemen, not to a sovereign who reigns over a vast kingdom, not to a merchant, but to a father who was a sailor, who had a passion for the sea and travelling. Until I was eighteen, he used to take me with him everywhere he went but my mother asked him not to take me with him any more but to leave me behind in Baghdad. She wanted me to marry and have children before I sailed again. My father obeyed her and left without me, while I rejoiced, for I had always imagined myself in the company of women, many, many women; young girls, young women, women in the prime of life, boasting to my friends that I lived with as many women as there are pebbles on the shores. Only their creator knows how many there are. My mother found me a beautiful bride whose father was a merchant. Though I had never seen her before, I fell for her instantly as I lifted the veil off her face and saw her shyly lowering her eyelashes and then, when I heard her soft voice, I fell more deeply in love with her. So we lived in peace and harmony and I took a job in a carpet store which belonged to a Persian merchant, looking after his shop when he was there and when he was not, for he used to travel for weeks and months before he came back loaded with many different kinds of silk and woollen carpets. Soon my wife became pregnant and in time gave birth to a son, whom I named after my father, and then she gave birth to another boy and she became busy with him and we continued living together, just as pigeons lived, serenading one another, playing and kissing.

Then one day she fell ill and kept tossing in bed like a serpent's tongue, in pain and unable to sleep. She drank boiled herbs and massaged her stomach with oils and placed scalding stones upon it, but her health did not improve. Then one night she woke me, saying that she was craving apples. I told her that I had heard of apples but I had never seen one. So the next day, on my way to work, I passed by the market and looked for apples, but found none. When I came home and told my wife, she sighed and turned away. "How I wish I could crunch one bite from an apple or even just smell it. Then it wouldn't matter if I died."

When I heard my wife's wish, I decided I would find her an apple, even if I had to go to Paradise itself, and I began asking here and there where I might find apples. But every fruit seller and farmer I asked assured me that I would find what I wanted only in Mousel, in the orchards of Haroun al-Rashid, the Commander of the Faithful himself. His orchards produced apples of every kind and shape, big and small, sugary and sharp in taste. I rushed to hire a mule and the journey took me several nights and days until I arrived and someone pointed out to me where Haroun al-Rashid's orchards were. I saw the apples dangling from trees as if they were precious stones. I carefully selected three apples and paid for each one of them a whole dinar! I wrapped them with more than one cloth, away from the rays of the sun or the wind, and then put them in a safe place in the saddle pocket as if I was hiding treasure. I rode back home immediately, without taking even a few minutes' rest, spurred on by an image of my wife running from her bed when she saw the apples in my hand. I imagined that she would hug herself with delight, and that the colour would return to her cheeks as she took the first bite. But when I finally placed the apples close to her face, instead of leaping with joy as I had imagined, she merely opened her eyes for a second, smiled at me and took the apples, laid them on the table next to her and went back to sleep.

I worried that my journey had taken too long. Then I promised myself that I would be patient and that in the evening I would help her to eat at least one of the apples. As soon as the time came to close the shop, I hurried home. My wife kissed me, thanking me as she pointed to the apples and then went back to sleep. There and then, I pleaded to Almighty God to save her, for it seemed that now only He could.

Next day, I again left for work, which distracted me from my pain and anxiety about my wife's health. While I was outside the shop spreading the carpets in the sun, a black slave, as tall as a bamboo reed, and as wide as a rowing boat, walked by, holding a single apple in his hand. I found myself hurrying after him.

"How did you get this apple, my good slave?" I asked him.

The man winked at me. "From my sick mistress. Her husband, whom she detests, travelled for two whole weeks in order to get her three apples. She gave me one—she would rather that I had one than eat it herself. This is what I call love, don't you agree with me?"

I nearly fell to the ground, but the echo of his words made me rush to the house, hallucinating, as I repeated over and over, "Oh God chase the devil off my back, and let me see three apples! Let me see three apples!"

Then another idea came to me. "Could it be that my wife tricked me by demanding the apple so that I would go away and leave her alone with her lover?"

I entered my house, touching my eye as I said to myself, "I swear by this eye that if I don't see three apples I will slice my wife open from one jugular vein to the other."

I entered her room and to my shock and ill-fortune and tragedy, I found that there were two apples instead of three. In my anger and frustration I nearly shook my wife awake, but instead I controlled myself, asking, "Wife, where is the third apple? I can only see two."

"I don't know," she said in a dull voice, without opening her eyes.

Her answer assured me that everything the black man had told me must be true. Very calmly I entered the kitchen, fetched a sharp knife and cut off her head. Then, as though I was a rabid animal, I cut her into nineteen pieces, wrapped her in a cloak, tied the four corners as if I was wrapping up dates, put everything beneath a carpet in a basket of palm branches, and sewed it in tight with red woollen thread. As if I was carrying a carpet, I bore it to the edge of the Tigris on my shoulders and threw it into the river. I stood and watched it sink to the bottom. Bending down again to the river, I washed my hands, as if I was cleaning off her deceit, and returned back home.

At this one of the merchants cried, "Oh God, speedy deliverer," but everyone else in the room couldn't decide if it was a cry of bewilderment or disgust or disturbance. The three merchants whispered to each other and then the third dervish went on with his tale.

Each time the horror of what I had done overcame me, I thought of the black slave, and then breathed a sigh of relief, and congratulated myself on my actions.

But when I saw my eldest son standing on the steps weeping, I choked with guilt and pity, for he loved his mother. But again this thought ignited my fury—how could she have deceived me and her two boys, in our own home?

Then my son spoke, and I realised he didn't yet know that his mother was dead. "Father, I'm afraid to enter the house. How I wish to God that you would forgive me. I stole one of my mother's apples to show to my friends. But a black slave snatched it from my hand. I hurried after him and pleaded with him to give it back, but he brushed me off. I tried to snatch it back from him, but his arm was too high. 'Please, respectable good man, give me back this apple. My father travelled nearly two weeks to get the apple for my sick mother.' But the man just walked away, throwing the apple in the air and catching it either in his hands or his mouth. I followed him, pleading with him until he stopped, slapped me on the face and threatened to drag me by the hair and tie me to a tree. Oh father, please forgive me, and ask my mother to forgive me as well."

Hearing this, I realised I had killed my wife in error. I yelled so loudly in agony that the pigeons trembled in their cages. I struck my face with all my might and threw myself in my son's lap, wailing and weeping as if I was a woman. My son, overwhelmed by my behaviour, asked, weeping, "Will my mother die, because she did not eat all three apples?"

His question made me weep even harder. I howled so loud that my father, who lived nearby, came rushing to see what was happening; he found me still at the entrance of our house. When I related to him what I had done he wailed, too, thanking God that my mother was already dead because she would have taken her own life on hearing this, for she adored my wife.

The three of us huddled in each other's arms, weeping; my younger son came in and joined us without asking what we were doing. We stayed as we were for three days. From time to time one of us would shout that we must take revenge on the accursed slave who had lied and slandered my wife but my father led me at last by the hand, as if I was a child, to the house. When I entered the house and saw the two apples still next to my wife's empty bed, I decided to kill myself. I waited until dark descended. Then I held the same knife up to strike it with all my might into my heart, but I stopped myself when I realised my selfishness. I was running away from my responsibility towards my two boys and fleeing from my awful crime. I had become obsessed with revenge, rather than a seeker of the truth. Now my two sons had ceased their crying and fallen silent, but they avoided meeting my evil eye. Realising this, I found myself plucking out my right eye, upon which I had sworn that if I did not see three apples I would kill my wife. I screamed in pain, soon all was dark and my consciousness left me.

When I came round I went to blind my other eye, but my elder son had hidden the knife.

"That's enough; you've avenged our mother," he said.

My sons went to live with my father. I left home to roam around Baghdad, atoning for my sins by helping the needy.

Today I met these two dervishes and sighed in relief as they talked about spreading goodness and how they had renounced everything to become Sufis. Their words made me feel at peace and secure.

When they told me that they had come to Baghdad to seek out the Commander of the Faithful, Haroun al-Rashid, in order to tell him their life stories and share their misfortunes, I nearly told them about my tragedy, but kept quiet since they didn't share with me what had happened to them.

When the dervishes decided to look for a place to spend the night, I found myself knocking at your door. Now, I thank you for your generosity and sympathy.

He bowed to the mistress of the house, who told him, "Stroke your head and go."

But the third dervish said, "By God, mistress of the house, grant me permission to stay and hear the tales of these merchants."

"You may stay, I have no objection," she told him.

A few seconds passed, and then minutes, and not one of the three merchants came into the middle of the room, but instead whispered among themselves. When the mistress of the house cleared her throat impatiently, one of them came forward.

The First Merchant

 have been sitting here, listening to the dervishes spilling, much like a running stream, their life stories with great honesty, and I have decided to remove my mask and reveal my true identity. I have never been a merchant, nor have I ever lived in Mosul, as I claimed to the honourable lady who opened the gate to the three of us, inviting us to be guests in this house. Exactly nine days ago, we walked disguised through the city, so my Master could witness the welfare of his subjects with his own eyes and hear the complaints of those treated unjustly. We saw an old man carrying a fishing net in his hand and a basket on his head, sighing a deep sigh which had no beginning and no end.

My Master asked him, "What has happened, old man?"

"I am a fisherman, sir, fed up with life and living. I've been trying my luck since midday but my net has caught nothing but water. For God's sake, sir, can you tell me what I can do for my hungry family? I return home each night and see them with open mouths."

Hearing this, my Master said to the fisherman, "Come with us to the river and try your luck once more. I will give you one hundred dinars for any catch you get, even if it is only small fry."

Greatly relieved, the old fisherman walked with us down to the Tigris and threw his net into the water. When he gathered the ropes and pulled the net in, we discovered that he had caught a heavy basket made of palm leaves secured with red woollen thread. To our horror, we saw a slain girl inside, hacked into many pieces.

At these words, the listeners whispered to each other as realisation stirred among them. Only the porter remained entirely bewildered. The third dervish held the hands of the other two in mortification. Ignoring the reaction of the gathered company, the merchant went on with his story.

When my Master saw her face, which was as beautiful as the full moon, a deep sadness overtook him. So deeply did he mourn her fate that tears fell down his cheeks. He turned to me, saying furiously, "Is it possible that our subjects are slain in Baghdad and thrown in the river beneath our very eyes? I want you to find me her killer. I want to avenge this girl. How else can I stand before my God and Creator on judgement day?"

As he continued, anger sparked from his eyes. "I will give you one week, no more, to find her killer. If you do not, I will hang you—as sure as you are Jaafar the Barmecide, my Vizier, and I am the Caliph, Haroun al-Rashid, Commander of the Faithful."

The whole company rose to their feet in amazement, apart from the porter who became increasingly frustrated, demanding of the others, "What's going on? What's got into you all?"

The merchant who had been so impatient to understand the reason for the strange behaviour of the women of the house, and whom the others addressed as "Master," stood and removed his turban, revealing his white complexion, which shone like silver, and a tall figure which inspired fear and respect. Now there could be no mistake: all in the room realised that they were before the Caliph Haroun al-Rashid in his sublime silk attire, imported for him from far-off China by his wife, Lady Zubeida. The merchant telling the story also shed his outer clothes to reveal the elegant form of Jaafar the Barmecide. Stunned, the three dervishes and the three equally astonished ladies bowed their heads in supplication. "Pardon us, pardon us, Commander of the Faithful, for the despicable and disrespectful way we have treated you."

The shopper grabbed the porter and threw him to the floor, face down. Haroun al-Rashid turned to Jaafar, and said, "Well, you lucky old dog of a Vizier, it looks as though the merciful one has shown you special kindness. What a remarkable coincidence. But do not rejoice quite yet. There's still the matter of the accursed slave, who was the cause of this calamity. You will be off the hook only when you bring him to me."

"Commander of the Faithful," Jaafar replied calmly, "if I might ask you to be patient and listen to the rest of my tale, I can guarantee you that it contains a more remarkable coincidence even than the revelation as to the killer before us now."

Haroun al-Rashid turned in surprise to the third dervish, who remained silent and simply shrugged his shoulders.

"You may continue," said the Caliph.

After the Caliph had given me a week to find the killer or die, I returned to my palace, and resigned myself to my fate. For three days I told myself repeatedly how impossible it would be to find the killer even if I were a magician, for how can one find a mustard seed in a dense forest? The feeling of frustration and sadness grew in me with every moment.

I confined myself to the house, awaiting my fate and the will of God. On the sixth day—this very day—I witnessed my last testament in the presence of judges and witnesses and then I gathered my family and bade them farewell, taking special care over my beautiful youngest daughter. This girl is like a shining star, so attached am I to her, and she loves me in return with the innocence and naivety of a child. She would often say to me, "Oh father, how I wish you were so small that I could put you in my pocket and take you out each time I missed you." I felt agonised at the thought of being parted from her, and I longed, in return, to become small enough to hide in her pocket.

At this bleak hour a messenger appeared, with a summons to see the Commander of the Faithful.

I was confused by this urgent summons, since I had one day left before my deadline. I feared that the Caliph was hastening the time of my execution. I reached for my daughter one last time. Squeezing her to my heart, I lifted her up, wishing that I could hold on to her until Doomsday and not part from her that night. As I did so, I felt something protruding from her pocket.

"What is that in your pocket, my darling child?" I asked.

From her pocket she took an apple and showed it to me. "Look, father, the name of our Master, the Caliph, is written on it and Rayhan our slave sold it to me for two dinars."

Everyone in the hall gasped, while Vizier Jaafar continued.

At the time, I didn't give the apple another thought but left my home and family with the heaviest of hearts. I went to prostrate myself before the Commander of the Faithful, knowing full well that he never goes back on his word and fearing his terrible justice. When I arrived before him he was sitting drinking wine and conversing with the wonderful comic poet, Abu Nuwas. This confused me, for he calls for Abu Nuwas when he yearns for distraction and relief from his worries. Abu Nuwas turned to me, cup in hand, with a playful smile and recited . . .

The third merchant stood for the first time and slowly revealed his true identity: he took off his coat to reveal his young and slender form, and golden locks beneath his turban, which he put back on his head as he recited:

> "Nuwas, dear friend, steel yourself, endure.
> So, Fate has dealt you a difficult hand
> But you've also had your ecstasies
> And God's mercy exceeds your anxieties—
> One atom of his forgiveness is vaster than the world.
> Man is only as God wills.
> His creatures cannot choreograph,
> He masterminds each epitaph."

Overcome by emotion, the third dervish cried out, "God is most great!"

Jaafar continued:

"My poor Jaafar," the Caliph said to me. "You have served me well for many years, how can I let you spend your last night on this Earth alone and full of the anticipation of death? Come, let us disguise ourselves as merchants and walk the streets of my city and see how the people live. It may comfort you to see the misfortunes of others, and who knows, we may chance upon a final adventure through which we can remember you with joy."

It is the Caliph's habit to walk Baghdad's streets in disguise, and we have experienced many extraordinary evenings in this way— but none more so than tonight. Our stroll had been uneventful and even rather melancholy, until we passed your mansion and heard voices and music and saw the lights burning so warmly. We knocked, hoping for diversion. We had no inkling that, thanks to the will of God, we would stumble upon the answer to both mysteries in one place. I trust, madam, that this fulfils our side of the bargain and that you will now pardon myself and my two companions?

The mistress of the house lowered her head in deep discomfort and Haroun al-Rashid laughed out loud.

"Now, Jaafar, you may be in the clear but please don't gloat at the embarrassment of others. You'll recall how you objected to knocking at the door, fearing that the people within were intoxicated and might insult me. How pleased I am that I insisted we enter, with Abu Nuwas, and that once inside we interfered in that which didn't concern us, despite your urging me to the contrary! We were threatened with death, but luckily for you, the third dervish, whose eye wound has not yet healed, confessed to his crime with great simplicity and courage. I have one more important matter to deal with, for which you remain responsible. Where is Masrur?"

"Your executioner is, as usual, at the gate waiting for your orders, Oh Commander of the Faithful."

He clapped his hands and in one second Masrur the executioner entered and bowed at the feet of the Caliph.

"Masrur, hurry and bring me Rayhan, the slave of the Vizier, as quickly as a flying bird."

As soon as Masrur left, the poet Abu Nuwas stood and bowed to the Caliph.

"Oh, Prince of the Faithful, may I recite a poem?"
The Caliph agreed with a gesture.

> "Apple tree, my apple tree
> You never suffer thirst,
> For your harvests are dreams, not fruit.
> You assured me that my lover's kisses
> Would sweetly abundant be
> But in return he received but a tasty nip.
> Don't rebuke me, I feel no shame,
> When the teeth and the tongue act as one."

The Caliph was quiet for a while and then he said, "Your poem is not appropriate, Abu Nuwas. Remember the apple led to a woman, in the prime of her youth, being slain!"

"Murder is evil; poetry divine. Good deeds chase away the bad," was the poet's reply.

The Caliph nodded in appreciation, and Abu Nuwas returned to his seat as Masrur the executioner came in, leading Rayhan the slave by the hand. Masrur bowed to the Caliph and made the overwhelmed and stunned Rayhan follow suit by pressing him down.

"Did you sell an apple to the Vizier's young daughter with my name carved on it?"

The slave's head was nearly touching the ground. Masrur lifted it up, and Rayhan, still kneeling, answered in a faint voice.

"Yes, my Lord and Master."

"Where did you find it?"

"I shall tell you the truth, my Master, because it is always safer and better than telling a lie, even though a lie might save me. I swear by God Almighty and his Prophet that I didn't steal the apple from the Vizier Jaafar's palace, nor the palace of the Caliph. I saw it in the hand of a young boy, and snatched it from him even though he pleaded with me to return it, running after me and telling me how his father had travelled two weeks in order to get his sick wife three apples."

"Go on with your story and don't stop," the Caliph commanded.

Shakily, the slave continued. "The boy followed me, begging me to give back the apple, and wouldn't give up until I threatened him. Later, when I was in the market, tossing the apple in the air and catching it in my mouth, a carpet seller asked me where I had got it from. Without knowing why, I lied and told him that my lover had given me the apple instead of eating it herself, even though her husband had travelled for two weeks to get it for her from Basra."

At this, the Caliph cried out, "Damn you, slave! Are you aware that your wicked lie branded an innocent mother of two young boys as a treacherous adulterer, and that she was hacked to pieces by her jealous husband, the carpet seller, who asked you where you got the apple? You lied to him, and in doing so ended her life while she was in the bloom of youth, leaving two boys motherless and casting him into such despair that he plucked out his own eye? Can you see that you are the cause of all of this? What will you do to atone for your sins?"

The slave cried and sobbed, and shook and trembled.

"Well, you can be sure that I will make sure you pay for it!"

The Caliph asked the third dervish to come forward. The third dervish bowed and kissed the ground before the Caliph, then remained on his knees.

"You have heard me tell the slave that he caused a woman to be slain, but this doesn't mean that you're relieved of responsibility for killing your wife in cold blood, without giving her the benefit of the doubt. You didn't even ask her if what you had been told was the truth, nor did you give her the chance to defend herself before ending her last moments on Earth. You slayed her like a butcher slays a beast and chopped her to pieces. And now I hope to avenge this woman who was in the bloom of her youth, by putting one of you to a worse death. And in doing so, I will quench the thirst for vengeance."

He was silent for a time, eyeing the two men. "And I will give my verdict, which will please my Glorious God, when I'm ready."

He turned to congratulate Jaafar. "Wonder of wonders, Jaafar! I cannot believe the haphazard coincidences of your tale, which exceeds anything imaginable in its absurdity. Can it be that your soul was in grave danger because you could not find the killer and yet the cause of the crime was under your own roof, laughing and playing all the while?"

He laughed uncontrollably, hitting one palm on the other, until the others gathered around him began to shift uncomfortably. When he finally regained his composure, the Vizier Jaafar said, "Allow me, Commander of the Faithful, to tell you that this extraordinary story of the three apples is nothing in its absurdity when compared to the tale of the hunchback and the tailor."

"I cannot contemplate a tale in which coincidences play a greater role than in this story of the three apples."

"Yes, yes—I assure you that this tale is more extraordinary. But I will relate it to you only on one condition."

"What is that?"

"It is this: if you agree that my tale is more remarkable than that of the three apples, then you will pardon my slave, Rayhan. He was born in our house and has grown up within my family. His error was great, but I believe he will learn even greater kindness and generosity from it."

The Commander of the Faithful thought for a moment.

"Come on, Jaafar, tell me the story of the hunchback and the tailor. If it is indeed more astonishing, then I will pardon your slave."

And so, as the Caliph settled down to listen, the ladies poured their guests more wine, lit more incense and returned to their seats. The Vizier cleared his throat. "I heard, Oh Commander of the Faithful, once upon a time, in faraway China, a tailor and his wife were returning home at the end of the day, when they came upon a hunchbacked man."

The Hunchback

he hunchback was extremely drunk, singing and playing the tambourine. The tailor and his wife were taken at once by this hunchback, amused and delighted by his appearance, which would lift the gloom from any heart. He had on a robe with wide, embroidered sleeves, and a tall green hat from which many coloured ribbons streamed down to his feet. The tailor and his wife were about to pass the hunchback, but then they stopped and invited him to come home with them and dine. He accepted the invitation, and the couple whispered to each other, "Oh we are going to have the best night ever with this sweet hunchback! He will certainly entertain and amuse us."

And they were right. The three of them had much to drink, bantered, joked and ate many dishes with the greatest appetite. But then the tailor crammed a big piece of fish in the hunchback's mouth and held it shut with his hand, saying jokingly, "You must swallow the whole piece in one go."

Unbeknown to him, the piece of fish contained a large bone, which stuck in the hunchback's throat, choking him. When the tailor saw the hunchback's eyes roll back in his head, he thumped him on the back, but instead of releasing the bone, the hunchback fell to the ground lifeless.

The tailor was stunned. He froze, murmuring, "There is no power and no strength save in God! How is it that I am the one who has ended his life! How can I forgive myself for what I have done?"

But his wife screamed at him, "Take hold of yourself! Haven't you heard the poet say, 'How can you sit and let the fire rage on? Such idleness brings ruin and destruction.'"

But the tailor, who was still in shock, said, "I don't know what to do."

"Hold him in your arms as if he was our child," his wife told him. The tailor picked up the hunchback and his wife threw her shawl over him, saying, "Let us take him to a physician in another neighbourhood."

When they were far enough away from the house, the woman started wailing, "Oh my boy, I wish that this smallpox had struck me instead of you!"

She stopped to ask about a doctor, and someone directed her to a Jewish physician. She knocked at the door until a maid came down. The woman pressed a quarter dinar coin into the maid's hand. "Give this to your master and ask him to come down as quick as lightning to see my child who is greatly ill," she pleaded.

When the maid went up the stairs to get the doctor, the tailor and his wife propped the hunchback on the stairs against the wall and ran away.

Meanwhile the maid gave the doctor the coin and bade him go down and see the sick child. The doctor hurried down the stairs in the dark, calling, "Bring me light!"

But he stumbled on the body of the hunchback, which rolled down to the bottom of the stairs. When the physician saw that he was dead, he cried, "Oh God, Oh Moses, Oh Joshua son of Nun, Oh Jacob! Help me, for instead of curing this wretched sick person I have killed him."

They lifted the hunchback and carried him up the stairs to his wife and he told her what had happened.

His wife was furious. "You are so naive, why did you carry him up here? Don't you know that when day breaks and this dead body is in our house, we will lose our lives? Quick, do not stand like a stick in a desert, let us carry him to the roof and lower him into the house of our neighbour, the Muslim bachelor."

So they carried him to the roof and lowered him very gently by his hands and feet through the ventilation shaft into their neighbour's kitchen. When the hunchback's feet touched the ground, they propped him against the wall, next to the window, and then they hurried back to their home.

Their Muslim neighbour, who was a cook, came home around midnight holding a lighted candle. He saw the hunchback standing near the window, and yelled, "Oh God Almighty! Only now do I discover the real thief: none other than a human being, made from flesh and bone, and not the cats and rats I'd always accused. Do you know how many cats and rats I have killed wrongly, and all the while you creep in when I am fast asleep and steal all the meat and the cooking butter given to me by my employer? But of course you are now lost for words."

Then he took a heavy club and thumped it on the hunchback's chest, and the body slumped to the ground. The cook came nearer and looked at the hunchback's face and saw that he was dead.

"There is no power and no strength, save in God the Almighty! I've killed him, may God curse the meat and the cooking butter. To God we belong and to him we return; wasn't it enough to be a hunchback? Why did you have to become a thief too?"

He carried the hunchback to the market, and when he found a dark alley, he set him on his feet against a shop door and ran back home. A few minutes later a drunk Christian tradesman wearing a turban came swaying left and right down the alley. He squatted to urinate and looked up to see the hunchback standing before him. Thinking that he was about to snatch his turban, as had happened the night before, the Christian tradesman called out, "Where are you, night watchman? Come and catch a thief!"

He punched the hunchback on his neck, knocking him to the floor. When the hunchback did not make a sound, but lay still, the tradesman was flabbergasted. Surely he hadn't killed a man with a single blow? He knelt down, and in his drunkenness, fell on the hunchback.

At that moment the night watchman appeared and saw the Christian tradesman on top of the hunchback.

"Oh God, a Christian is killing a Muslim," he shouted. He lifted the tradesman off the hunchback and when he saw that he was dead, he seized the drunken man, bound him and took him to the Governor's house.

The Governor locked the tradesman in a room and asked the watchman to bring the dead man and leave him in the same room. The next morning, the Governor went to his King, who was King of China, and described how a Christian tradesman had killed a Muslim in the market. The King immediately ordered that the tradesman be hanged.

The executioner set up a wooden gallows and put a rope around the Christian tradesman's neck. The tradesman, whose drunkenness had left him, to be replaced by reason, wept.

"I swear by the Almighty that I barely hit the hunchback," he cried out, but to no avail. Just as the executioner was about to pull the rope tight around the tradesman's neck, the Muslim cook appeared.

"Stop, don't hang him! This man didn't kill the hunchback, it was I!"

And he described to the Governor what had happened the night before, saying, "Is it not enough that I have killed a Muslim? Now a Christian will be killed instead of me, and I will never again live in peace."

So the Governor ordered the executioner to release the Christian and hang the Muslim cook. The hangman wrapped the rope around the Muslim's neck, but the second he was about to hang him the Jewish physician appeared, crying out, "Stop! Don't hang him, this man did not kill the hunchback, it was I!"

And he told the Governor what had happened, how a woman had brought the hunchback to his home, claiming that he was an ill child, and how the doctor had stumbled on him in the dark, killing him. "And so I carried him to the roof and lowered him into the house of the Muslim bachelor next door, and left him there."

Hearing this, the Governor ordered the executioner to take the rope from the Muslim cook's neck and put it around the Jewish physician. But just as the executioner was about to pull the rope, a tailor made his way through the crowd. "Stop, don't hang anyone but me, for I was the one who killed the hunchback," he shouted.

And he in turn told the Governor what had happened, and how he had choked the hunchback in jest, and how he and his wife had then left the hunchback with the Jewish physician and fled. Hearing this, the Governor told the hangman, "Go ahead and release the Jewish doctor and hang the tailor."

But the executioner said to the Governor, "To tell you the truth, oh respected Governor, I am so tired of stringing up this one and releasing that one, now the Christian, now the Muslim, now the

Jew, now the physician, now the cook, now the tradesman! Thank God there is an end to the matter."

Then he released the Jewish physician and wrapped the rope around the tailor's neck. But just as he pulled the rope tight, a man approached saying, "Stop and don't hang this fellow." But this time, instead of continuing, "I am the killer," he addressed the tailor, the physician, the cook and the tradesman.

"I am one of the King's chamberlains. I must take all of you to the King, because the hunchback you've killed was none other than the King's favourite clown to whose company His Majesty was addicted. He was entertained by him every single night, and when the clown failed to show up last evening, the King ordered us to look for him high and low. We discovered that he had been killed, and now His Majesty wants to hear from you exactly what happened."

Soon, the four men were brought to the King of China and kissed the ground before him. The hunchback lay in the throne room, stretched out on a grand bed with his head on a silk cushion.

Each one of the four men told the King his story. Tears fell down the sovereign's cheeks. "Oh my beautiful hunchback, you were funny even in death." The four men sighed in relief when they heard the King's kind words.

Then the King addressed the entire company, saying, "Has anyone heard anything funnier than the story of the hunchback?" And then the King shook his head, as if he remembered something particularly funny about the hunchback because he smiled and laughed a great laugh which allowed the four men to laugh with him, then the whole court dissolved in laughter. The Christian tradesman, encouraged, came forward, restraining a chuckle and he knelt down, kissed the ground before the King and said, "Oh King of the Age, would you allow me to tell you a funnier story even than that of the hunchback?"

"Go on, tell me," was the King's reply. And the tradesman began his story.

When I was about to go into the tavern last night, I saw a well-known thief leading a donkey. I joked with him, saying, "Don't tell me, good thief, that you've stolen this donkey!" He answered, "But of course I did! And you're going to be amazed to know that I snatched it while it was being led by its owner."

The thief continued to brag: "I did it in clear daylight! Am I not known as the thief who can rob lashes from the eye? I love to be challenged, and today I was walking with another thief, who is not nearly as accomplished as I, and he challenged me to steal the donkey, which was being led by a muleteer ahead of us."

I immediately asked the thief to walk on until we reached a fork in the path, and then I took off my shoes, and gestured to him to do the same. We approached the donkey soundlessly and I removed the halter from the donkey's head very carefully, gently freeing the animal and handing it to my companion, who led it away down the other path. Then I put the halter over my head, put on my shoes, and allowed myself to be led by the muleteer, mimicking the noise of the donkey's hooves. When the donkey and my friend were safely out of sight, I froze and refused to move, no matter how hard the muleteer tugged on the halter. Eventually he looked around, and when he saw the halter on my head instead of on his donkey, he trembled and shook with fear.

"Oh! God Almighty, what is going on? Who are you and where is my donkey?" he cried out.

"I am your donkey, but my story is a strange one!" I answered. "I returned home one day so drunk that when my pious mother saw me, she flew into a rage and scolded me, repeating over and over, 'Repent my son, repent and abandon your evil behaviour and come back to God Almighty.'

"In my drunkenness I too flew into a rage, and began to beat her with a stick. She cursed me and pleaded with God to punish me, in whatever way the Almighty wished. So God transformed me into a donkey, and then someone saw me in an alley and took me to the market and sold me to you. I was your donkey until a few minutes ago, when my mother must have suddenly thought of me, felt pity, and blessed me before God Almighty, who out of generosity has returned me to what I was before, a human being!"

When the muleteer heard my story he cried out: "There is no might and no power except with God the Omnipotent!" He quickly released me from the halter with shaking hands, and sank to his knees. "Forgive me, brother, and I beg you in God's name not to hold me responsible for treating you as a beast of burden, for riding you and loading you with the heaviest of stones, and above all, for hitting you every time you slowed down."

He asked if I could find my way home, and I replied that my house wasn't far away. When we reached his house, we parted. As soon as he went inside, I burst out laughing.

Then I pricked up my ears, not donkey's ears, but those of a thief, and listened to his wife speaking to him inside their home.

"For a split-second, I didn't recognise you without your donkey. Where is it? And why do you look so sad?"

I heard the simpleton sighing as he told her what had happened. She exclaimed, sighed as well, and pleaded with God to pardon them both for treating me as a donkey, saying that she would distribute alms in the neighbourhood.

Two days later my friend and fellow thief and I took the donkey to the market to sell, and who did I see? The same muleteer, trying to buy a donkey. I hid and watched as he recognised his donkey.

"Damn you! I can see that you've taken to the bottle again, you ill-omened fellow. You've returned to Satan once more, and you must have beaten your mother again too." The poor donkey must have recognised its master because it brayed and brayed.

But the muleteer put his mouth to its long ears and shouted, "Now stop hee-hawing at once. You won't succeed in making me feel sorry for you. I'll never buy you again, you wretched, drunken mother-beater."

The Christian tradesman reached the end of his story, laughing uproariously, and the three other men laughed with him. Eventually he composed himself, and asked the King with great confidence, "Is my story not more astonishing and entertaining than that of the hunchback?"

But the King of China pouted and yawned. "No it isn't, and since you have failed to entertain me like my precious hunchback used to, I must hang you all for his death."

Then the Muslim cook came forward, kissed the ground before the King of China, saying, "Oh, happy King. If I tell you a fantastic story, one more astounding than that of the hunchback and that of the Christian tradesman, will you pardon us?"

"Yes, get on with it."

Then the cook rose and told his story.

As I have said before, Oh King of the Age, I am cook to an honourable master, who invites and gathers every Friday night many judges, religious men and dignitaries to hear a recitation of the blessed Qur'an. After everyone reads the Fatiha for the soul of their dead we spread a banquet table, with many dishes I have prepared, and the men gather around my famous ragout. This dish of mine contains a secret ingredient, for my grandmother follows the bees to seek out a rare kind of saffron, which tastes like angel's food with its strong aroma, and picks it for me.

Last evening, I stood beside the table, proud and erect, in case the guests needed me. My master came forward with his cousin, who for many years had lived in foreign lands. But when the cousin looked at the table, he covered his eyes and moaned as if in pain.

"What is wrong with you?" my master asked in surprise.

His cousin pointed at the ragout and turned away as if he had seen his worst enemy. I held my breath, in fear that an insect or even a mouse had fallen into the dish.

"I have taken an oath not to touch ragout, because if I do, I must then wash my hands forty times with soap, another forty times with potash and finally forty times with galingale."

Still astonished, and now a trifle irritated, my master said, "Go on, cousin, have a taste of this formidable ragout and then wash your hands as many times as you wish."

Clearly feeling pressured and embarrassed, especially since the guests had gathered around him, filled with curiosity and bewilderment, my master's cousin sat down and stretched a trembling hand to the ragout. He began to shake all over, but this didn't deter him; he dipped it reluctantly in the ragout. But the food kept slipping from his hand, no matter how hard he tried.

Finally my master exclaimed, "Cousin, I don't recall that you were born without thumbs!"

"No, my generous God Almighty didn't create me without thumbs. I am afraid that losing them is connected to this ragout."

When my master and all the guests demanded to hear his story, the cousin began.

*　　*　　*

It seems that I have no escape from facing my tormented past: I am descended from a family of most prominent merchants, stretching back to my great-great-grandfather. But my father didn't follow suit, he spent his days drinking and playing the oud and hopping from one concubine to another until he lost all his money and left his business in great debt. But when he died, I wasn't deterred from reopening the shop, and traded by selling and buying very modestly to make ends meet even with no capital. Early one morning, when mine was the only shop open, a lady riding a mule, led by one slave and followed by another, with a eunuch walking at her side, stopped and entered the shop while the eunuch stood guard at the door. She removed her veil, and I glimpsed her face and encountered beauty itself. Then she asked me to show her my finest wares.

"I've none that would satisfy your extravagant tastes, for I'm poor, my lady, but as soon as the other shops are open I'll get you only the best from each of them."

And this is what I did: I got her everything she wanted, at a cost of more than five thousand dirhams. Then she stood up and bade the eunuch to load her purchases on the mule, mounted the creature, and left.

As she disappeared on the horizon, I sighed with grief and lamented my luck, because not only had she failed to pay me, and I now owed the other shopkeepers five thousand dirhams, and would have to persuade them to wait to be repaid, but the beautiful creature had also taken my heart.

For a whole month, I reproached myself for not asking the eunuch or her slaves about the identity of the woman. Then one morning, to my utter surprise and joy, the woman reappeared with her entourage, entered my shop, unveiled her face and smiled at me, telling me that she had come to pay me the money that she owed. In reply, I could produce only a moan followed by a sigh.

"Are you married?" she asked, out of the blue.

"No, I am not," I answered, and I wept.

"Why are you weeping?" she asked.

I mumbled, unable to speak, and she stepped out of my shop. As he paid me, I asked the eunuch who she was, and he told me that she was none other than lady-in-waiting to the Lady Zubeida at the Caliph's palace, charged with purchasing all the goods of the Lady and doing her errands. The Lady treated her like her daughter, for she had brought her up since she was a little girl.

The despair must have shown on my face, for how could I ever reach such a woman? I asked the eunuch if he would be the go-between, offering to pay him some dirhams. He laughed.

"She is more in love with you than you are with her. That's why she didn't pay you the first time she came: she wanted to see you again."

He walked out of the shop and I accompanied him.

"I'm going to tell you why I wept: it is because I have fallen in love with you," I found myself saying to her.

She ignored me, and instead addressed the eunuch, saying, "Soon you shall carry my message to him."

She mounted her mule, leaving me to spend a sleepless night.

Next day I went to my shop even earlier than usual and waited for the eunuch. He soon appeared, saying, "She told Lady Zubeida all about you, describing how you had trusted her with the money the first time you met, and asking Lady Zubeida's permission to marry you. Lady Zubeida wants to see you and decide if you are a good match. It's not easy to enter the palace; but if you succeed you are alive and if you are caught out you are dead. Do you think it is worth trying?"

"I'm ready to face every danger in the world to be with her," I answered quickly.

The eunuch told me to wait for him and my lady at the mosque by the Tigris River. I arrived early in the evening, and waited all alone until dawn, when I saw the eunuch disguised as a servant and my lady step out of a boat, which was filled with boxes and baskets of goods bound for the harem of the palace.

My lady wept as she hid me in a big basket which was made of palm tree leaves and locked it, and then the eunuch put me on to the boat, among all the chests and baskets. The boat sailed for a short time before I was lifted up, probably on to the shoulder of a slave, and I heard an angry voice yelling, "Come on, open everything you have. Not one thing, not even a tiny ant is allowed to enter the harem of the palace without inspection."

The servant stood still, waiting for my basket to be checked, and I panicked and wet myself, and my urine ran out of the basket. I clutched my heart, waiting to be undone, when I heard my young lady say to the angry voice:

"Chief! You ruined me. What shall I tell Lady Zubeida when she sees that her dresses are stained and spoiled! I put a bottle of holy water in among the dresses and it must have tipped over and made their colour run."

"Take the basket and go," the angry voice answered.

I was lifted up again and as I sighed with relief, I heard voices saying, "The Caliph, the Caliph."

My heart stopped beating as I heard the Caliph say to my lady, "So many chests you have, what is in them?" And I heard the voice of my lady reply with all the courage I lacked: "Garments and clothes I purchased for Lady Zubeida."

"Open all of them."

And my young lady answered with even more courage: "But Lady Zubeida insisted that no one should see their contents."

But the Caliph only became more determined to see what was inside the chests. He ordered the guard to open them one by one, and when it was the turn of my basket and I was set down before the Caliph, I wept silently as I held my head in my hands and blocked my ears, so that I would not hear the sound of the sword striking my head.

"I beg you, Commander of the Faithful, not to open this particular basket except in the presence of the Lady Zubeida, because in this is her secret," I heard my lady say, and the ferocious throbbing of my heart nearly broke my ribs.

As I bade my life goodbye, I heard the Caliph order the eunuch to carry all the chests and basket to the harem quarters.

Soon my lady opened the basket and asked me to climb out and go upstairs, then enter the first room on my right. I did what I was told, and in a few moments she came in and said, smiling, "You made it, my hero, and Lady Zubeida is on her way to meet you. I pray to God that she will like you so that you will win my hand and be the happiest of men."

The door opened and twenty high-bosomed young women came in, followed by Lady Zubeida. One of them fetched a chair, and as she sat down, she cried out, "Bring him over!"

I came forward and kissed the ground before her and she pointed to a chair facing her. She asked a few questions about my family and my work, and seemed pleased with me, because she said: "I raised this girl like my daughter and I think you are fit for her, but I must consult the Caliph to see if he will permit the marriage."

That same day my love stole a few moments and came to tell me that the Lady Zubeida had secured the blessing of the Commander of the Faithful. Our marriage contract would be drawn up the next day, and the wedding ceremony would take place a few days after that. Overjoyed, I jumped in the air like a little boy. And from that moment on, I boiled with great passion and desire to be with my bride.

On the day of the wedding, my lady was taken to the baths by her maids, to prepare her from head to toe for her wedding night, and someone handed me a meal, which consisted of ragout cooked with cumin and decorated with pistachio nuts and pine seeds. I fell on it and ate the last pine seed, wiped my mouth and waited for the night to grow darker, while the maids held candles, parading my lovely lady through the Caliph's palace, receiving presents and congratulations as they sang and beat tambourines.

Finally the procession entered my rooms and the maids disrobed my bride and let her long hair fall on her white body. I hurried to her as soon as we were alone and took her to the bed and into my arms, unable to believe that we were together.

Suddenly she screamed and screamed, rousing all of the maids in the palace, who flung themselves upon the door, asking, "What is the matter, our sister?"

I sat trembling and sweating, asking myself what had I done to her, other than squeezing her to my heart?

"Just take this madman far away from me!" she shouted.

"What have I done to you, that you think that I am a madman?" I asked.

"Did you eat ragout spiced with cumin without washing your hands, you mad madman! How dare you think that you can consummate marriage with a lady like me, while your hands smell of not only cumin but saffron as well!"

"Throw him to the ground," she said to her maids, and in the blink of an eye I was thrown down, and my lady whipped my back and buttocks until finally she cried, "Take him to the chief of police and have him cut off the hand with which he ate the ragout."

I hid my hand with the left one and repeated, "There is no power and no strength, save in God, the magnificent, what a tragedy, what a calamity, wasn't it enough that I suffer such a painful beating? Now I must lose my hand altogether because I ate ragout spiced with cumin and saffron and forgot to wash afterwards? God curse this ragout, and all the cumin and the saffron on the entire Earth!"

The maids interfered on my behalf, and kissed their lady's hands, saying, "Forgive him for our sake and above all for our God's sake; he didn't harm you after all, his sin was that he forgot!" But she cursed me, yelling, "Mad madman." Then she roared like a tornado, "I curse you over and over and still I cannot believe that you didn't wash your hands after eating the ragout, I can even still smell the cumin. No, no, I can't forgive you."

Then she ordered her maids to take hold of me, took a sharp knife and cut off my two thumbs. I lost consciousness as her maids tried to staunch my blood, while others poured wine into my guts. When I came to my senses, I wept, and pledged out loud, "I promise that as long as I live, I will not touch or go near a ragout without washing my hands a hundred and twenty times."

"Bravo! Bravo! You've learned your lesson," my lady cheered. But then she continued: "No, no, I'm not able to forgive and I won't, just leave this palace and don't show your face again."

I gathered my belongings as the blood dripped from my two thumbs and she left the room with rage and disgust. I left the palace and Baghdad as well, for she had struck at the heart of my manhood and trampled on my integrity. I knew that if I remained, people would point and whisper wherever I went, saying, "Look at this man, who on his wedding night stank of ragout cooked with cumin so strongly that his bride pushed him away from her, and punished him by cutting off his two thumbs and kicking him out."

The Muslim cook tried in vain to study the expression of the King of China, who had his hand pressed to his forehead, as if he was thinking about the story. When he didn't comment, the Muslim cook said, "Oh King of the Age! I hope that you found my story more fascinating than that of the hunchback?"

"Did you see me laugh or even smile while you were telling it? By God! Your story is no more astounding or entertaining than that of my lovely hunchback. So be assured: you four shall face the hangman."

Then the Jewish physician stood up and kissed the ground before the King.

"Oh happy King, I am going to tell you, with your permission, a story which is more amusing and delightful than all of these stories, even the story of the hunchback, and then by the grace of God you may be moved to spare us."

The King fell silent, while not only the four men but the whole court held its breath, before at last he spoke: "Go ahead and let us hear it . . ."

A few hours before the hunchback was brought to my house, I was at the herbalist's where I buy deer musk to use as an aphrodisiac for my patients. While the herbalist was weighing half a kilo out, his wife appeared and said to her husband, "Maybe our doctor could help you." Her husband ignored her, and when she tried to address me, he shouted and yelled at her and tried to push her back behind the curtain, but she refused to leave him alone.

"He is a doctor, after all," she reasoned.

Embarrassed by the situation, I asked, "Can I help you in any way?"

The herbalist put the musk in my hand, refused payment, and followed me out of the shop.

"I must apologise to you for my wife's behaviour," he said. "I'm fine. I don't need any help from you. I am a little embarrassed to talk to you about this, but you are a doctor. You see, I've stopped sleeping with her, because of three wishes I made three months ago. As I say, I am fine, I haven't lost it, but my anger towards her makes me freeze. Let me tell you what happened."

The herbalist began:

It all began when I sat on the porch looking at the heavens, praying and pleading with the angels on that special night, the sacred night when the doors of heaven stand open and the angels grant one believer three wishes. To my utter astonishment, I was chosen. An amazing light shone on me, and I yelled, "Oh God, the Magnificent, I am here, I am here!"

Then I cried out to my wife, "Quick, quick, I've been granted three wishes, what shall I wish for?"

My wife pointed at my penis and then opened her arms and stretched them as far as she could, and so I asked, with great passion, "God, enlarge my penis."

My penis started to grow and grow until it tore off my underpants and it became so big and heavy, like the stalk of a gourd, that I lost my balance, and fell down flat on my face. When my wife tried to help me to stand up, I found myself dragging her by the hand inside, so that I could make love to her straightaway with my new penis.

But she screamed as if I was a rapist, and ran away, taking refuge under the bed. When I crouched down to talk to her, my penis hit the floor and I shrieked in pain and screamed at her, "Why are you running and hiding from me? Wasn't this what you wished for, you lusty lascivious woman?"

"But I am so scared and terrified of your new penis, and I don't want it as big as it is now," she said.

She remained under the bed, refusing to come out, until she heard me calling to heaven: "Oh God, rescue me from what you have bestowed on me and free me from it."

In the blink of an eye my penis was gone and I found myself with a smooth surface down below, like a cheek.

"What a shame! I have no choice but to leave you, as I have no need of you as you are now," said my wife.

"But don't forget, ungrateful wife, it was you who made me waste two wishes, instead of allowing me to aspire to anything I might desire in this world or the next. Now I am left with the third and final wish."

"Pray to God to restore your penis to the size you were born with, no more no less," she insisted.

And so I prayed to the open heavens, and was granted my final wish.

When the Jewish physician had finished his story, the King yawned an even bigger yawn, saying, "Nothing in this story took my breath away and you cannot even compare it with the hunchback's, so I must hang all four of you. Your only hope is the last story, from you, tailor: the chief offender. Tell me a more amazing, diverting and entertaining story than that of the death of my beloved hunchback, and you and all these other fellows will be spared."

"Yes, Your Majesty," said the tailor, and he began to tell his tale.

It happened, King of the Age, that before I met the hunchback yesterday evening, I was invited to a luncheon banquet at my friend's house. I got there early, and eventually nineteen other guests arrived. Last of all, a lame young man arrived and shook all of our hands one by one, until he reached a barber called The Silent One. Instead of saluting him, he recoiled and screamed in horror.

"God save us from this ugly face and from that tongue of yours, which is as long as a snake. God save me from this unlucky man who made me lame and homeless."

All of us recoiled at the tactless, arrogant young man's outburst, especially since The Silent One, who was probably old enough to be the young man's grandfather, hung his yellow face and gazed at the ground as he heard these curses.

"For God's sake! Tell us why you chose to humiliate this old man, and spoil our plans to amuse ourselves with good food and wine and entertainment," one of the guests asked the young man.

And so the young man told us his tale. He started by telling us that this old man he had insulted was the reason for his fleeing his hometown of Baghdad and travelling as far as China and living here, for he had pledged an oath not to remain in the same city as the old man. Seeing him at this banquet with us had made him lose his temper. He went on to tell us that his father, who was one of the richest men in Baghdad, died when the young man reached manhood and left him a big fortune, but soon he discovered that God had made him a misogynist, with no time for women, until one day he caught sight of a young woman out walking with an old woman and fell in love with her. He followed her home and discovered that she was the daughter of a judge known to be a very strict father, who had his daughter watched constantly.

He returned home in deep distress and fell into bed, boiling with fever. "Oh how agonising to be in love," he cried out.

Eventually the young man regained his strength. The old woman, whom he'd seen with the girl, found him standing by the judge's house, looking up at the window in the hope that his dream girl would appear and he might catch a glimpse of her, and she agreed to help the young man. At first the girl refused to listen to the old woman when she pleaded with her to meet the boy, but she pestered the girl every day, telling her that the boy had fallen ill, that his family had given up on him, and that if she continued to refuse to see him the young man would surely perish and die.

The girl finally agreed to allow him to visit her home for one hour, during the hour of prayer, when her father would be at the mosque.

On the appointed day the young man asked his servant to get him a barber to shave his head. He was relieved on hearing that the barber's nickname was The Silent One, since he couldn't stand people bothering him with chatter.

But as soon as the barber entered the room, he asked, "What is wrong with you, my lord? You're very thin and your face is yellow."

"I have been ill," the young man replied.

The barber took an astrolabe from his leather bag, saying, "I pray to God to make you well and cure everyone you know."

He took the astrolabe to the courtyard and looked into the eye of the sun for a while. "Today is Friday the eighteenth of Safar, in the year six hundred and fifty of Higra," the barber said, "and the seven thousand three hundred and twentieth year of the era of Alexander. Eight degrees and six minutes have passed of this day, and our planet, according to the astrolabe, is between Mars and Mercury, meaning this is the best time for shaving your hair. But I can see something else: you're intending to meet somebody who has a bad spirit and is not to be trusted. How I wish you would not meet that person!"

"I would like you to shave my head, not pester me with your wretched predictions. I am not asking you to consult the stars, only to cut my hair. Get started at once or I will send for another barber."

The barber apologised immediately. "Take it easy, my lord, it seems that you're not aware of how lucky you are. You have asked for a mere barber, and God has sent you not only a barber, but also an astrologer, a physician and a scholar, a linguist and a grammarian. A barber who knows about logic, disputation, arithmetic, algebra, science and history, as well as theology and the Hadith of the Prophet according to Islam and al-Bukhari. And I should tell you that I've read all books and digested them, and studied the science of nature. So you must thank God for sending me to you. Do please bear in mind that when I suggest that you follow my advice, I mean that of the stars. And all of this comes free of charge, because of my affection and esteem for you, which is beyond compare. And I am obliged to help you, for your father loved me not only because of my wisdom, but also my lack of curiosity and because I kept to myself. People call me The Silent One, while my six brothers were famous for their chatter. Take our eldest, Baqbuq, 'The Prattler,' the second, al-Haddar, 'The Blabberer,' the third, al-Buqaybig, 'The Gabbler,' the fourth, Abu-Kalam, 'The Chatterbox,' the fifth, al-Nashshar, 'The Braggart,' and the sixth, Shaqayiq, 'The Noisy.'"

At this, the young man felt his gall bladder might explode at any minute. "You're going to finish me off today! I have changed my mind. I don't want you to shave my hair any more, just take four dinars and go."

"What kind of talk is this? I am not going to stretch my hand and take from you even one piaster, since I haven't served you yet and I am about to do so. It is my duty to help you even if you don't offer me any money."

And then he recited some lines of verse:

"I visited my Lord one day to cut his hair
Entertained him with tales of glorious kinds, clever mortals,
And all that came into my head.
He was ecstatic and flattered me saying:
'Your knowledge is beyond compare!'
'Oh no,' I replied,
'You are the well of wisdom
For lesser men like me,
You are the Lord of grace and munificence
The epitome of wisdom, wit and excellence.'"

The young man opened his mouth to shout at the barber, but the man quickly said, "Oh, I see that you gasp in awe and sheer delight, because your father, God bless his soul, did the same thing when I had recited to him those very verses. I still remember how he called to his servant: 'Give this barber one hundred and three dinars and a robe of honour which would be worthy of him,' he said. And when I asked your father, God bless his soul, not once but a thousand times, why he had given me one hundred and three dinars, his answer was, 'One dinar for your astrological advice, another for your beautiful conversation, a third for the bloodletting, and one hundred dinars for your beautiful praise of me.'"

Hearing this, the young man burst out angrily, "May God show no compassion to my father's soul for knowing the likes of you."

But the barber laughed. "There is no God but God Almighty. Glory be to him who changes not; it seems that your illness has made you foolish. It is known that people become wiser with age, but you're excused, since I am worried about you. And I should tell you that it wasn't only your father who never made a decision without consulting me, but your grandfather before him. As the poet said:

> 'Before you embark on a new course of action,
> Always put your faith in trusted friends!'

"Be assured that you won't find someone more experienced than I. Here I am, ready to serve you without weakness or lassitude. I can see that you have become bored and annoyed with me, but as I've said before, you are excused."

Vexed and worried that he was going to be late for his meeting with the young woman, the young man tore his robe open and slapped his chest. The barber came forward and began to sharpen his razor slowly, stopping from time to time, and each time the young man looked at him, hurrying him, the barber would sharpen his razor once more.

Eventually the barber shaved a few hairs, before stopping and saying, "Whosoever said that haste was the work of Satan was right. But you could always tell me why you are in such a hurry?"

"Don't interfere with what doesn't concern you! Just hurry up; you're tightening up my chest."

"But aren't you aware that in care there is safety and that in hurrying you risk regret? Now, try to open your heart. Tell me why you are in such a hurry. I worry that this haste of yours will harm you."

And then he put the razor down and took the astrolabe out to the courtyard.

"Still three hours left till the end of prayers," he said when he returned.

"I wish you would swallow your tongue, for you have really exasperated the hell out of me."

The barber came forward, shaved a few more hairs and then said, "Rush, rush, rush, confide in me and tell me the reason you are hurrying and remember that your father and grandfather, God bless the souls of both of them, didn't take one step without consulting me."

"I have to go to a party at the home of one of my friends and I don't want to be late."

When the barber heard the word "party" he said, "Oh God! I forgot—'Let us hope that death will forget me'—that I have invited some friends this evening, and I have forgotten to prepare food for them."

"Don't worry about it," the young man replied. "I have plenty of food and drink to give you, on one condition: that you hurry and finish cutting my hair."

"Oh, bless you," the barber replied. "But could you please tell me what you're giving me, so my heart will rest at peace?"

"Ten fried chickens and a whole roasted lamb," the young man replied.

"Could you ask the servant to show it to me?"

The young man called his servant, who in the blink of an eye brought everything to the barber. "Thank God the food is indeed here and ready, but I don't see any wine."

"Don't worry, I have two flagons of wine," the young man told him.

But the barber insisted on seeing them. When the servant brought them, he said, "By God, what an excellent fellow you are, and how generous. But since we have the food and drink, what about dessert and fruit?"

The servant rushed to the kitchen and came back with plenty

of dessert and fruit, but the barber wasn't satisfied yet. "We have food, wine, dessert and fruit. What remains is only the incense."

The servant brought him a box full of incense and the barber knelt down and exclaimed as he checked the contents: "Amber, musk, myrrh and . . ."

The young man interrupted him. "Take the whole box and hurry up and finish cutting the other side of my head."

The barber continued to check each item, and the young man, terrified that he would be late for the girl, found himself pulling out his remaining hair in anger and frustration. The barber drew nearer and shaved a few hairs and then stopped, saying, "I don't know, my lord, should I thank you, or your father? For my party will be possible only because of your generosity. But to tell you the truth my friends whom I have invited don't deserve all that I will offer them. They are all decent fellows—the porter Sa'id, Zenut the bath keeper, Salih the corn dealer, Sallut the bean seller, Akrasha the grocer and Kari the groom. They are all delightful and charming and you would call none of them unsympathetic or drunken or gloomy or meddlesome. They are all quite like your servants, who mind their own business, but each one of them has a melodious voice and a special dance of his own. The bath keeper dances and sings 'Oh mother, I am going out to fill my jar.' The bean seller sings even better than the nightingale and he dances to this song: 'Oh wailing mistress, you have not done badly.' The grocer dances and sings to the rhythm of a drum. Those friends of mine are so much fun they could distract a hungry bear from his food. Oh, I've an idea! Why doesn't my lord go to his friends another time and come with me, so he can enjoy himself, especially since he is so emaciated. Besides, who knows? Maybe at the party one of his best friends might upset him and make him suffer dearly."

The young man laughed in spite of his irritation. "Thank you for your advice, I promise that I will accept your invitation another time. But now I beg you to hurry and shave the rest of my hair, for my friends must be waiting for me."

"How I wish that you would meet my friends this time, for postponement is like the robber of time; but if you insist I could always give my friends all that you have donated to the party and leave them to enjoy eating, drinking and entertaining each other while I go with you. For there is no formality between me and my friends."

The young man tried to keep calm. "I am going to go my way and you'll go your way," he said.

But the barber answered quickly, as if his answer had been waiting under his tongue. "God forbid that I leave you and let you go on your own."

The young man said, "Oh fellow, this party is very private and I don't think you will be able to get in."

But the impudent barber said, "My lord, it seems that you are meeting a woman, since if you were really going to a party you would take me with you, for by now you know that a man like me will be the life and soul of any party. I would bring gaiety and joy even to a funeral. But I beg you to listen to me. If you are planning to meet a woman, you must tell me, because I am so crafty that I can help you to meet her and enjoy your time together. You will put yourself in great jeopardy and danger if you enter her house in the light of the day. And do not forget that you are in Baghdad and the Governor is known for his ruthlessness and severity."

The young man answered, disgusted now. "Aren't you ashamed of making these insinuations?"

The barber shook as if the young man had wronged him. "Why do you scold me when all I want is to help you?"

The young man suddenly felt afraid that his family or a neighbour might hear their conversation. So he kept quiet until the barber finally finished shaving his head. Then he tried to outsmart the barber, saying, "Go ahead and take the food and drink and everything to your friends and hurry back, so I can take you with me."

But the cursed fellow said, "I think you are trying to trick me and chase me away so you can go on your own and throw yourself in a trap and calamity: a disaster from which you cannot escape. I want you to wait for me and promise not to go on your own, so I can guarantee your safety."

"I promise I will wait for you if you hurry back."

All of a sudden the muezzin called for midday prayer, and the young man panicked and became desperate and rushed to the girl's house like lightning. When he arrived, he found to his good luck that the door was open. He rushed in and saw the old woman waiting for him.

"What kept you? The girl is worried that her father will be home soon."

The young man cursed the barber, but he hurried to talk to the girl, who snapped at him: "I don't understand! I thought you were dying to meet me, but when I agree, you have the indecency to arrive late?"

He tried to explain what had happened to him, but it was impossible for anyone to comprehend his saga with the barber. They had exchanged only a few words when they heard her father's voice echoing around the house, and realised he had come back from the mosque. The young woman trembled and asked the young man to go and hide on the second floor where the women servants lived. He did what he was told, and then he thought of a way to flee. He hurried to the window to see how high it was in case he could throw himself to the street. To his horror, he saw the impudent barber waiting below, and realised that, rather than taking the food and drink to his friends, he had followed him there.

Now it happened that at that moment the judge began to beat one of the maids for doing something wrong and she began to scream. Then a male slave came to her rescue and the judge beat him too, and the male slave screamed in agony as well. The cursed barber thought that the judge was beating the young man and he began to wail and tear his clothes and throw sand on himself, pleading for help. A crowd gathered around him, asking what was happening. "Someone is killing my Master at the judge's house," he screamed. He sent someone to fetch the young man's family, his servants and his friends and neighbours and soon everybody arrived. The young man couldn't believe his eyes, as the number of people below in the street reached nearly ten thousand, wailing as they pulled their hair and tore their clothes.

"Alas for our Master, he was so young," the barber cried, pointing at the judge's house, whereupon the judge opened his door. The barber cursed him with the worst curses: "How dare you kill our Master, you pig?"

"Who is your Master and what's the matter with all of you people?" the judge shouted.

The barber answered. "You've beaten the greatest of men and you must have killed him and hidden him. I heard him weeping and crying with pain and agony over the wall of your house."

"But what did your Master do in order for me to beat him and kill him? And why did he come to my house in the first place?"

Hearing this, the young man bit his lips, terrified that the barber would divulge his secret.

"Don't pretend that you don't know, you cursed man, I know everything. I know that your respected daughter loves my Master, and he loves her and I know that when you came back from the mosque and caught them, your good sense departed from you instantly, and you took revenge to protect you and your daughter's reputation. By God, no one will disperse this crowd except the Caliph himself. He must intercede in this case personally and give us back the young man, dead or alive."

The judge was humiliated and embarrassed. He opened the door wide. "If you're telling the truth then go in and get him."

The young man quickly looked around for a place to hide but only found a wooden chest. He pulled the lid down and held his breath while the barber searched the entire house; he went up to the maids' quarters and when he saw the wooden chest, he lifted it on to his head and hurried with it out of the house. The young man, inside, trembled and shook. Perhaps the barber would never let him be so long as he lived? At this thought, the young man opened the lid and fell on the ground, breaking his leg. He had golden coins hidden in the sleeves of his shirt, which he scattered among the crowd, and while many men were busy collecting the gold he fled into the alleys of Baghdad, in spite of his broken leg. The cursed barber ran after him, shouting, "They tried to deprive me of you, Master, they tried to finish the life of a young man who is the benefactor of my family, my children and my friends, unaware that I love you because of my loyalty to your father and grandfather. Oh, how I thank God for helping me to win over the judge and pull you from his grasp as if I was pulling a hair from dough. No, don't hurry, my Master, you don't need to run away, for if it wasn't for me you'd be finished. I hope that I won't live except to take care of you. I beg you to stop. Haven't you learned a lesson from what happened? You were so stubborn and went on your own. How I thank God that I didn't trust and believe you when you promised to wait for me. The truth is that I sent the food, the wine, the dessert and incense with one of your servants and I followed you step by step and I saw you entering the judge's house."

Hearing this, the young man got so exasperated with the barber that he wanted to beat him to death. He tried in vain to flee, running left and right in the crowded markets, but nothing could divert the barber, who was running with the speed of a young man. When the barber had nearly caught up with him, the young man took refuge in a shop in the market and told the owner his story. The barber tried to enter the shop, but the owner drove him away. "I am going to wait for him outside even if it takes days and nights," the barber shouted.

The young man put his head in his hands, thinking that the barber had become like a wart attached to his skin. He would never be rid of him! At this thought, instead of falling into a rage and taking his revenge or having a weeping fit, he called witnesses and made a will, leaving his money to his family. He sold his house and he left the shop, pledging to roam in God's open and wild world, fleeing his horrid pursuer. Eventually he settled down here, in China.

But soon enough his dream turned to a nightmare when he entered the party and saw the cursed face of the barber, whose tongue is like nonstop frogs croaking, who made him lame and chased him far away from his people and country.

Once we heard this tale of woe, we turned to the old barber and asked him if what the young man had told us was true. The barber lifted his head and said, "I should like to ask you a question before I utter one word. Have you heard the proverb, 'Beware of him to whom you've done Good'? This proverb fits this young man perfectly. If it wasn't for my wisdom and understanding of human nature, he would have perished by now—he injured his leg but didn't lose his life. By God, I was never curious or talkative; I out of all my six brothers was nicknamed The Silent One, while my eldest brother's name was Baqbuq, the second al-Haddar . . .'"

At this the lame young man fled, blocking his ears, and the guests left one by one. Even I left with my friend, who had hosted the party. I returned home and when I told my wife what had happened, she reproached me because I had left her for most of the day at home and insisted I take her out into the heart of the city. I obeyed her wishes and it happened that on our way back we saw a hunchback, reeking of wine, singing, beating the tambourine. He was so delightfully funny that we could not stop watching him. We invited him home to dine with us so we would have an amusing evening. I found myself stuffing a piece of fish into his mouth and he choked on a bone and when I thumped him hard on his back, trying to save him, he fell to the ground dead. I took him with my wife to the Jewish physician's house and contrived to get rid of him . . . And you know how the story ends.

The King of China shook his head with joy and wonder. "The story of the young man and the troublesome and intruding barber is more enrapturing and exhilarating even than the story of my dearest hunchback. Now I want you to bring me the silent barber, for I am longing to see him and to hear him talk. After all, it is he who has saved the four of you from death. Then we will bury the roguish hunchback and build him a tomb."

The tailor hurried to his friend who had hosted the party in order to get the barber's address, but when he entered the house he found that the barber was still there, talking to many parrots and other birds in cages. When the barber saw the tailor he was overjoyed.

"How happy I am that a human being is going to listen to a crucial moment in my story. I would like you, rather than these parrots, who keep mimicking me and interrupting my tale, to hear what I have to say. For reasons of which I am not aware, everybody abandoned this house, the guests and even the master of the house and his entire family, leaving me alone to tell my stories to these talkative and noisy birds."

The tailor took him by the hand and hurried back to the King. The barber stood before him, unsure of why the King of China wished to see him. The King started laughing when he saw that The Silent One was ninety years old with a white beard and eyebrows, floppy ears and a long nose.

"I want you, oh Silent One, to tell me one of your tales."

But the barber said, "Oh King of the Age, by God tell me what is the story of this Christian, this Jew and this Muslim, and why is this hunchback stretched on a bed fit for kings, and what is the cause of this gathering?"

"But why do you ask, when it is you who are supposed to tell me a story?"

"I ask in order to assure Your Majesty that I am not nosy or curious and to prove to you that I am innocent of the accusation that I am talkative. In fact I am a silent man."

The King told him what happened to the hunchback, and the barber came over to where the hunchback was lying and sat on the bed, taking the head of the hunchback on to his lap. He drew his face closer to the hunchback's and he started laughing and laughing until he fell on his back, and then he said, "For every death there is a cause but the story of this hunchback should be recorded in letters of gold."

The King of China was intrigued and puzzled. "What do you mean, Silent One?"

"I swear by your health that this hunchback is still alive."

He took from his belt a jar of ointment and applied it to the hunchback's neck. Then he asked for an iron stick and made two servants hold the hunchback's head while he inserted the iron stick in the hunchback's mouth. Then he took a pair of tweezers and thrust them into the hunchback's throat and removed the piece of fish dripping with blood.

At this, the hunchback gave an enormous sneeze, which was heard all over the silent palace, jumped to his feet and shook his head.

"What is going on here?" he asked.

"Oh my beautiful hunchback, can it be that you lay unconscious for a night and a day before this Silent One brought you back to us?"

The hunchback quickly asked for his tambourine and when it was given to him he started playing it at once, singing and dancing.

"But Your Majesty, you haven't told us when and how you met the hunchback, or do you prefer that I tell you a tale?" The Silent One asked the King.

"Not today, Silent One," said the King of China, "I'm exhausted."

With that, Jaafar finished his story of the hunchback and the King of China, and the Caliph clapped his hands with wonder and delight.

"Jaafar, this story of the hunchback's adventures and The Silent One is extraordinary and contains more absurd coincidence even than the story of the three apples."

Then he turned to Masrur, saying, "Slave."

Masrur brought forward Rayhan, who bowed and kissed the ground before the Caliph.

"You must stop behaving like an arrogant and foolish young fellow. I know that you didn't mean harm but nevertheless you've created this tragedy. I am going to fulfil my promise to Jaafar and forgive you, but not without conditions. You must spend some hours with the children of the innocent, dead woman, every day. When you hear them talk, or laugh, or cry, you will remember that you are the reason they are motherless."

Then the Caliph said, "The third dervish!"

Masrur brought the third dervish forward, who knelt and kissed the ground before the Caliph, then rose to his knees.

"Do you accept that you're responsible for your crime?"

"Yes, my lord," said the third dervish, burying his face in his hands.

"One should never act on what one hears from others, but seek and discover the truth for himself. Since you've punished yourself by plucking out your eye, and since you've become a dervish, and to be a dervish is to forgive, and because you are the father of two young motherless children, I will let you go."

The third dervish kissed the ground before he stood up and let Masrur lead him aside.

Everyone sighed in relief that the night, so nearly at an end, had concluded without imprisonment or death. They waited for the Caliph to stand up and leave at any second with Jaafar, Abu Nuwas and Masrur. But he reached for a cup of water, drank it, frowned at the three women, piercing them with a look.

"You three ladies have heard during this gathering, which wasn't planned, and couldn't have been predicted, episodes and stories which have happened to some of us. Stories which have entertained, bewildered, and others which have darkened our hearts and filled us with regret and sadness.

"Now, I want each of you, followed by the other, to open up, despatch and spill your secrets. Let us begin with you, Mistress of the House. Tell us, why did you stress, as soon as we entered your house, not to question what went on, making sure that we read the inscription on the door, 'Speak not of what concerns you not, lest you hear what does not please'? But what you really meant to say, was, 'one word from you about what you have seen and you're dead.'"

The Caliph poured himself water, brought it to his mouth but then, enraged, he failed to drink. "Could you explain to me," he said, "where this violence comes from? Why did you pounce on and thrash those bitches until they bled? You, flogged lady, why did you sway and yelp in pain, and fall into a swoon, when you heard that song and melody on the oud? We were horrified to see the scars on your body. And now, you third lady, tell me, why have you ignited your sisters' fire rather than extinguishing it?"

The Caliph fell silent and sipped his water.

A heavy silence fell on the room, everyone taken by surprise.

The ladies had become as pale as the colour of quince. They trembled and shook, realising for the first time the consequences of their earlier threats, especially the mistress of the house, who was the brains behind it all, and who'd decreed the rules.

She rose and said, "Oh Commander of the Faithful, how we wish that we had cut out our tongues instead of firing threats and accusations. And how I wish I had cut off my two hands instead of summoning my seven slaves with a clap. I beg your forgiveness, your wisdom and integrity to spare us from unburdening our hearts and revealing our motives and reasons which forced us to break the law of the land. To unveil our secrets would be the same as twisting daggers in our hearts, and I assure Your Lordship that it will result in horrible, strange and bizarre stories that no one will believe, other than thinking we are three lunatic women."

The porter said under his breath, "It is true, life is but a bunch of secrets." The Caliph cut through the rising excitement in the room by ordering the mistress of the house, "Go on with your story, we're all ears."

As soon as the mistress of the house found herself, forced, into the middle of the room, Vizier Jaafar stood up, saying: "Be aware that you are in the presence of the seventh son of Abbas al-Rashid, son of al-Hadi, son of al-Mahdi and the brother of Saffah (the butcher), son of Mansour. You must reveal your secrets frankly to the Caliph, and speak only the truth, even if your words burn like fire upon your tongue."

The woman nodded, her eyes cast down reverently, and began.

The Mistress of the House's Tale

y case is so strange, and my tale so bizarre, that if I engraved it with needles at the corner of my eye, it would be a lesson for those who wish to consider it. My Caliph, those two bitches are none other than my bewitched sisters, and I must whip them three hundred times each night in order to keep them alive.

But let me start at the beginning, when we were five sisters enjoying the love and tenderness of our caring parents. Then my father, the great merchant, died and we divided the fortune he left us between us and our mother. Soon our mother joined our father in death and so we divided her money equally among us five sisters. As soon as the period of mourning ended my two elder sisters married, took their share of the money and left Baghdad with their husbands to settle in a foreign country. I remained at home to care for my two youngest sisters, postponing the idea of marriage until they matured and immersing myself in working as a merchant, continuing my father's business. Two years later, one of my elder sisters returned home, dressed like a beggar in tattered clothes. Shocked and filled with pity,

I embraced her and asked what had happened. She wept and told me that her husband had wasted all their money, sold their house and disappeared from the face of the Earth. I took her in, cared for her, served her unconditionally and even shared my money with her. When I thanked God that the black storm had passed over our family, my other elder sister collapsed on our doorstep one day, barefoot. As she sobbed and struck her face she told us that her husband had plundered all her money and deserted her in that foreign land without even a morsel of bread. She had wandered from one country to another until she reached Baghdad. I squeezed her to my bosom as I had done with our eldest sister, showed her love and the utmost kindness, and then divided my money with her too.

"You're much wiser and more insightful than us, though you're younger, and now we feel that you have taken the place of our mother, may God pray for her soul. We promise you with all our hearts that the word 'marriage' will not cross our lips again," my sisters told me, weeping.

"Let us hire a ship and go to Basra with our merchandise and trade there, for we must depend upon ourselves and not on men," I told them.

They accepted my offer and suggestions, and when we came back victorious, having made a big profit, they thanked me and were grateful for my kindness towards them.

Two years passed, during which we enjoyed great stability and prosperity. Then one day, my sisters shocked me with disastrous news: they had decided to marry for a second time because they didn't fancy living without husbands.

"After all God created the animals in the world in twos; every creature in this universe gets married, even mosquitoes and lizards," they told me.

I reminded them that they had tried marriage, and that it had inflicted upon them great pain, poverty and degradation. But they would not heed my advice. They each married, without my consent, and took their share of the money while I continued to look after my two younger sisters.

What I had feared and foreseen came to pass, and my two elder sisters returned in a worse condition even than before. They apologised and asked my forgiveness, swearing by the precious Qur'an, which each of them held in her hand, that if ever they uttered the word "marriage" again, I was to cut out their tongues in revenge. They then threw themselves at my feet, wailing and weeping.

"We don't expect you to take us back, other than as your servants," they cried.

I found myself feeling great sorrow and pity for them. "You are after all my two sisters, my flesh and blood, and nothing is dearer to me in life but you; you are to me as were my departed parents."

And so I took them back as I had the first time, to my bosom, my house and my business. Soon I observed that their disappointment and pain made them immerse themselves in work and business with great dedication, resulting in our making even greater profits.

One evening, when we five sisters were sitting on the terrace, away from the maids, counting our money, one of my elder sisters sighed and said, "What's the point of this great fortune, if we are not married?"

Before I could answer, the other sister moaned, "I agree completely; life without a man is like a kitchen without a knife. We know full well that we were unlucky twice, but who can say? Perhaps we might be lucky the third time and meet the best of men."

When I heard this I nearly snapped at both of them, but since our two younger sisters were with us I calmed myself and sought to offer advice.

"Am I not younger than both of you? Yet I will not consider or contemplate marriage, and do you know why? Because I have learned a lesson: there is little that is good in marriage. It would be next to impossible for me to find an honest man of great integrity, well-mannered; a real gentleman who would honour me and appreciate me and love me for my own self and not for my money. The time has come for me to open up and confide in you. My heart does indeed throb and beat with the desire to fall in love and secure myself in the stability of marriage. But where is the man who would not deceive me and steal my money? Show him to me, for God's sake!"

As I have said, we sisters were sitting on the terrace facing our orchard, which was filled with trees and flowers, looking out as the sun began to plunge below the horizon. As I finished speaking, an enormous bird, larger than any I have seen or dreamed I might see, gave a high cry and flapped its wings, which were the many vibrant colours of the peacock, in our direction. I turned to my elder sisters.

"Look at its huge wings; aren't they like those of an angel? Perhaps it's a beautifully coloured angel seeking to rescue you from your own thoughts!"

The five of us laughed, while the giant bird flew towards me and hovered, fluttering its wings vigorously and uttering strange cries, soft and loud at the same time.

"This bird is no angel, but the man you are looking for!" my elder sisters cried out, as we laughed again. The bird flew away and joined a flock of these strange and enormous creatures, with their huge, brightly coloured wings.

I forgot completely about this bird until a few days later, when I went down to the manna from heaven trees by the pond, to find out whether the manna was ripe. In the distance I could see the enormous, colourful bird drinking from the pond. To my astonishment, I watched as the bird started to shake and shake, until a man emerged from beneath its feathers.

I put my hand to my mouth, gasping and suppressing a scream of confusion and amazement. I walked towards him as though hypnotised, feeling no fear. The man was looking at the house and did not seem to have noticed me. He was not like any other man I had ever encountered, he was so beautiful.

"Praise God who resembles no one," I murmured, for I had never seen a man as handsome as he. He had a face like the crescent moon, with rosy cheeks and eyes like those of a *houri*, as if God had created him to bewitch and enchant.

I calmed myself, and didn't try to catch his attention, but waited and watched as he walked very carefully towards our terrace. Then he entered his feathers again and flew away, leaving me to stare at the sky, speechless.

When I climbed into bed that night and shut my eyes, I saw only him, as if he stayed beneath my lids the whole night long. In the morning, I rushed to the pond but neither the bird nor the man was to be seen. I found myself checking the pond several times during the day, to no avail, until dusk fell. To my disappointment I then saw ten birds instead of one at the pond, playing, drinking and taking off and landing on the water. Eventually all of them flew away and my heart sank. But the same bird flew back, landed, shook and shook, and when he had become a man, he saw me standing not far from him. He smiled at me and I reached out and touched his feathers, which were soft and beautifully decorated.

"Who are you and what are you doing here?" I asked him.

"But have you forgotten that you yourself invited me? Did I not hear you say the other night, as you sat with your sisters, 'Where is the man who would not deceive me and steal my money? Show him to me, for God's sake?' I am that man you called for, and I hurried to comply with your wishes, of that you may rest assured, my beauty."

He took my hand in his and when I recoiled and moved away, he said, "Do not be alarmed. Here is my oath: my eye will not look at one dinar of your money and my hand will not touch one piece of bread from your table. On the contrary, I am planning to have you sleep in a bed of gold, eat from golden plates, and bathe in water of gold."

"But who are you really?" I asked, as I tried to still the hundreds of butterflies which fluttered in my heart in spite of myself.

"When I saw you, I lost my senses, for you took my breath away. My brothers and I come often to the pond in your orchard towards evening to drink from its fresh water. Yesterday evening I reached the pond earlier than usual. As I waited for my brothers, I heard voices. I felt curious, since I was accustomed to the stillness here, and found myself following the sound until I saw you like a rose among these women. I listened to the entire conversation with your sisters, and found myself marvelling, not at your beauty and charm, but at what I heard you saying and for your dazzling personality. I went back home and couldn't sleep because I kept thinking of you, and so I came back to you, for my heart now is aflame."

His words scared me even more, and my mind started to play tricks on me. Perhaps this man was planning to make me fall in his trap, only to suck my nectar, then desert me exactly like the four men who had disgraced my two sisters?

I froze, not knowing what to say. The man took things out of his wing, and I stood overwhelmed as he produced jewels, among them pearls as big as pigeon's eggs, saying, "Now do you believe that I want you for yourself and not for your fortune?"

He bowed and kissed my two hands and my feet. "I will be your obedient servant until Doomsday. I wish to marry you according to the rule of God and his Prophet."

At these words, I changed my opinion of men in the blink of an eye. I took him to a cave in our orchard, and there we kissed like Adam and Eve, and to my surprise I let him lift up my dress, and what would happen between a man and a woman happened between us, while I prayed to God to forgive me, assuring the Almighty that we would draw up our marriage contract first thing in the morning. Soon I found myself drowning in ecstasy and pleasure for the first time in my life. I then slept at his feet, and when I woke we sat content and fulfilled, holding the sun and the moon together. I asked him once more: "You haven't told me who you are. Are you the son of a prince bewitched, one of the greatest merchants, or a nobleman?"

"I will reveal my identity to you on one condition: you must promise me that no matter what your ears hear me reveal, you will never leave me."

I clasped my heart, and I felt myself break into a sweat as I said, "I promise on my memory of my parents that I will never leave you, unless you tell me you're the Shaytan, Satan himself."

The man laughed. "God save us from Satan, I am the son of the King Azraq Blue, the King of Jinnis, the enemies of Shaytan Satan, and my father lives in the Alakroom Citadel, and he has six hundred thousand jinnis, who dive in the deepest seas and fly in the vast sky. I have nine brothers, each of whom carry the name of our father, Azraq Blue, and we fly here and there in God's wildest world."

I caught my breath and said, "Glory to God, the omnipotent, the Almighty, the powerful."

Then I thanked God for sending me this flying man.

He took my hand, saying, "Come with me, let us fly together to my palace which is built in the air, and can be reached by neither human beings nor jinnis other than my brothers, who would take you as one of them."

All of a sudden, reality hit me. What was I thinking, falling in love with this man, now that I knew he was a jinni? Dazed and confused, I found myself saying, "I do not wish to go to any palace, either in the clouds or on the ground. I will live only in the house which my father built for us, and in which I grew up. You are probably not aware that I am the head of this family and I am an accomplished tradeswoman, as well as being responsible for the well-being of my four sisters. How can you ask me to fly away with you, and give up all that my God has bestowed upon me? I am certain that I would soon miss my sisters and Baghdad and then I would regret what I had done and cease to sleep peacefully and happily in your arms."

I started to weep, feeling sorry for myself. Life had finally smiled at me and I had fallen in love with the man of my dreams, whom I thought I would never find in teeming Baghdad. But then he turned out to be the son of the King of Jinnis!

"But how will I leave my brothers? Why did my heart flutter only for you, a human being? How could I cease to be a jinni?"

Then we wept together, embraced and wept even more, knowing that we were making the decision to separate; that our love was forbidden. We kissed and hugged and bade farewell to each other, and then hurried back and embraced again and again. He wiped my tears, I wiped his tears and then I ran home, stopping to look back just once more, to see him fly up and disappear.

I couldn't stay away from the pond. I checked again and again, and each time I saw that neither the man nor the bird was there,

I was plunged into melancholy and sadness. My eyes looked constantly to the heavens and my ears strained to hear the rustling of a wing.

When my love became an unbearable torture, I left my bed one night and ran to the pond, not caring if any of my sisters saw me. To my sheer bliss I saw my love waiting for me. He fluttered his wings, jumping in the air before he left his feathers and held me in his two arms. As we stood face to face with our lips touching he spoke: "I tried in vain to be away from you, but I will vanish and die without you."

I gazed into his beautiful, sad eyes and the thought that I would not be able to see them night and day made me weep and choke. But Azraq Blue embraced me and dried my tears with his hand.

"Please stop crying, my lovely. I shall be the one to leave my family and come and live with you as a human being, for I cannot live for another instant away from you."

I squeezed him to me, kissed him and kissed him again, and felt that I was finally in heaven. We agreed that he would knock at our door the next day and introduce himself as a merchant from Basra, asking for my hand.

"See you tomorrow if God wills," we said to each other, and I hurried back home, wishing that the night would pass quickly. I was woken by a great commotion and then some tapping at my window. It was Azraq, in the form of a bird. I opened my window and with my help he squeezed himself through and fell to the ground with a thud. Once inside he took off his feathers and we embraced each other and he told me that he could not bear to be parted from me, even for the rest of the night. We became like an orange to its navel. As we whispered words of love, I heard my two elder sisters at my door, asking if I was all right, for they had heard someone at my window. I answered them, pretending that I might have talked in my sleep. Azraq and I froze for a while, until we heard only silence. Then we embraced so strongly that each of us gasped for breath.

Early in the morning, before he left, Azraq asked me, "Do you have a safe place to hide my feathers?"

"Don't worry, I'll make sure that no one will set eyes on them," I told him.

"I would like to hide them myself, for these feathers are my power and soul," he said.

But I laughed, saying, "Don't worry, no one will put them on and try to fly with them."

"No human could fly with them, but as I told you, the feathers are my power and my soul. If even one feather is damaged, all of them would be broken and then I would lose my power to fly and . . ."

I interrupted him. "Then I will be the one who will interfere with your feathers, so you will stay with me for ever and ever."

He smiled as he hugged me and with great patience he said, "What I mean is that if I lose my power of flight, I will lose my power as a jinni, and I will lose my power to be a man. Then I would soon disintegrate into ashes."

"Let us hide them in the safest place so you won't become ashes," I said playfully, since I was certain that what he feared would never happen. I pointed to a closet. "My father's closet, where I hide everything which once belonged to our parents, as I fear that my sisters will lose things."

I took a golden bracelet from my wrist and straightened it and the bracelet became a key. Azraq was so surprised that I said to him, "You see, Azraq, humans can be inventive too!"

We laughed as I opened the closet with the key, and then together we laid the feathers inside, wrapped in one of my coats.

We locked it and twisted the key until it became a bracelet once more and I put it on my wrist.

Azraq then climbed out of the window and, after a short time, there was a knock at our door. One of the maids rushed to tell us, we five sisters, of our visitor. I was the last one to appear. Azraq asked about our parents, I wept and so did my two younger sisters while the elder two sat, poised and steely, looking at Azraq with great suspicion. Azraq then asked who was the oldest of us, and asked for my hand in marriage. I interrupted and asked for a moment with my four sisters. When we were alone, I said: "This man seems to be from a good family, serious, capable and honest. I would like to marry him."

My two elder sisters weren't surprised at all; they didn't even remind me that I had changed my mind about marriage and men, while the two younger sisters exclaimed, "Oh, sister, how happy we are for you! We had a feeling that you would never agree to marry and live with a man, but this beautiful man has changed your mind in one second."

So I married Azraq Blue according to the rule of God and his Prophet. I wore a dress my bridegroom had presented me with, decorated with so many precious stones that I needed several maids to help me to walk.

My two elder sisters asked why we had never heard of such jewels on our trips to Basra, while my younger sisters said, "Your dress is a slice of heaven."

Days and nights passed, as I plucked one honeycomb after another, meaning that I was completely immersed in passion and love. But other things did not go as smoothly as our love, because my husband's brothers never ceased trying to woo him back to them. They appeared at dusk each day and flew around until midnight, shrieking and screeching the loudest cries, which made Azraq weep.

"I am between two fires," he would say, "your love and their love. My brothers and sisters insist that I should return to them, fearing that in time I will become a human being and lose my powers as a jinni."

I felt great pity for him, and I offered him the chance to leave with them, putting my grief and heartache aside. But his answer to me was instant: "I cannot be away from you and so I have decided not to see them again, because being with them causes me sorrow rather than joy."

My two elder sisters, meanwhile, were eaten up with envy because I had found the man of my life. They never ceased to show their dissatisfaction with everything around them and their unhappiness, blaming me for preferring the company of my husband and resenting him for taking me away from them. I decided to accompany them on a business trip to Basra, but Azraq told me that he could not bear even the distance of a tiny strand of hair to fall between us. My elder sisters threw a tantrum, accusing me of being selfish, and so I advised them to go and look for husbands themselves; this time perfect husbands who would love and care for them, adding that maybe they'd be lucky the third time. My sisters searched high and low for husbands, asking matchmakers, going to the public baths every day, but nobody would marry them. I became accustomed to hearing them cry and sob at night, mingled with the shrieks and strange cries of Azraq's brothers.

How I wish that my elder sisters had kept on lamenting their luck and weeping instead of plotting and scheming to destroy my love for Azraq Blue! And how I wish that Azraq's brothers had not lost their senses and become violent! They began to throw mud and stones at our house; they would attack anyone in sight, even our gazelles and cats. We all became prisoners in our own home, and my two elder sisters complained, while my younger sisters looked everywhere for their nests, assuming that the birds' violent behaviour was because they were protecting their eggs.

Azraq Blue finally agreed to go and be with his brothers for one night, to try to calm them. He pleaded with me to accompany him. I refused, insisting I had no doubts whatsoever in my heart but that he would return to me. In the first hour of the morning, when everything was asleep, we hurried to the pond and before he entered his feathers he kissed me three hundred kisses. Then he flapped his wings, and flapped them even harder. For a moment I thought that he had forgotten how to fly, or he was changing his mind, but like a raging beast he kept trying and then searching his feathers, swearing in the way I had only heard him when he dreamed that he could no longer fly. Now that day had come to pass: Azraq couldn't fly. He took off the feathers, yelling, "I can't fly, I can't fly, someone must have damaged my feathers. I have lost the power to fly."

"Try, try again," I urged him. "No one knows about your feathers, and the key is always around my wrist."

He tried once more and then he took my hand and hurried towards the house, panting and cursing until we reached our bedroom. There, he rushed to the closet and started to inspect it, from the outside, very carefully, as if he was trying to find a flea on the back of a camel. Then, with all his might, he pulled the closet away from the wall. To our horror and agony, we saw that the whole back of the closet had been removed.

"I knew it! Your two sisters have interfered with my feathers. They must have heard me that night, when I flew to your room and hit the window; they heard me tell you about my feathers and how I could lose my power. Oh God Almighty, help me."

Then, still holding my hand, he led me to my elder sisters' room, flung the door open, and when they saw Azraq they screamed, mortified that he was still alive.

"Give me back the feather you have plucked. Now!" he demanded.

But my two sisters kept hugging each other and screaming.

I pleaded with them, crying, "Please, give him the feather and we will forgive you."

"What do you mean? What feather are you talking about?" asked one of my sisters.

Azraq spoke again, and this time with the greatest fury: "Give me back what you took from my wings."

"Come on, you ungrateful sisters, give him back the feather you have," I shouted.

My sisters looked at the door, desperate to escape, and Azraq spoke again, only now his voice was weaker.

"Do what your sister is asking of you, or you will regret it."

One of them spoke, saying, "This is the first time that we have seen your feathers and we don't know what they are for!"

I grabbed both of them by their shoulders and shook them, weeping. "For the love of our parents, give him the missing feather. Don't you realise how much I love him, how I cannot live without him? Do you want me destroyed?"

"But you have us. We will live, all five of us together, like we did before he came."

"I love you more and I'll always love you no matter what happens," my husband said, drawing me to him. Then he turned to my sisters and said in a shaking voice, "This is the last time I will ask you. Return the feather, or I'll cast a spell which will transform you into two dogs."

"I don't think you're able to do anything, you have lost your power," one of my sisters said.

He began to murmur some words in his language and then he spoke.

"You two ungrateful sisters, I am going to spare your wretched lives for the sake of your sister. But now leave your human form and become two black bitches."

"No, Azraq Blue, no! Wait! Let them give you the feather first, please don't despair."

But it was as though my sentence helped his power, because my two sisters were transformed into two barking dogs.

I threw myself at his feet, pleading with him, "But they have to give us the feather."

"They must have destroyed it and I can't afford to waste more time. Now, my love, you must give them three hundred lashes with a whip each night, and if you don't they will die."

Then my man, my bird, my jinni, fell down on the floor and didn't move.

"But you're a jinni, you must survive. How can I send a message to your brothers?" I beseeched him.

My Azraq Blue whispered, "Not without my missing feather and not without me."

I tried to take him out of his feathers, in the hope that he might survive as a man, but inside I found nothing but ashes.

I fainted, and when I came back to my senses I found my two young sisters beside me and the two dogs licking my hands and barking. They scampered to the cupboard in the hall and lay on their backs, their four legs in the air, then came back and licked my hands once more, barking violently while nosing their heads in Azraq's feathers.

I stood and took the feathers, cradling them in my arms, to the pond, wishing that Azraq's brothers would come and return him to life, even if it were only as a bird. I called in my loudest voice and then in my softest, but there was no answer. I laid the feathers down and searched the pond for another feather or something of his or his brothers which might help, but found only his footprints. I sat by the feathers in the stillness of the pond until early evening, when his nine brothers landed and circled around him. Then, instead of reviving him, they took him by their beaks and flew away with him.

I felt like a dead tree. How I wished I could live in the cave which had witnessed our first love. I dragged myself to the house to find my two bewitched sisters still barking and trying to jump up at the cupboard door in the hall. My two younger sisters were in great distress because they couldn't calm them; they had offered them food and water and a mattress to sleep on. When they saw me, the dogs started to howl, now attacking the cupboard.

I thought that perhaps my poor bewitched sisters were terrified, knowing that as soon as night descended, I would lash them with the whip that was in the cupboard. But when the cursed time came, and I flogged them, forcing my hand time and time again so that I would complete the three hundred lashes, instead of collapsing from the pain and the wounds inflicted on them, the two dogs yelped and howled and once again jumped at the cupboard.

Perplexed, we three sisters opened the cupboard door wide, and began taking out its contents: bottles of rose water, a lute . . . Soon one of us held up a fan made from peacock feathers, and the two dogs produced the strangest yelps, now driven almost to insanity. It didn't take us long to find, hidden among the feathers, one single feather belonging to Azraq: the feather which killed him and destroyed our love.

My two sisters were trying to give the feather back, so they might be forgiven and become human again, not realising that it was too late!

I removed the feather from the strong thread which bound it to the fan's handle and held it to my breast. Then, clutching it, I opened the window, calling at the top of my voice, "Azraq, Azraq, brothers of Azraq, here is the feather!"

I called, weeping and wailing, for hour after hour, until I lost my voice.

Eventually I let my two younger sisters take me to bed, clasping the feather in both hands, before resting it on my pillow. From that night onwards, the feather and I have never been parted.

"Here is my complete story, Oh Commander of the Faithful. You've witnessed the whipping of my two sisters until they bleed. I carry on doing that every night, fearing that if I disobey Azraq's orders they will die. That's why you saw me weeping when they wept, drying their tears for them with my handkerchief, asking their forgiveness. I am certain that they are aware I have no choice but to inflict this pain and torture on them."

The Caliph was both shocked and amazed at the tale of the mistress of the house. He turned to the flogged girl.

"Now tell us the cause of the marks on your chest and sides," he asked her.

And the young woman came forward and began.

"Oh Commander of the Faithful . . ."

The Doorkeeper's Tale

Oh Commander of the Faithful, I was living quietly and peacefully with my two sisters, the mistress of the house and the youngest one, and also, of course, my two elder sisters, who had by this time been turned into dogs by the jinni.

One day, an old woman came to the door of our house, kissed the ground before me, and said, "I am a stranger to Baghdad and I have moved with my orphaned granddaughter to your neighbourhood. We have no one to invite to her wedding tonight, and so I implore you to honour us by accepting our invitation and thereby mend our broken hearts, for a wedding celebration without guests is like heaven without people."

She wept, and I felt sorry for the old woman and her granddaughter. "Let me assure you, my lady," she said, "all the ladies of this city will attend if they hear that you are going to be there."

"I too am an orphan," I said, "and so I will attend the wedding for the sake of the orphaned bride, and the Creator."

The old woman bent and kissed my feet. "Don't trouble yourself, my lady, I shall come and fetch you around suppertime."

I dressed myself for the celebration in one of my elaborate

gowns, which cost one thousand dinars, put on my pearls and gold jewellery and then made up my face, and sprinkled myself with musk and perfume from head to toe.

The old woman arrived to find me waiting with my maids. She smiled broadly, kissing my hands. "Every lady I invited has accepted, and now they are all waiting for you," she told me.

I smiled back. What the old woman had said was true: I was famed throughout Baghdad for my enormous inheritance and prosperous lifestyle. For when our parents died, they left us five sisters a great deal of money, and my sister, the mistress of the house, who looked after my other sister and me, had capitalised on our inheritance through her success in taking over the family business.

We set out, the old woman leading the way, while my maids walked behind me. Soon we stopped at a clean, swept alleyway, shimmering like a mirror, with a golden lamp above a grand door. The old woman knocked at the door and a slave opened it; silk carpets were laid everywhere and candles lit from the door to the hall. The sumptuous furniture was encrusted with precious stones. And yet I was puzzled to hear no clamour of a wedding; neither the beating of tambourines, nor singing, nor the melody of the oud.

A beautiful young lady approached and greeted me, and I noted that she was not dressed as a bride. Seeing my puzzlement, she spoke at once. "I have a brother who is far more handsome than me. He noticed you on several occasions and admired your beauty and so he made enquiries and learned that you were the daughter of a great merchant, now dead. He is the head of our clan and he has decided to seek your hand in marriage. What do you say?"

I had fallen into a trap and I was completely alone. "But then who is the old woman?" I asked.

"She is the one who raised my brother. I hope you will forgive her for playing this trick on you, for she adores him."

The girl clapped her hands and a door opened and a handsome man emerged, dressed in clothes fit for a prince. I was attracted to him immediately, but as we sat together and talked, I was captivated. Seeing our harmony, and that we were in love, his sister clapped her hands once more, and a witness and a judge came through the same door. The marriage contract was drawn up and signed.

"Now, I want you to take a solemn oath never to look or talk to another man, under any circumstances," the young man said to me.

He handed me the divine Qur'an and I swore to obey his wish, thinking all the while, why would I give another man even a glance, when I had such a handsome and sweet husband?

I sent my maids back to my two sisters to give them the happy news, while we spent the best of sensual nights together. If anything, his behaviour became more ardent with each day that passed. He showered me with love and favours. We lived in happiness for a whole month, until one day I asked his permission to go to the market and he consented, on condition that the old woman accompanied me.

The old woman suggested we go to a shop owned by a young man who had every fabric one could desire. Once inside, I asked the old woman to have him show us his best stock.

"Ask him directly," the old woman said.

"Have you forgotten that I have sworn and promised my husband not to look at or utter a word to another man?" I whispered.

"Show us the best fabrics you have," the old woman said to the young man. The owner immediately brought out, from a wooden box, sequined fabrics of such splendour and beauty that I gasped in amazement.

I whispered to the old woman to ask the price of three which I most desired.

To my mortification, he answered, "These three cloths are priceless. I will not sell them, for either silver or gold, but only for one kiss on this lady's cheek."

At this I took a few steps back in horror, exclaiming, "Oh, God forbid!"

"Your husband forbade you to look at or to speak to a man, and you won't be doing either. Just turn your face to him and he will kiss it. That's all, unless you've really changed your mind about having these beautiful fabrics," the old woman whispered in my ear.

I yielded to temptation and turned my face to him. But the man sank his teeth into my cheek, with all his might, and bit off a piece of flesh. I screamed and passed out.

When I opened my eyes, I found myself clasped to the bosom of the old woman, outside the closed fabric shop. Seeing that I'd come to my senses, she said sadly, "Oh my lady, God has saved you from something even more horrible. Get up, let us hurry home."

I cried in terror when I heard the word "home." Weeping, I asked, "What am I going to tell my husband happened to my cheek?"

"He's not going to pay attention to your face," the old woman reassured me. "Just pretend that you are not feeling well, cover your face, and I'll dress your wound with ointment. You'll be cured in no time."

Encouraged, I rose to my feet and we walked back home, where I hurried to my bed and covered myself.

"Oh darling, what's the matter?" my husband asked when he saw me lying there.

"I have a horrible headache," I answered weakly.

How I wish I hadn't lied! He hurriedly lit a candle, lifted the covers and saw my wounded face. "What happened to your soft cheek?" he asked.

"I was in the market with the old woman buying fabrics, when a camel carrying firewood bumped into my face in the narrowest passage and the wood cut my veil and cheek, as you can see."

"Tomorrow I will go to the Governor myself and ask him to hang every camel driver in the whole of Baghdad," my husband said.

"No, my lord, we must not hang innocent men and bear the guilt of their death," I pleaded, in great agitation.

"Tell me again what happened; who actually harmed you?" my husband asked.

"I was on a hired donkey and when it wouldn't budge, his driver tugged very hard, and it stumbled and I was thrown to the ground and as luck would have it, I landed on a piece of glass, which cut my cheek."

"I promise you that as soon as the sun rises I shall be standing before Jaafar al-Barmaki, demanding that he hang not only every single donkey and donkey driver in this city, but also every sweeper."

On hearing this I changed my story again. "But my Lord, this was not what happened to me. I don't want you to kill innocent people and beasts because of me."

At this point, my husband started to lose patience. "Tell me, then, what really happened to you!"

I begged him to drop the matter: what I had suffered was my fate. But he kept insisting, pressing me to tell him what happened. I became more and more evasive and vague, but I could feel my cage constricting. At last, exasperated, I mumbled the truth.

My husband gave a great cry that shook the house and brought three slaves running. He asked them to drag me to the middle of the room. The slaves pulled me from my bed and threw me to the ground. My husband ordered one of them to sit on my chest, the other to hold my head and the third to draw his sword. Oh Commander of the Faithful! The three slaves granted his wishes at once.

Then my husband spoke to the slave bearing the sword. "Strike her, Sa'd, and cut her in half. Then each of you shall carry one half to the River Tigris and throw her to the hungry fish. This is her punishment. And to anyone else who breaks the oath and fails to follow my orders, I say the following." And he said angrily:

> "If I'm betrayed in love,
> I kill, despite my soul's destruction,
> Better to die nobly than challenge another,
> To sleep in the arms of my own cherished lover."

Staring, filled with hate, he again ordered the slave to finish me off. The slave, now sure my husband meant it, bent low and asked me, "Do you have any wish? For this is your end, my lady."

"My last wish is that you get off me and let me speak to my husband," I said.

The slave stood up. I raised my head and realised that I now faced death; once I had been high and powerful; now I was disgraced. I wept and choked with sobs and tears. My husband looked at me with fury and disgust and said:

> "You dared to leave me for another
> And repay me with mocking disdain?"

Hearing this, I wept even more, looking up at him as I said:

"You said you'd love me for ever,
Then smashed your vow like an unwanted vase,
Leaving my innocent love bleeding
With all trace of trust receding."

His look was ferocious, as if my words had been like knives in his chest, and he continued:

"I didn't leave her for another,
Oh no, her sins framed her fate.
God condemns duplicity
And cautions against its debate."

I pleaded for my life, but he yelled at the slave, "Go ahead, cut her in half, and rid me of her, for she and her life are worthless to me."

At this, I lost any hope that I might survive, and saw that my life was at an end, for his heart had become a steel fortress. Shivering and trembling, I nearly lost consciousness, when I was roused by a commotion behind me, and the voice of the old woman, like the roar of a cyclone. She threw herself at my husband's feet, wept and pleaded with him.

"Forgive her, my son, don't kill her. By the breast that nursed you and reared you, I ask you this, not for the sake of this worthless woman, but for your own sake, because he who slays ultimately shall be slain. Go on; drive her out of your sight and life completely."

She wept more tears, and implored him to set me free. Finally he relented. "But I will not let her go without branding her with a permanent mark on her body," he said.

He ordered the slaves to strip off my clothes and sit on me. My husband took a quince rod and within seconds whipped me all over my body, so hard that I wanted to die with the pain. Then he told the slaves to take me home under the cover of darkness and leave me on my doorstep.

My two sisters wept for me. The mistress of the house treated me with ointments and drugs, but nothing helped the pain or the marks on my body or the wounds to my soul. I stayed in bed for months and when I eventually recovered, my body remained disfigured, as you have witnessed, Oh Commander of the Faithful.

One morning I ventured out to visit my husband's house. But alas, I found it ruined and the alleyway a rubbish heap. Distressed, I went back home and swore never to think of him again, nor any man.

That night, and every night which followed, my two sisters, the black bitches, are flogged. Each time the whip falls on their bodies, my old wounds are reopened and ooze, and I writhe in pain, and sorrow drenches my heart.

In this way I lived in quiet seclusion with my two sisters, and the two bitches, until today, when the youngest sister, our shopper, allowed the porter, who carried home our goods, to stay for supper . . .

"This is my story, my Caliph."

The Caliph gestured to the flogged sister to sit. Then he asked the shopper to come to the middle of the room. "It seems that you have a story as well, for I noticed how you sang with such pain and disdain. Am I right? Tell me if you too have suffered a calamity at the hands of a man?"

The third sister, the shopper, began. "Oh Commander of the Faithful . . ."

The Shopper's Tale

h Commander of the Faithful," she said, and then fell silent, lifted her shawl from around her shoulders and secured it on her head. But then she began crying softly, wiping away her tears with the hem of her shawl.

"Oh Commander of the Faithful, with your permission I will abstain from telling my story."

"Everyone in this room has told his or her story," said the Caliph. "Remember that when I entered this house in disguise, with the Vizier and Abu Nuwas, the three of you sisters threatened us with death should we not reveal the truth about ourselves. Now go on and tell your story."

"With your permission," said the shopper, "I should like to emphasise that I will achieve nothing by telling my story, other than to cause embarrassment to others present, and so I . . ."

But the Caliph interrupted her and ordered her to begin, and so she did.

Upon witnessing the suffering and pain of my four sisters at the hands of their husbands, I pledged to lock my heart with a key and never to think of love and marriage. But bad luck and destiny lay just around the corner. Yes, Oh Commander of the Faithful, I was dragged by the tide of fate and nearly died like a bee drowned in her own honey. I say honey, because I was soaking in bliss and the happiness of love, living in the Caliph's palace, of all places.

The Caliph looked intrigued and confused as the shopper continued.

I was invited to attend a large banquet to celebrate the circumcision of the only son of my cousin. To my surprise a lady came in, glittering from head to toe, and even before I heard women whispering to each other, "Lady Zubeida, Lady Zubeida," I thought to myself, who could this gorgeous woman be except the Queen?

I learned that my cousin had made a vow to slaughter one hundred sheep to give to the poor if Lady Zubeida attended. I should mention here that when asked to play the oud, I played as if only the sky was the limit, and this pleased Lady Zubeida and she asked if I might sit beside her. I bowed and kissed her hand as I had seen the others do.

"Your dress is out of this world, it's a sheer delight, like a poem," she said to me.

I was wearing one of my sister's dresses that Azraq had given her, with beasts and birds embroidered on it in red gold. I told her it was my sister's.

"But where did your sister buy it from? I haven't seen anything like it before."

I fabricated an answer, telling her that the dress had been given to my sister by a sorcerer and once belonged to a princess who had died of love. Lady Zubeida, with tears in her eyes, asked if I was married.

"Oh, Lady Zubeida, I will never fall in love or marry."

She was horrified. "Never say that," she replied. "You're still in the prime of your youth and life is ahead of you. I'm sure when you meet the right person and your heart dances and rejoices you'll forget your vow and pledge yourself."

I smiled, thanking her for her kind words and her interest in me.

"And I have just the right person in mind. Let me work on it."

That evening, when I returned home, I thanked God that Lady Zubeida had been distracted by all the other women, and had forgotten all about matchmaking. But I couldn't have been more mistaken, for early the following morning a eunuch arrived at our house and invited me to the palace for dinner. The idea of a prospective suitor filled me with dread, but once I was in the palace, I entertained her and her slaves by singing and playing the oud. Each time I began to make preparations to leave, she insisted I stay, until, in the early hours of the morning, my fingers could play no more, and I had no voice left to sing and the eunuch led me to where my maids were waiting for me.

But all of a sudden the eunuch left, as a man approached.

"What are you doing alone here at this hour?"

He smelled like all the delicious fragrances of the garden.

"I was playing the oud for Lady Zubeida," I replied, "and my maids are taking me home."

"Are you the lady whom I heard competing with the nightingales and the sparrows?"

I blushed and smiled.

"I swear you are now shaming the flowers and roses with your beauty. The stillness of the night carried your voice and playing to me when I was wandering in this garden, because I couldn't sleep. Now I've put a face to the voice, I am struck double by insomnia."

Hearing this, I was sure this man was the suitor that Lady Zubeida had talked to me about, especially since the eunuch and my maids had disappeared when they saw him, leaving us alone.

The Caliph now exclaimed with great confusion, interrupting the shopper's story, and asking her to reveal her face. She did so, and when he recognised her, he gasped and shook his head in disbelief, gesturing to her to sit back down, which she did. The Vizier hurried to the Caliph and kissed his hand, and whispered into his ear. The Caliph thought for a moment, then nodded, and addressed the shopper.

"Come back to the centre of the room, and continue with your story."

The shopper came forward again, letting the veil hit on the sides of her head, as she continued.

When I heard this suitor speak, I registered how his manly voice matched his looks. Who could he be? I watched him as he cut a sprig from a tree, which he presented to me. The fragrance of Queen of the Night enveloped my heart. But then I remembered my vow never to marry.

"I wonder where my maids have gone," I said.

"They must have gone to bed, assuming you're staying here," he said, but then he laughed, and shouted out, "Who's there?"

We heard the footsteps of my maids and he left me, disappearing into the darkness.

When I was safely in my bed, I congratulated myself on avoiding fate, because my suitor would think I wasn't interested in him.

But the next evening, another eunuch knocked at our door, and said that he had come to take me to the palace.

I assumed my summons came from Lady Zubeida, but when we arrived at the palace the eunuch directed me elsewhere, leaving me in a room full of books and cages of birds.

To my surprise, my suitor came in. He poured wine for us both, smiled and when I refused to drink, he opened a cupboard and brought out an oud.

"Can you sing 'O! How I Would Like to Lie on Her Lap, for One Year, One Month, Or Even One Hour'?"

"I regret to say, sir, that I don't know that song."

He laughed mischievously. "This isn't a song, but how I feel. And now, let me kiss you, so that I might cool the fire which has been in my heart since last night."

I looked at the pattern on the carpet, willing myself not to give in to the desire to be kissed, and reminded myself that I had taken an oath never to love or marry. When this didn't work, I sought refuge in memory, picturing my unhappy and distraught sisters, but to no avail: I still longed to kiss this man.

Then I thought that if I drank wine, I might pretend that I was acting under the influence of drink. So I swallowed my cup of wine and then another, and when he did the same, desire took hold and my suitor drew me to him.

"By God, I am in love with you too, but there is no way you can reach me, for I have vowed to myself to remain chaste," I said, making for the door. "I beg you not to mention anything to Lady Zubeida."

"What do you mean?"

"If she knows I refused you, she'll be furious with me," I told him.

At this my suitor laughed and laughed. "On the contrary, she'd be delighted. For Zubeida happens to be my cousin and my wife!"

I gasped and my hands shot up to my mouth. Could it be that this man was none other than the Commander of the Faithful, Haroun al-Rashid? Then, as if I was dreaming a beautiful dream, I asked, "But why didn't you reveal your identity the first night?"

He laughed like a little boy. "I was enchanted that a woman who didn't know me might fall in love with me, as a person, not as the Caliph! Besides, I was terrified that you would disappear if you discovered my identity."

As I shook and trembled, I asked him if he had read the piles of bound books on the open shelves.

"Not all of them, but many," he answered. Then he took my hand and we sat and talked about music, science, astronomy and poetry, and he was surprised by my knowledge.

Then sleep overcame us and I slept on one couch while he slept on another. In the morning, when I woke before him, I smiled happily.

"I have broken my oath, but will never regret it, because the Caliph is not like any other man."

He awoke, and rejoiced to find me still with him, and we kissed.

Then I showed him what I'd embroidered on to my underwear, beneath my dress: *I promise you, body, not to let any man touch you, so you will be free from suffering.*

He kissed me on my forehead. "Let me assure you that you'll never suffer with me. Just give me one month, and then I'll draw up a marriage contract."

The Caliph settled me in a beautiful apartment within the palace, with ten women slaves to tend to me. Our days stretched into nights, and nights into days, until we became inseparable, like fish and water.

*   *   *

The mistress of the house and the flogged sister whispered to one another and gasped in horror at what they heard, while the shopper continued with her tale.

When the Caliph left me my heart would count the seconds till his return, and when I combed my hair before him, he would say to me, "Why are you deserting me?"

Then one day Lady Zubeida sent her eunuch with an invitation to dine.

The shopper's voice trembled, and she paused, then forced herself to go on with her story, swallowing hard. The Caliph and the Vizier exchanged glances.

I accepted the invitation, but my eunuch ran after me.

"Must you go, my lady?"

"Yes, I must, I don't wish to make an enemy of Lady Zubeida."

Now I realise that the eunuch, in his way, was trying to warn me. For it was known throughout the palace that Lady Zubeida had stopped eating and drinking for a whole six weeks, as the Caliph's visits to her became briefer and less frequent, while his concubines saw neither hide nor hair of him.

It wasn't only the Caliph's relations with his women which were under strain from his wish to remain constantly at my side. Ministers from the government assembly complained that he was neglecting public affairs, venturing out of the palace only for Friday prayers. Jaafar al-Barmaki, the Vizier himself, tried to reason with him, drawing his attention to the growing dissatisfaction.

"My obsession with her is beyond my control, my heart is totally ensnared," the Commander of the Faithful replied.

Jaafar persisted, however, advising the Caliph that he could resume his public affairs without jeopardising our relationship. "She will always be there, waiting for you, Oh Commander of the Faithful."

He suggested a hunting trip, and the Caliph agreed to go, for one night only.

All of this had been hidden from me; I knew nothing of it at the time. The Caliph kept me apart, alone and cocooned, and in this way he robbed me of all power over my fate.

The night before he left, we embraced and embraced, as if we were parting from each other for ever—which of course we were.

Lady Zubeida welcomed me at dinner with much admiration, as I bowed and kissed the ground before her.

"Peace upon the Abbasid Lady, who descends from the Prophet; let us pray that God Almighty may protect you for now and for ever," I said.

"I had forgotten how beautiful you are!" she said. "No wonder my cousin cannot keep the distance of a hand between you."

I was ecstatic when she continued, "He tells me that he will soon take you as his wife."

Then she led me to a sumptuous banquet, prepared as if for a hundred, not just the two of us. She offered me an exquisite Chinese dish with a fish pattern, saying, "You must taste this *battareck*; it is a rare dish beloved of my cousin al-Rashid."

I took three mouthfuls out of respect for the Caliph. As soon as I swallowed, my eyes became heavy, I felt the earth spinning, and I lost consciousness.

I came to my senses in unbearable, silent darkness. My limbs ached, and when I tried to stretch them, I found they were trapped. I lifted my head and it hit something hard.

*   *   *

"Oh, my darling sister!" the mistress of the house exclaimed.

I screamed, certain that I was buried alive in a tomb. Then to my relief and salvation, I heard the voice of a man.

"Open up, open up, I'm not dead!" I shouted.

"Oh God, there's a jinni in this box. Oh angels, come and rescue me!"

Then a second voice said, "You're hallucinating. This box is as still as a rock, smash it with a big hammer."

"No, for God's sake! Don't use a hammer, I'm begging you."

The two men cried out in surprise.

"Let's leave it and go," one of them said. "I'm really scared, I can hear someone coming."

I heard them running away as footsteps approached.

A new voice said, "In the Name of God the Compassionate, the Merciful; in him I trust."

I felt the box lift and then I heard the sound of mule's hooves hitting the ground for what seemed an eternity, but in reality can't have been longer than half an hour.

Then the box was pulled off the mule and we entered a house. The man's footsteps were muffled by carpet, the box was put down gently, and I heard him try to open the lock, as I held my breath. When he finally succeeded and lifted the lid, he muttered to himself again, "In the Name of God the Compassionate, the Merciful; in him I trust. By God, what is this sleeping *houri* of Paradise doing in this box? Who put her here?"

I opened my eyes, and looked up at a young handsome face.

"Where did you find me?" I asked.

"In the graveyard," the man replied. "I was visiting the grave of my mother, who passed away two days ago. I saw two men trying to open this box, and when they heard me approaching, they ran away. Come, sister, let me help you out of this wretched box."

I gave him my hand, and as I stood and took my first step, I nearly fainted. He opened a bottle of rose water, and smelling it helped me retain my balance, but I was very weak, and trembling.

"Here is the bathroom, let me get you some towels and heat the water for you," he said, as he led me to a door. I thanked him and then looked at myself in the mirror and cried with all my heart; and when I thought of the Caliph I wept more.

The Caliph held his head in his hands and shook it in disbelief, but the shopper carried on.

I wanted to shout, "Get me to the Caliph straight away."

But instead I thanked this stranger, bathed and dried myself. When I reappeared, he showed me a table on which there were a few dishes of food. But remembering what had happened at my last meal, I began to weep again.

"Don't cry, sister; just try to eat in order to regain your strength."

"Thank you, and God protect you for your kindness and good deeds, but I'm not hungry."

And so he prepared some tea. "Now tell me, who are you? You are adorned in so much jewellery and yet whoever put you in the box chose not to rob you."

I hesitated. Should I tell this man, with his kind eyes, obviously from a good family, who I really was? I decided to be honest. I told him I was the Caliph's fiancée, and to my surprise, he raced from the room. I followed and asked why he was troubled.

"How can an ordinary human being be in the same place as the fiancée of a lion?"

"What do you mean by that?"

"Isn't the Caliph a lion amongst men? How can I breathe the same air as the woman he loves?"

"You rescued me," I said, "and for that the Caliph will be grateful to you."

He showed me to a room where he had prepared my bed. He asked me if I needed anything else before he left to spend the night at his sister's house. I asked his name, and he said he was Ghanem bin Saeed. I asked him for his occupation and he told me that he was a merchant. Then he left, but I couldn't sleep. I was scared that I would find myself back in the cemetery, locked in the box. And I wondered how a great woman like Lady Zubeida could have carried out this evil crime, just like a common criminal? What had she told the Caliph when he'd returned from his hunting trip and I had disappeared? When the sun finally rose and I was still alive, I fell into a doze. I slept late, until I heard Ghanem knocking at my door.

He told me he had risen early and visited the auctioneer who sells items from the palace. From him he had heard a rumour that I had been drugged and put in a box, which was auctioned while still sealed. Next he had visited the mosque and prayed next to a pious, elderly eunuch who had been working at the palace for a long time. After they had recited the Fatiha for the souls of their dead, Ghanem had cried for his mother. Then they had walked together, and Ghanem had given the old man a few dates, taking one for himself and pretending to choke on the stone. The old man had hit Ghanem on the back saying, "Careful, young man. The other day the Caliph's favourite choked on a morsel of food and dropped dead. There is no power but God the Merciful."

"The Caliph must be devastated," Ghanem replied.

"He has cried rivers, the Tigris and the Euphrates together, and everyone in the palace wore black, following Lady Zubeida's wishes. She even constructed a tomb for the poor young woman inside the palace itself. A friend of mine told me he saw the Caliph clutching the grave, crying and reciting as even the stone wept upon hearing him:

> " 'Tell me, unflinching grave,
> Has her beauty faded?
> Or her radiant smile evaporated?
> Timeless grave, where neither sky nor gardens bloom,
> How do you stay true
> To ephemeral flowers as well as the full moon?' "

Ghanem told me how the eunuch's eyes filled with tears at these lines.

We both fell silent when he'd finished recounting this tale, and I struck my face and wept. I had been erased from the Caliph's life. He would mourn me for a while and then forget me. Anger began to bubble in my chest, like boiling water, as I thought how the Caliph had accepted what he was told without investigating my death or asking for witnesses. He hadn't even asked for my tomb to be opened, by the measure of two palms, so that he might touch my leg or bid me farewell.

As if possessed, I hurried to the door, determined to seek out the Caliph and shame Lady Zubeida and everyone who'd assisted her in her devilish plot. But Ghanem hurried after me. He kissed each of my hands, and threw his arms around me, saying, "Remember to put your trust in God. Didn't the Almighty send me at the crucial moment to save you?"

His words were like a river of rose water, which calmed and soothed me. I thanked God for him. He showed me the goods he'd brought, laying out beautiful clothes and garments and four different sizes of embroidered, expensive slippers before me.

He disappeared into another room for a moment, and handed me a pair of earrings, each in the shape of a hand holding a flower, with a diamond ring on one of its fingers. I gasped at their beauty.

"Try them on. They were my mother's. She made me promise her to give them only to the woman I fall in love with and marry."

I didn't take the earrings. "I am completely lost, Ghanem. I think you are the loveliest man I've ever met, other than my father, but I must remain true to the Caliph."

"I understand."

At this, I held him tight for a moment, and laid my head on his shoulder, but we quickly separated, and he started to prepare food. I had no appetite, for I was beginning to doubt that I was really alive, since I had a tomb engraved in my name. Ghanem persuaded me to eat from one dish, and then another, until I felt sleepy and tired. When I awoke the following morning, I found him waiting for me. He told me he must go to work and leave me on my own, instructing me not to open the door to anyone.

As he left I heard hooves clattering in the alley and smiled. I prepared supper with the chicken and vegetables he had bought, to surprise him. As I worked, I reflected on how peaceful his house was, and how satisfying life was without the clamour of the palace and the jealousy and competition and the mistrust felt in every part of the royal court, from the slaves to the nobles. I went into the bathroom to prepare myself for Ghanem's return and saw the beautiful earrings laid out for me on a towel. I tried them on and found myself wishing that I had met him before I had fallen in love with the Caliph. When Ghanem came back from his work, we sat together and ate. I handed him back his earrings, saying, "I am still loyal to the Caliph, although my heart flutters when I see you."

"I beg you to take them, so you'll remember me when you wear them."

I drew close to him, and he held my hand and kissed it, saying, "The Caliph is the luckiest man in the world. Can I suggest that I confide in the old eunuch who frequents the mosque? I will tell him everything that's happened to you, that you are still alive, and listen to his advice."

He drew closer to me, and seeing the vein in his temple throbbing, I wanted to hug and comfort him but held back.

"It's no use," I said. "I'm still loyal to the Caliph."

In the morning he promised he would ensure that the happy news did not reach Lady Zubeida before it reached the ears of the Caliph.

"Farewell, my lady, God be with you and remember me in your prayers. Who knows, God might answer and send me a wife as trustworthy as you."

"Will you not return to say goodbye?"

"When the Caliph sends someone to fetch you, it is better that I'm not present." I rushed to him and pressed him to my heart, but he drew back and kissed my two hands. Then he disappeared, before instructing me to leave the key under a jar in the garden.

I prepared myself for a summons for the palace, but nobody came, and I nearly set out to find Ghanem at his sister's house. After a while I fell fast asleep. Suddenly the door was broken down and soldiers stormed through the house, expecting to find us together in bed. When they couldn't find Ghanem, they began to destroy the house, as I screamed and yelled at them, saying, "My rescuer never slept here."

They continued their rampage until nothing was left unbroken. Throwing my things into a cart pulled by an old mule, they took me with them. With such disrespect I feared the worst, and I was right. I wasn't met by Jaafar, or even by my eunuch or my slaves at the palace, but I was led like a criminal into a pitch-black cell, with an elderly woman as my keeper.

"No, no!" cried the mistress of the house. "There is no will or power save in God." But the shopper carried on with her tale.

I cried out, over and over, pleading with my captors, and telling them that they would be sorry when the Caliph found out how I was being treated. Finally, after twenty-four hours of captivity, the old woman who sat in the corner watching me, and shooing away the rats, said, not without sympathy, "Listen, we're only executing the Caliph's orders."

She told me that the same old eunuch whom Ghanem had asked to pass on the news to the Caliph, had gone in turn to a trustworthy concubine whom he knew very well, and who he knew hated Lady Zubeida. He confided in her that I was still alive and asked for her help. She agreed but any plan she may have been forming was destroyed by her loose tongue. This concubine happened to be the Caliph's favourite masseuse. She was massaging the Caliph's shoulders as he snored deeply and she couldn't resist whispering the secret to another concubine who was massaging his feet.

The Caliph had leaped up and shouted, "Did I dream, or did I hear that my fiancée is still alive?"

The concubine babbled something, but the Caliph shouted impatiently, "Where is she?"

Hearing that I was at Ghanem bin Saeed's address, the Caliph called for Vizier Jaafar.

"I have been mourning an adulteress. Find her and imprison her."

When I was brought to the palace and thrown into a cell like a witch, he called Lady Zubeida and accused her of lying to him. She had no choice but to confess and tell him the whole story, blaming her deep love for him, which had made her dangerously jealous of me. He forgave her, and kept me locked in the cell and who knows why? Perhaps he believed that when a woman and a man are together under the same roof, Satan will be the third. Or because of the rumours which were circling around and about the palace that I had betrayed him, in the Caliph's mind, I had become used goods.

When I heard that he had forgiven Zubeida, I was devastated and I screamed at the Caliph's betrayal. "One day, Oh Commander of the Faithful, you'll stand in the hands of a just ruler and the judge will be your God and angels your witness. They will all acknowledge your injustice and show you that you treated badly the one who never did you harm."

I repeated these lines to the Commander of the Faithful day and night, murmuring to the walls, to the rats, then shouting them out loud until the rats scuttled away in fear. I stopped eating and drinking. Ghanem came to me in my dreams, shaking his head in disbelief at what had happened, but then he would disappear and I would wake, crying out, "No, don't go now, stay with me," and stretching out my hands to catch him.

Seeing that I was becoming insane and delirious, the woman keeper took my head in her hands, recited a few verses from the holy Qur'an, and asked me if I had a family. I wept and repeated over and over the names of my four sisters until the woman whispered to me to pretend to die, so she could take me back to my sisters. Half dead anyway, I pretended to fall down dead.

I heard the keeper telling the guards to go immediately to the Caliph and inform him of my death.

The guard came back a few hours later and said that the Caliph had forgotten that I was imprisoned and that my body was to be returned to my family. As I cried silently, the woman wrapped me in sheets and placed my body on a mule with the help of the driver. She made her way to my home and knocked at our door. As soon as someone opened the door, she hurried away.

My sisters couldn't believe that I had finally returned; they thought that someone had kidnapped me. Hearing this, I told them that I had indeed been kidnapped by a lunatic man, who thought that I was his sister. He had put me in a cellar and his old wife had managed to rescue me by faking my death. I kept the truth in a well I dug deep in my heart.

The shopper looked at the Caliph, who was still resting his head in his hands.

"This is my story, Oh Commander of the Faithful, but I have one final thing to say. I could not agree more strongly with what Your Lordship said to the third dervish; that one shouldn't act upon what he hears till he is certain that it is the truth. And even then, always to act with mercy."

The shopper went back to her seat, and her sisters wrapped their arms lovingly around her, while the people in the room looked at the Caliph, awaiting his reaction. But the Caliph continued to rest his head in his hands as the audience fidgeted.

The Reaction of the Caliph

he Caliph was saddened when he heard the shopper's story. The more he thought about the matter, the more it became clear to him that he wanted to right the wrongs of the past, and he said, with great determination: "You three ladies have suffered enough pain, worry, loneliness and isolation. You have lived without husbands or family, in total seclusion, as if waiting for death, while each of you is still in the prime of youth."

The Caliph was interrupted by the barks and yelps of the two bitches, and addressed the door behind which they were locked. "Don't worry, wretched bitches; you haven't left my mind since I heard your yelps and whimpers and saw your tears."

He turned to Jaafar. "I want you to find someone able to deliver these two women from the spell they're under. I am certain we can win over the jinnis with the help of God the Almighty."

Masrur came forward, bowed to Jaafar, and whispered a few words. Jaafar turned to the Caliph. "The slave Rayhan claims that he learned witchcraft from his aunt; he has memorised the one hundred realms of magic and he would like to help the two bitches."

"Rayhan, try to save these two sisters from the spell they are under, which has made their lives one of torture."

Rayhan bowed and kissed the ground, and then addressed the mistress of the house, his eyes cast to the floor. "Come, my lady, hand me the feather of your husband, the jinni."

The flogged sister went and fetched the feather and handed it to the slave.

"I need a flame," he said.

The flogged sister brought him a candle. Next he asked for the two bitches to be brought to him. The shopper and the porter went to the cupboard and brought out a dog each. They stood before Rayhan, who took the feather and lit it, so that it burned up and disappeared into the ether.

"Owner of this feather," he said, "appear before us now; as a spirit or in the flesh, wherever you are, in the depths of seas or in the skies, in the folds of the earth, or on top of mountain peaks."

At this, the house began to tremble and the jinni Azraq appeared in the room as a shadow. The mistress of the house took a step towards him, but Rayhan stopped her with his hand. Then he closed his eyes and muttered a spell, intoning the talismanic words: "We need you, oh jinni, who cast a spell and turned these two women into bitches. Please, lift your curse and release them from their misery, for they tried to give you back your feather, too late, and they and their sisters have suffered enough for their crime."

Azraq appeared fully before them now, as handsome and beautiful as ever.

"Peace be upon you. It seems that repentance has lightened your hearts. In the name of Almighty God and his covenant, be yourselves again."

The two bitches shook and trembled, and stood up as two

women, in their nightgowns, just as they had looked when Azraq cast his spell on them. Everybody gasped.

"God is great!" the porter yelled, breaking the silence, and the room filled with great commotion and excitement.

The mistress of the house ran to Azraq, who gazed at her, then disappeared. She held her breath, hoping he might appear once again, adjusting her shawl so that he might see her beauty. When he did not materialise, as she had so fervently hoped, she felt a great anger engulf her. Why had he never appeared to her before, so that they might exchange a few words and glances, as he had been able to do tonight? But she stopped dwelling on him as her four sisters rushed towards her with all the joy and euphoria in the world. The five sisters held each other in celebration of their reunion and the elder two sobbed, touched their faces and their nightclothes, unable to believe they were free at last.

The shopper ran to her room and brought out two big shawls and silk dresses, and helped her sisters to put them on, as the mistress of the house whispered to them about the Caliph and Jaafar. Then she presented them to the Caliph and the two sisters knelt before him, and thanked him, kissing his hands.

They wept till Jaafar interrupted, indicating they should compose themselves, and sit back down. Then silence fell as the Commander of the Faithful spoke.

"Splendid work, Rayhan; may God reward you with every good wish for delivering these two ladies from their spell and torture and I am going to reward you. And now do you think you could discover who wronged the flogged sister by robbing her of her rights?"

The slave bent and kissed the ground before the Caliph.

"I will give it a try, guided by Almighty God," he said and then he called to the porter. "Brother, fetch me a bowl of water, to which you have added just one drop of oil."

The porter fetched a bowl while the flogged sister held the shopper's hands and rested her head on her sister's shoulder, closing her eyes. Once again, Rayhan uttered a spell and talismanic words, looked into the bowl for a long time and then gasped, swaying in disbelief.

"Oh Commander of the Faithful, he is . . ."

"Spell it out, slave; who is it?" shouted the Caliph, growing impatient.

"What can I say? The man is the nearest of all men to you. He is al-Ameen, your son, the brother of al-Ma'mun. He married her secretly but legally."

"Masrur, go and fetch me al-Ameen at once," shouted the Caliph. Then he turned to Jaafar.

"The events of this evening resemble life itself: filled with harmony, the sublime, and with great contradictions—hate and love, tyranny and freedom, bliss and torment, loyalty and betrayal. Can you imagine the contradictions of fingers which play the oud and others which clutch the whip? Nights of music and melodies and others filled with sobbing and wailing?"

"Not to forget nights drinking wine and nights drinking water," whispered Abu Nuwas. Everyone in the room heard him and suppressed a laugh.

The Caliph was about to respond when his son al-Ameen entered, curious to know why his father had asked him to come to this unknown house, rather than visit his quarters at the palace. He was even more perplexed to discover the Caliph, Jaafar and Abu Nuwas in the presence of three dervishes each with an eye plucked out, and five beautiful women who were neither slaves nor concubines.

The Caliph addressed his son. "Look at these five sisters very carefully; perhaps you recognise one of them? Ladies, assist him by pushing your scarves aside so he can see your faces."

Al-Ameen recognised the flogged sister instantly. "Yes, my lord, this lady is my wife. I married her after I had heard about her charm and beauty and I tricked her with the help of my old nurse and a slave girl. She accepted my offer and I married her immediately and secretly before only witnesses and a judge. Then we separated and each went our own way."

"Yes, my son. The lady told us the reason behind your separation—and we have seen her whole body, bearing the indigo and black bruises of a brutal flogging. If her story is correct, and you are indeed the one who caused her wounds, then I order you to seek her forgiveness by marrying her under a new contract, rather than abandoning her, tormented by her dark and agonising memories."

"To hear is to obey, my lord."

The Caliph turned to his Vizier. "Jaafar, summon the judge. All in this room shall be witnesses. Dervishes, come forward."

The three dervishes kissed the ground before the Caliph and knelt.

The Caliph looked at the first dervish. "Aziz, I shall appoint you the chief of the eunuchs in the women's quarters of my palace and give you horses and money."

"To hear is to obey, my lord," said Aziz.

The Caliph turned to the second dervish. "You, prince, I want you to wed the mistress of the house. I shall make you a chamberlain and give you money and a palace of your own in Baghdad."

"To hear is to obey."

Then the Caliph addressed the third dervish. "You, carpet seller, shall marry one of the elder sisters, now freed from her spell, and

I shall appoint you a member of my inner circle and give you a palace in Baghdad and money."

"To hear is to obey, my lord."

The Caliph looked round. "And you, porter." The porter copied the dervishes' actions and knelt before the Caliph. "You are going to marry the other elder sister, and I shall also appoint you as chamberlain and shower you with wealth."

"To hear is to obey, my lord—but I would like, with your permission, to marry the mistress of the house, for I fell in love with her the moment I entered this house."

The Caliph smiled. "Then we shall marry you to the mistress of the house and the second dervish shall marry the elder sister."

The second dervish and the porter answered as one. "To hear is to obey."

"Long live the Caliph!" the porter added. "I promise you, oh lord, that if God rewards me with boys, I am going to name each one of them Haroun al-Rashid in your honour."

Laughter echoed around the room, but soon everyone fell silent, for they were curious to hear what the Caliph's verdict would be regarding the shopper.

Without a trace of hesitation the Caliph said, "Praise be to Almighty God, who saw that my path crossed with my lady's path once more upon this Earth. Now I am going to atone for all the miseries and the upheaval she went through by pledging my love to her once more, and ask for her hand in marriage, showering her with the wealth she deserves."

Everyone looked at the shopper, who stood up and approached the Caliph and bowed before him.

"I should like to thank the Commander of the Faithful, who is famous for his wisdom, tolerance and fairness, and who always looks after the well-being of his subjects. I am greatly indebted to him for his generosity and sympathy and do not forget the honour he has bestowed upon me. But it is impossible for me to marry you, Oh Commander of the Faithful. Not out of revenge or lack of gratitude, God forbid, but because I and my pain have become one, and I do not wish for a life other than the one I am living, without a man. I feel now that a big chunk of my pain has disappeared at the return of our two elder sisters from their hell and so I am sure that I can endure what life remains to me."

The Caliph was clearly stunned by the shopper's response. He cleared his throat several times, but not a word was uttered. When the mistress of the house rose, he was visibly relieved, clearly assuming, as did all the men in the room, that she would scold her foolish and ungrateful sister.

"I hope my lord will allow me to express my gratitude, and to say how touched I am with his noble intentions. Your generous heart seeks to enable us to begin new lives and leave our miseries behind. But I find myself following my sister's decision, for I do not wish to marry the porter, nor anyone else. My happiness does not lie with a man. Before I married the jinni Azraq, I had decided that I would never give my heart to a man. How I wish I'd stood by my instinct, rather than suffering every second of those years! Not only did I see my two sisters turned into bitches, but I was forced to whip them each night until they bled. To place me in this position was the ultimate cruelty and betrayal."

The flogged sister stood. "I stand, Oh Commander of the Faithful, with my slain heart, for I am certain, without doubt, that I can never again be with a man. These feelings are beyond my control, for a bad thing never dies. I abide by the proverb, which says, 'Never marry your old lover or your ex-husband.' But

I thank you, with what remains of my heart, for your sympathy and consideration."

The flogged sister remained standing, awaiting the reaction of the Caliph, but when several minutes passed, and the Caliph remained silent and still, she returned to her seat.

The two elder sisters stood, and one of them spoke while the other one nodded her head in agreement.

"Oh Commander of the Faithful, we did to our sister, the mistress of the house, what a wild animal might do to a hand offering food: we grabbed both hand and morsel. This happened because a seed of evil grew up inside my sister and me, and eventually ruined us. But one must ask the question: how did we become the soil which grew the seed? My answer is that the men we married not only squandered our money, but abandoned us as if we were two flies on a heap of garbage. And so I pray, Oh Commander of the Faithful, that you will forgive my sister and me for not fulfilling your wishes and marrying for a third time."

When the two elder sisters returned to their seats, everyone in the room waited for the Caliph's response. Would it be fury, or understanding? Eventually he spoke:

"Allow me to praise each of you ladies for your courage and self-assertion; but you shall do as you are told. I want you to view your tormented past as a nightmare, and look now to the future with joy in your hearts, and fresh hope. With God's protective eye upon you, you have long years to live and you must have men alongside each of you, to ensure your well-being. The loneliness of the old is like death itself; and if you reach those years without husbands or children you will feel great bitterness and resentment."

Without giving them a chance to respond, the Caliph turned to Jaafar. "Are the judge and witnesses here?"

The Vizier bowed to the Caliph. "Allow me, Commander of the Faithful, to remind you that you are the great believer in fairness and justice. Let us leave these sisters to live as they wish, especially since they are scrupulous and lead decent and dignified lives. What is more, one shouldn't forget how accomplished they are as businesswomen and merchants and how faithful and loyal they've been to the memory of their parents. Isn't it enough that they have suffered so at the hands of men? Now you want to plunge them back into wedlock, which might immerse them yet again in misery and pain?"

The Caliph became angry. "Scrupulous? They nearly killed the seven of us in cold blood, when we questioned their beating of the bitches. And, what man here would cause them further pain, now we've heard their agony? Myself? My son al-Ameen? The dervishes or the porter?"

Giving the porter another look, the Caliph said, "The porter may appear insolent, but he won't treat the mistress of the house with anything other than fairness and goodness, since I shall be his brother-in-law after I have married his wife's sister."

The shopper stood up. "Pardon me, Oh Commander of the Faithful, if I say, once again, that I shall not under any circumstances marry, nor spend the night under the same roof as a man, even in a separate room."

"My lady, the night is nearly over and you've spent it in the company of seven men; no, I mean, six men and two half men," said Abu Nuwas, indicating himself and the first dervish.

The Caliph smiled at Abu Nuwas's wit but then he flared up. "Why is it that men are always the accursed ones? Who thought of that diabolical plot: a man or a woman? Who drugged you and locked you in a chest, sold you and constructed a tomb, and ordered everyone in the palace to mourn by dressing in black? And, what about the man who loved you, and mourned you as never before, or since?"

"Oh Commander of the Faithful," the shopper answered, "the wiles of a woman and not a man were behind that dreadful scheme, but I blame the man whom I loved and lived with, not as a wife, but as a concubine, even though I am from a distinguished family. I blame him, not because he didn't investigate fully when he heard of my death, but because when he learned that I was alive, rather than talking to me in order to establish the truth (as he has blamed the third dervish for not doing), he cast me out. How can I trust men, when the man I adored, and whose honour I protected even when I was shaking with fear, forgave the one who was behind the diabolical plot to kill me? And then threw me into the darkest prison, presuming I was an adulteress? All too readily he accepted that I was damaged goods; and thus he would do anything to protect his honour."

"That's it," the Caliph stormed, for now he felt the shopper had gone too far. "Enough. You've squeezed my last drop of patience. You and your sisters either do as I order or, be very sure: you will face death."

Silence fell on the room like a dark cloud. The five sisters moved closer together to each other, as if taking refuge and warmth, and the eldest sister, who hadn't uttered a word all evening, spoke.

"We plead with you, Oh Commander of the Faithful, to forgive us. We are unable to obey your good wishes, for we regard men as a deadly disease."

Abu Nuwas, fearing for the lives of the five sisters, jumped up as if he'd been bitten by a snake and addressed the impatient, impulsive Caliph.

"Would the Caliph permit me to show the ladies how women are more deceitful than men? Just remember what Satan says: 'I teach men what I learn from women!'"

The Caliph seemed to welcome Abu Nuwas's intervention, for he gestured to the poet to continue.

It is known that men are hard on women. They torture them and distrust them, and at the same time they are disloyal themselves. This is all true, although let us not forget that women are not incapable of cruelty; nor are they to be trusted. One could say that their behaviour is identical to that of men, but they differ in their approach. We men are not crafty and wily like women. Men confront women with great aggression, while women can take you very easily to a river, yet bring you back thirsty. Women are crafty because they are capable of sewing knickers for a flea. A woman may tire, even as her tongue keeps lashing at you, but her mind remains as focused as ever, as she sells you eggs without yolks. Trust women? Trust me if I tell you not to trust them, for a woman without a keeper is like an orchard without walls. Women can snatch the black kohl from one's eyes; they ignite a flame and then call "Fire!" There are three things one cannot trust: the horse, the sword and women.

He laughed and continued to speak.

Let me tell you about Baqbouq, our neighbour! He attracted the attention of strangers, because of the size of his ears. All who knew him loved his innocence and childlike approach to life, even in his twenties. Once the herbalist kicked him out of his shop, because Baqbouq had insisted he mend the broken wing of a butterfly lying in the palm of his hand. As he sat outside the shop, a beautiful woman slave came out, and said, "Why don't you come to our house, which is heaven itself? If you put your butterfly on a particular rosebush in our garden, its wing will mend, for the petals are known to cure anything, from wounded fingers to toothache." When Baqbouq smiled happily, she said, "I have some pain in my neck, and my heart is telling me that if you give it a kiss, it will be cured." Hearing this, Baqbouq was very embarrassed, having only ever touched his mother's hand.

He rose, and followed the slave until they reached a house with a garden filled with trees and shrubs. "Is this the heaven people talk about?" Baqbouq asked, and the slave laughed. Then, instead of leading him to the rosebush or letting him kiss her neck, she made him sit in a big hall. Her mistress, who was far more beautiful than the slave, welcomed him, and asked her slaves to lay a table with food. In no time Baqbouq was eating, overjoyed and surprised, not only by the quantity of plates before him, but also by dishes he'd never dreamed existed: stuffed pigeon and the tongues of birds. The lady began feeding Baqbouq by hand, and the poor fellow thought that this was how rich people ate. When he tried to feed her, she choked with laughter and looked to her slaves, who giggled. She gave Baqbouq a cup of wine, and then another, and then she drank one herself, becoming playful and flirtatious. Soon Baqbouq was convinced the beautiful woman was in love with him. How he wished his mother could see that God had answered her prayers and found him a woman to marry! His five cousins had refused him, and the seven girls from his neighbourhood, and even the ugly spinster who was balding. And now look at him! But when he bent his head for a kiss, the beautiful woman slapped him so hard on the neck that he wept, and then seeing him crying, she laughed and her slaves joined in. Even the slave who'd brought him to the house was laughing. He rose up in anger to leave, but he couldn't remember which door he'd come in. Everyone laughed, confusing him even more, saying, "It's this door," or, "No, don't believe her, it's this door." Finally the beautiful slave took him by the hand, and said, "My lady slapped you because she is head over heels in love with you."

"What do you mean? Do you hit someone when you are in love?" Baqbouq asked.

"Your mother loves you and she must have hit you from time to time," she answered.

Innocent Baqbouq smiled and returned to his chair beside the lady, who hit him twice more, before her slaves joined in too, as the lady congratulated the beautiful slave, saying, "Good girl, I've never seen anything better than this one!"

Eventually Baqbouq couldn't take the violence any more, and fainted. The lady ordered her slaves to sprinkle him with orange blossom water and to burn incense. When he came round, the slave said to him, "My lady was testing your patience. Now she knows that it is as great as a camel, she has decided to reward you."

With that the lady gave Baqbouq a brief, quick kiss near his mouth, which made him spin around like a dog chasing his tail. "I am your slave, my lady," he told her, "do whatever you want with me."

"Let my slave dye your eyebrows and pluck your moustache," the lady said. But Baqbouq objected strongly, "It's all right to dye my eyebrows, but plucking my moustache is going to be too painful, and I couldn't endure the pain."

"God created me with a huge appetite for fun and to be merry, and whoever joins in with me will ultimately win my heart and body."

"But I'm scared. My moustache has lots of hair."

The slave whispered to him, as she gave him a cup of wine, "Be patient, soon you will take everything you wish and desire of her; if you're not patient, you'll lose everything you've endured already."

Baqbouq accepted reluctantly, closed his eyes and pressed his two hands to his chest, sobbing, even before the slave had touched him. When she did, he cried out in pain and fright and didn't stop till she'd finished plucking his moustache. Then she dyed his eyebrows while he sat, happy as a clam, counting the seconds before he could be with his lady.

Finally, the lady sat beside him and pretended to kiss his reddened eyebrows. "But where has your moustache gone?" she asked.

"Don't tell me you've forgotten already that it was plucked out, didn't you hear me cry like a bull?"

The lady laughed and giggled. "Oh yes, I remember now."

Then she stroked his beard, and sighed. "How I wish that you could get rid of your beard, so that your face is as smooth as a plum." Baqbouq was annoyed, but excited by her touch at the same time. "If I get rid of my beard, everyone in the market will laugh at me," he said. "No, no, I'd better not."

But the lady held his hand and stroked her own face with it. "Can you feel how delicate my skin is—like a rose petal? It scratches very easily, even when the soft breeze touches it, so you can imagine what will happen if your beard rubs my face when we are kissing, licking and embracing."

Baqbouq looked at her with love, infatuation and, above all, lust, but remained silent. The slave whispered, "Are you mad? Don't you see how passionately my mistress is in love with you? Be patient, you're nearly there, you're about to have her and in a day or two your beard will grow back. Now lie down for me and don't think about anything except the blissful time you will have with my lady."

So trusting Baqbouq put his faith in her and in God, and let her shave off his beard with a knife. Then, feeling something on his face, he asked, "What are you doing?"

"Applying an ointment to help your beard grow tomorrow," she answered.

She took him by the hand, back to her mistress, who, when she saw his painted face, laughed and giggled, saying, "I am delighted! You look so handsome, like a real prince. You have won my heart and all of me, with your patient and sublime nature. Let me, beloved, see you dancing, so I become excited and lustful. What will arouse me and turn me on is a handsome young man like you swaying and shaking his hips."

Baqbouq felt proud of himself for the first time in his life. He danced without any rhythm or tempo, which made the lady laugh hysterically. She began to throw cushions at him and her slaves joined in, hurling potatoes and lemons. Every time he ducked, the lady made him dance with her, until he was bent over like a monkey suffering indigestion. The lady began to take off her clothes but Baqbouq was too embarrassed and overwhelmed to respond. The slave whispered into his ear, "My lady is intoxicated now, wait until she is in her underwear, and then take off all your clothes and follow her."

When the lady had stripped down, she cried out, "Catch me if you can!" Baqbouq stripped off as if his clothes were on fire. The lady called out, "Do you really want me?"

"Yes, yes, yes," Baqbouq replied. "Come and get me," came the reply. She ran from one room to the other, as Baqbouq ran after her panting, his penis hardening, encouraged by the slaves who called out, "You've nearly reached her!"

He ran from one room to another like a rabid dog, drooling, his penis jutting out like the branch of a tree. Then, running after her, he found himself in a dark room and felt he was running on wooden boards, but nothing could stop him now, he just wanted the woman. All of a sudden, the floor broke and he fell down and found himself in the leather market. When the traders saw him fall down among them, totally naked, with an erect penis, without a beard or moustache and with red, bushy eyebrows and a face as red as a baboon's bottom, they beat him with leather, laughing, until the poor fellow lost consciousness. Then they put him on a donkey, parading him through the market to the chief of police, who asked, "What is this and where did you find it?" "He dropped and fell from a chamberlain's house like this," the merchants answered.

Baqbouq was given one hundred lashes, and then he was ordered to leave Baghdad for good. When Baqbouq's two brothers found out what happened, they came to me to ask me for help, knowing that I visit the Commander of the Faithful from time to time. I hurried to the Wali himself, describing the gentle nature of Baqbouq, who wouldn't even tread on a dead ant, assuring him that someone must have played a trick on him, and the Wali pardoned him, and let me take him back to his family. From that day, until now, Baqbouq has never crossed the threshold of his house. He is unable to trust anyone, man or woman; not even me, who helped him.

Abu Nuwas, coming to the end of his tale, looked round at the sisters. "Now, my ladies, I urge you to confide in me with all the humanity you hold and conscience you carry within you. Can the actions of that disgraceful, whimsical and spoilt lady be described as mean, vile and lowly? Surely he suffered the ultimate injustice at her hands, because he was what people call an idiot? In my opinion, he suffered as all of you have, because of the cruelty of a woman. And I want you to imagine what would have happened to him if I hadn't asked the Wali to pardon him. He would have become a fugitive, away from his home and city, exiled and alone in the wilderness, not only with no money or food or roof over his head, but with no love, care or sympathy."

Dalila the Wily

he audience shook their heads in sorrow for poor Baqbouq.

"My brother, the fisherman, is Baqbouq's neighbour," said the porter. "You've forgotten, my dear poet, to add that Baqbouq has never stopped repeating, 'Why, why, why,' his breath rattling in his chest like a slaughtered beast!"

The poet turned to the five sisters, whose expressions remained blank. "Baqbouq's story is nothing but a few mint leaves with which to whet the appetite. The main dish is most certainly mischievous Dalila the Wily."

To the great surprise of all who were gathered in the room, one of the elder two sisters stood up.

"Oh Commander of the Faithful," she said. "Would you permit me to tell the tale of Dalila the Wily myself? My family knew her so well."

"Yes, you may," answered the Caliph.

She cleared her throat, but Abu Nuwas interrupted her, barking like a dog.

"Would someone stop this infernal dog from barking?" said the Caliph, with great irritation.

But the eldest sister simply ignored the commotion and began her story.

Dalila's husband was in charge of rearing carrier pigeons for the Caliph. When he died, his salary of a thousand dinars was stopped, as well as the two meals provided for him, his wife and two children each day. Dalila tried in vain to get a pension, even a quarter of her husband's salary. But her request was declined and so she was forced to seek employment, working here and there as a maid to make ends meet. She worked every day without ceasing until she became old.

It happened one day that she heard of two men who had come from Cairo to Baghdad and played confidence tricks and grew in influence until they found their way to the Caliph himself, who appointed them commanders of the right and left flanks of the district just outside the walls of the city. They were given money, food and above all respect, which in Dalila's opinion they did not deserve. She decided that she would exact revenge for her ill treatment, playing confidence tricks with great craftiness and deviousness in order to win her reputation in Baghdad and thereby claim the salary of her late husband. She swore that news of her feats would reach not only the Wali, but the Caliph himself.

"I will show them that I am the only person able to milk an ant!" she said to herself, and then she dressed up like a Sufi in a woollen gown which reached her ankles, with a wide belt around her waist and a woollen jubba on her head. She wrapped prayer beads and worry beads around her neck, filled a jug with water and laid three dinars in a cloth across the rim.

Then, covering her face with a thin veil, she strolled through the streets calling, "Allah, Allah!" But behind the veil, her eyes, like two eagles, were hunting constantly for prey. "What trick can I play now, and on whom?" she murmured.

Dalila made her way through the poor alleyways and slums until she reached the better part of town, where the influential and rich lived. Her senses alive, she scanned the streets until she spotted an arched door inlaid with marble. She stopped and looked at the house, calling out louder, "Allah, Allah, Allah!"

A beautiful young lady, surrounded by her maids, looked out of the window. When Dalila spotted the girl's elaborate clothing and glittering jewellery, she decided she would lure her out of the house and strip her of everything in which she was attired. She began to whirl like a dervish, her white woollen robes swirling as she turned until she looked like a dome of light.

"Come, you saints of God, let us be blessed by your presence," she intoned, as she turned.

When the gatekeeper of the house heard Dalila, he hurried to kiss her hand, but she refused, saying, "Keep away, lest you spoil my ablution. But I shall let you drink from my jug, so that you might be blessed."

She twirled the jug in the air, shaking her hand until the cloth fell and the three dinars dropped at the gatekeeper's feet. He picked them up and handed them back to her.

"These worldly things don't concern me," Dalila said loudly, so the beautiful woman would hear, and she indicated that the gatekeeper might keep the coins.

"This is indeed a heavenly gift," said the astonished gatekeeper.

Dalila ignored him, sprinkling drops of water in the direction of the woman's window.

"Come, saints of God!" she implored, "and bless these women!"

"Go and ask her ladyship if she wants the Sufi woman to bless the house. She is clearly a woman of great power and devotion," the excited gatekeeper said to the maids at the window.

As Dalila continued her devotions, a maid came down, kissed her hand and took her into the house to meet her mistress.

Once inside, the young lady rushed towards Dalila, offering some food.

"I eat only the food of Paradise, and then only five days in the year," Dalila said humbly, eyeing the woman's jewellery from beneath lowered eyelids.

Hearing this, the young woman asked all her maids and slaves to leave them. Dalila sensed that something was bothering the girl. She closed her eyes, and holding the girl's hand, murmured, "I can sense that you're worried about something, so confide in me, my daughter, and I'll try to help you."

The young woman began to weep. "My husband is the Emir Shar al-Tariq, Prince Evil of the Road," she murmured. "We've been married one year, and I haven't yet borne him a child. Yesterday he pushed me away when I approached him, saying that a man who leaves no sons or daughters will not be remembered. Then he accused me of being barren, unable to conceive, and said that he would start looking for another wife tomorrow. I defended myself, telling him that I had ground up so many medicines that every mortar in the house was worn away, and that I am not at fault. But he shouted at me, saying sleeping with me is like carving in stone," said the girl, weeping even harder.

Dalila, extremely happy to hear this, stroked the girl's hand in sympathy.

"I weep because I don't wish that flat-nosed mule, with his useless sperm like farting soap bubbles, to divorce me and rob me of all this wealth."

"Did he say tomorrow?" Dalila said. "Then we must hurry. Prepare yourself, and I'll take you to Sheikh Abu al-Hamalat, whose name describes how he carries everyone's problems in his heart and as a burden on his shoulders. If we go to him now, and you convince your husband to sleep with you tonight, you will conceive a daughter or a son."

"I swear that I'll fast for a whole year if this Sufi woman is not a holy saint!" said the gatekeeper, as Dalila and the young woman left in a great hurry, hand in hand.

Dalila, the holy saint, was thinking all the while, "How can I strip the girl of her jewellery and clothes, when the streets and alleys are so full of people?"

She said to the girl, whose name was Khatun, "Walk behind me, my daughter, because the people will stop me to kiss my hand, and burden me with offerings, but don't let me out of your sight."

Dalila led Khatun to the merchants' market, using all her antennae to sense those who were attracted by Khatun's bejewelled ankles and tinkling hair tassels. She spotted a handsome young merchant, too young even to shave, called Master Hasan, and indicated that Khatun should wait opposite Hasan's stall. Then she approached the young merchant.

"Are you Master Hasan, son of the merchant Muhsin?"

"Yes, but who told you my name?"

"I've been seeking a bridegroom for my daughter and many honourable people suggested you. Look at that beauty in the distance. Isn't she like a fairy princess? Her father, my husband, died and left her a fortune. I'm following the wise saying, 'Look for a husband for your daughter, but never for your son,' and so I would like you to marry her."

Master Hasan glanced at Khatun, and sighed a hundred sighs.

Seeing this, Dalila's heart stopped racing, and she said, casually, "I shall open another shop for you, and shower you with money."

Hasan smiled. "Well, my mother is constantly offering to find me a bride, but my sole condition is that I will only marry a girl I have first seen for myself."

"I guarantee that you'll see her naked," said Dalila, smiling, "if you follow us."

Dalila walked off with Khatun following, and Hasan quickly closed his shop, bringing a thousand dinars to pay for the marriage contract.

"God in heaven, tell me where I should take these two to strip them?" Dalila said to herself.

As soon as she cast her eyes back down she saw a dyer's shop. The owner, Hajj Muhammad, was sitting outside, eating figs and a pomegranate. He lifted his head at the sound of Khatun's anklets.

Dalila sat on the empty chair beside him, and asked, "Are you Muhammad the dyer?"

"Yes I am, what do you want, Sheikha?" Muhammad replied, his mouth filled with figs.

"Honest people have directed me to you, as it's known that you have two rooms you rent out from time to time. Do you see my daughter, with my son behind? He's walking at a distance, because he's so ashamed that we're homeless. We have been advised by our builder to leave our mansion for a month while it is repaired, because hundreds of rats have gnawed at the wood, and it's in danger of collapsing. Do you think we can lodge with you?"

Hajj Muhammad handed her three keys. "Here is one key for the house, the second for the hall, and the third for the upper floor," he said.

Dalila thanked him, went to the house, unlocked the door, and when Khatun followed her inside, she said, "This is Sheikh Abu al-Hamalat's house. Go upstairs, take off your veil and wait for me."

Hasan appeared and she said to him, "Wait here in the hall, while I go up and get my daughter ready for you, as I promised."

She winked and went up to find Khatun, who said, nervously, "I need to see Sheikh Abu al-Hamalat immediately, before other people arrive and recognise me."

"In a moment," replied Dalila. "But first, there's something I must explain. My son is one of the Sheikh's helpers, but unfortunately he is an idiot, and he can't differentiate between summer and winter, hot or cold, and so he remains half-naked all year round. He pulls the earrings off every beautiful woman who comes to see the Sheikh, tearing their earlobes, and then he cuts off their clothes with scissors. So take off your jewellery and clothes quickly, and I'll keep them safe for you."

Khatun handed over her jewellery and clothes, so that she stood in just her shift and her drawers.

"I'm going to hang these on the Sheikh's curtains, so that you earn an even higher blessing," Dalila said, hurrying away to hide Khatun's clothes, and then going back down to Hasan, who was waiting as if on hot coals.

"Where have you been? Where's your daughter?" he demanded.

Dalila began to weep.

"God curse Satan, who put jealousy and envy into the hearts of our neighbours," she cried. "For they saw you entering our house and asked me who you were. When I told them, proudly, that you were my daughter's bridegroom, they said, 'Is your mother so tired of feeding and clothing you that she's decided to marry you off to that leper?' My daughter was very taken aback, but I have convinced her that they are wrong. However, she has made it a condition of agreeing to marry you that if you insist on seeing her clad only in her shift and drawers, then you too must be half-naked."

Hasan was enraged. "Let her see if I'm a leper or not," he said, tearing off his fur hat, and all his clothes, so that he was clad only in his drawers and an undershirt which revealed a glimpse of his chest and his arms, which were as white as silver.

Dalila took away his clothes and the thousand dinars, assuring him she'd keep everything safe and that she would go and get her daughter. Then she rushed from the room, gathered Khatun's clothes and wrapped everything in a bundle, and fled the house, locking the couple in behind her.

Making her way through the crowds to the perfume market, Dalila bought a bottle of amber perfume and left it and her bundle with the owner, promising to return for it later. Then she hurried back to the dyer and told him she was on her way to collect her furniture. She gave him a dinar to give some food to her children who were still in the house, famished, suggesting he join them for lunch.

Next Dalila hurried back to the perfume stall, took her bundle from the shopkeeper and returned to the dyer's shop. She said to the boy left in charge, "Your master has gone to the kebabji to get my children grilled meat and bread; go and help him, so you too can get something to eat. I will wait here and mind the shop.

"Mind the children eat well!" Dalila called after him, laughing as she thought of Khatun and Hasan, naked and waiting for each other in separate rooms.

But in fact, Khatun and Hasan had already met. Khatun had grown tired of waiting for Dalila and had gone downstairs and discovered the half-naked Hasan. Assuming he was Dalila's lunatic son, she fled, but he cornered her.

"Have a look. Now do you think I am a leper?" Hasan shouted, lifting his shirt.

Khatun screamed in terror.

"Why are you screaming? Could it be you're deranged and that is why your mother has tricked me into marrying you?"

"First of all, this woman is not my mother. My mother is in Basra and I am married. But aren't you this woman's lunatic son?" Khatun said.

"Me? The lunatic son of that fraudster? She has tricked me out of 1,000 dinars and my clothes!" Hasan shouted.

"She fooled me into believing she was bringing me to meet Sheikh Abu al-Hamalat, who would help me conceive. Now she's made me strip off, and stolen my clothes and jewellery," Khatun said.

"But you were waiting across from my stall, exchanging glances with her. I'm holding you responsible. You must return my money and clothes."

"Well, I'm also holding you responsible for my clothes, but mainly for my jewellery, which is worth not hundreds but a thousand times more than your clothes," Khatun replied.

The two of them went on arguing, not daring to leave the house without their clothes, while not far away Dalila was looking around the dyer's shop.

"I had better hire a donkey," she thought to herself, "because there's so much to take that I won't be able to carry it all."

She approached a man passing with a donkey, and asked if he knew her son the dyer, and he confirmed that he knew him well.

"My poor son is now penniless," Dalila told him. "He's been thrown into prison for bankruptcy and so I must hire your donkey and return his stock to his creditors. While I'm gone could you assist me by taking all these jars and vats and destroying them?

That way, when the court sends someone to investigate, they'll find nothing left here."

Dalila handed the donkey owner two dinars.

The man thanked her. "The dyer's always been good to me," he said. "Like mother, like son. I'll help him by making sure that nothing remains."

Dalila left, the animal so heavily laden that it nearly buckled beneath the weight.

When the dyer returned, despatching his boy to take the food to his tenants, he saw streams of dye trickling across the ground outside and found the donkey owner in the process of smashing open the last vat.

"Stop! Stop! Are you crazy?" the dyer screamed, holding his head in disbelief.

"Praise the Lord! You've been released from prison. Your mother told me everything."

"My mother? My mother died twenty years ago!" screamed the dyer.

Having managed to extract what had happened from the donkey owner, the dyer began to weep. "My dyes, my shop, my vats, my jars, my goods, my customers!"

"My donkey! Get my donkey back from your mother!" the donkey owner wailed.

"Didn't I just tell you my mother's been dead for twenty years?" shouted the dyer, grabbing the man by the neck.

"If she wasn't your mother, why was she looking after your shop?"

"Because she's lodging in my house, she left her children there this morning," the dyer yelled.

"Well, let's go to your place and find her. She must return my donkey! He is my only friend and my source of strength."

They raced to the dyer's house, but found it locked. They managed to break in through the kitchen and surprised Khatun and

Hasan, who were exhausted from bickering and were standing together half-naked.

"What are you doing together, you incestuous degenerates?" shouted the dyer. "And where's your dog-faced pimp of a mother?"

"And where did she take my donkey?" shouted the donkey owner.

Hasan regaled the dyer with the evil trickery of the old woman, while Khatun tried to protect her modesty. But as she shielded one part of her body with her hands, she revealed another.

"Woe is my shop!" the dyer wailed, when Hasan had finished. "All is lost: my jars, vats, the goods and my customers!"

"Oh my donkey, my donkey, someone bring my donkey back to me!" yelled the donkey owner.

Finally the dyer pulled himself together. "Let's go and look for this con-woman and take her to the Wali, or to the Caliph himself," he said.

But Khatun and Hasan didn't move.

"Well, what are you waiting for?" the dyer shouted.

"Do you want the wife of the Emir Shar al-Tariq, Prince Evil of the Road, to walk through the street naked?" Khatun asked.

"Isn't it a disgrace to arrive at this house fully clothed and leave it undressed?" said Hasan.

So the dyer found them some clothes, and Khatun rushed back to her house, while Hasan and the others went to the Wali. Furious at their account, the Wali ordered the three men to find the disgraceful old woman and bring her to him, saying he would force a confession from her, even if he had to pull her tongue out with it.

So the dyer, the donkey owner and Hasan went looking for Dalila. They searched every alley and every market, but she was nowhere to be found. They split up in order to search different areas, and finally the donkey owner recognised her, despite the fact that she was now dressed from head to toe in black.

"Just tell me one thing: were you born deceitful? And where's my donkey?"

Dalila began to weep. "Forgive me, my son! I beg you to conceal what God conceals. There was a reason for everything I did, but let me get your donkey first. You are a poor man and you rely on your donkey for your livelihood, and I left it with the barber."

They walked back through one market after another until they reached a barber's shop.

"Just wait here and let me ask him politely to give you back your donkey," said Dalila.

She approached the barber, weeping, kissing his hands, and weeping some more until he asked what was wrong. She dried her tears and pointed at the donkey owner.

"Look at my only son," she said. "Who would think he was crazy? He fell ill with a high fever a week ago, and woke up this morning asking about a donkey, although he's never owned one. No matter what I say, he repeats, 'Where's my donkey? Where's my donkey?' I've taken him to doctors and they say the only cure is for two of his teeth to be pulled out and his temples cauterised. And you were recommended as the person to do this."

Giving the barber a dinar, Dalila said, "Please, call my son and tell him you have his donkey."

The barber, overcome by Dalila's distress, said, "OK, leave him with me, you poor mother. I swear I'll cure him, and if I fail I'll walk round Baghdad in a set of donkey's ears."

Dalila thanked him and left.

"Hey, son, come and get your donkey," the barber called.

The donkey owner raced to the shop, happily, saying, "Where is he?"

"Come with me, poor fellow, and we'll get your donkey," said the barber, leading the man to a dark room at the back of the shop, where two of his workers were waiting. They knocked him down, tied his hands and feet, pulled out two of his teeth and cauterised his temples.

"What are you doing, you crazy barber?" the donkey owner shrieked.

"This is so your mother can have a break, you crazy, deranged, donkey lover, from hearing you ask, night and day, 'Where's my donkey?'"

"She's not my mother, she's a con-woman," shouted the donkey owner.

But the barber and his workers only laughed.

"May God bring this evil woman nothing except deadly disease and misery, and punish you for what you've done to me," shouted the donkey owner, and he punched the barber in the face and pushed his way out of the room.

But the barber and his men followed him into the street, kicking and punching him without respite, until passers-by came to his aid, and the young merchant Hasan and the dyer came running to help him.

The donkey owner sat wiping blood from his face, and describing what had happened, when suddenly the barber shrieked, "Help, help! Catch that woman. She's robbed my shop! Look, everything has gone!"

He threw himself at the donkey owner. "Hurry up, take me to your mother before she sells all my combs, razors and scissors! She's even stolen my coat."

"How many times have I told you, she isn't my mother!" the donkey owner screamed. "She's a fraudster and she stole my donkey."

"And she stole a thousand dinars and my clothes," Hasan yelled.

"How I wish she'd only robbed me, like all of you! She's ruined my shop and my business for ever," yelled the dyer.

So the barber closed up his empty shop and the four men headed to the Wali and begged him to provide them with ten armed men with whom to catch Dalila. They returned to the spot where the donkey owner had spotted her, but not a single woman passed by. But they were determined to find Dalila, and they kept looking until midnight when they came upon a blind man, who, as soon as he passed them, stopped shuffling and sped away.

"You can't fool me," shouted the donkey owner, and he chased after the blind man, who broke into a run. All the men joined the chase and finally Dalila was caught.

They took their captive to the Wali, but he was throwing a party, and his guards wouldn't let Dalila's captors enter. They were told to wait by the door. The donkey owner was particularly anxious, explaining to the guards that Dalila was a woman who could trick a snake out of its pit and had to be watched every second. But the guards refused to listen, saying that there was no way the old woman could escape.

Dalila pretended to fall fast asleep, snoring loudly as she stealthily watched Hasan, the barber, the donkey owner and the dyer, until eventually they each dropped off to sleep. Then she stood up and approached a guard.

"Son, I am a fraudster and I know the Wali will soon lock me in prison," she said, clutching her crotch. "But I am desperate to relieve myself, and I don't know how to when these men are stuck to me like a nail sticks to the finger."

Sure enough, the four men jumped at the sound of her voice, alert at the danger of losing their prey.

"See what I mean?" Dalila said. "If I could, I'd pee out of my mouth, but I just don't think it's going to be possible."

The guards discussed it amongst themselves at some length. Finally, the toughest of them spoke to her. "I'm going to take you to the harem quarters, where you can do your business, while I wait for you at the door. Do you understand?"

Dalila nodded. "God protect your mother," she said.

Inside the harem, Dalila quickly saw that many slaves were asleep, but a few were still drinking wine and conversing. She picked one who seemed a bit tipsy and gave her five dinars.

"Daughter," she said, "I have brought the four Mamlouk slaves for the Wali from my husband, the slave broker, who is ill. My husband is worried the slaves will escape, so he told me to take them straight to the Wali. I asked the guards to hand them to the Wali, but they refused, because the Wali has guests. Do you think the Wali's wife would take them? I must return to my husband."

The slave led Dalila to the Wali's wife, who was being entertained in the next room. Dalila fell on the hand of the Wali's wife, told her the story, and asked her to examine the slaves before paying the thousand dinars. The Wali's wife glanced out of the window, saw the four men waiting there, and gave Dalila the money. Dalila thanked her, and then asked the slave who'd helped her to let her out of the back door in case the slaves gave her trouble.

Later, when the Wali entered the bedroom, his wife asked him if he liked the four Mamlouk slaves his slave broker had sent to him, but the Wali denied knowing anything about them. The wife told him she'd paid a thousand dinars to the broker's wife and that the men were at the door with the guards.

The Wali went down to the door. In the dark, he failed to recognise Hasan, the donkey owner, the barber and the dyer.

"Mamlouks," he said. "You work for me now, come inside."

"But we're not slaves, Wali," the men answered.

The Wali interrupted, saying, "My wife assures me that she bought the four of you this evening for a thousand dinars."

"But our respected Wali, we are the men who were conned by the old woman and you gave us ten armed men to help us find her, and we brought her to you."

"Where is she then?!" shouted the Wali.

The four men and the guards looked at each other. Finally one of the guards spoke up.

"One of us took her to the harem's quarters to relieve herself."

At that very moment, Emir Shar al-Tariq, Prince Evil of the Road, appeared.

"My wife has been tricked by an old woman who took all her jewellery and clothes and left her half-naked. I hold you personally responsible for allowing an old woman like that freedom to move through your city. And so I must ask that you return my wife's possessions immediately."

Hearing this, the four men plucked up courage to address the Emir, telling him how they too had been conned by the same woman.

But the Wali turned on them. "Yes, I should thank you four men, for it was you who helped that fraudster find her way into my home and con my wife out of 1,000 dinars. That little old woman has made a fool of my guards! Look, one of them is still waiting for her by the harem door."

At this, the Emir Shar al-Tariq laughed so hard that his moustache nearly covered his nose and eyes. The barber began to laugh as well, then the dyer, Hasan, the donkey owner and the guards.

Then the Wali laughed, his wife laughed and her maids and slaves laughed as they gathered at the windows.

Then, of course, the Wali promised to catch Dalila even if his men had to break down every door in the city. And the very next day, the Wali fulfilled his promise, because Dalila was found, with no difficulty at all, in her own home.

She was brought before the Wali, and when he confronted her with the number of people she'd conned, Dalila corrected him.

"But Wali, you forgot to count your guard, who I left waiting outside the door to the harem. That makes eight people, not seven."

Then she told him that she would return the stolen goods, including the donkey, on one condition: that they take her to the Caliph himself. And so Emir Shar al-Tariq and the Wali agreed to take her before the Caliph, and she regaled him with her escapades.

When she finished speaking, the Caliph asked, "Why did you play all these tricks?"

"In order to prove to you, Oh Commander of the Faithful, that I am capable of mastering skills greater than those of the two men who were appointed by your lordship as the commanders of the areas outside of the city walls, and that therefore I should be allowed to remain within your court, and to receive once more the salary of my dead husband, who was in charge of your lordship's carrier pigeons."

Much amused, the Caliph asked the old woman her name.

"Dalila."

"Dalila the Wily?" said the Caliph, and he gave the order that her husband's salary be given to her every month.

And it was said that when the Caliph was on his own with Jaafar, he said to his Vizier, "Dalila the Wily may have lied, tricked and stolen, but I am greatly impressed by her courage, intelligence and wit."

And then he laughed and laughed, especially when he recalled how Dalila had managed to trick none other than the wife of Emir Shar al-Tariq and the Wali's wife.

The Demon's Wife

To everybody's surprise the Caliph now stood and addressed the room.

Your Caliph has a story to tell you, about the wiles of women. As you know, King Shahrayar witnessed to his horror his Queen taking part in an orgy with her slaves. His mortification was complete as he watched one of the slaves fall on her as she parted her thighs, and making love to her while calling her a slut.

He fled his kingdom with his brother King Shahzaman, and roamed the world together for the love of God, having each sworn a vow that they would not return until they had found someone whose misfortune was even greater than their own.

They journeyed day and night, in disguise, through barren wilderness and green lands, sleeping on grief, waking up in sorrow, enduring their pain. Only when they reached the sea and a green meadow did they come to a halt. The expanse of water gave them an even greater feeling of loneliness. They sat together, talking over what had befallen them, when they heard a great cry coming from the sea, which made the waves tremble. The water parted as a black pillar emerged, spiralling taller and taller until it touched the clouds high above.

The two Kings hurried to an oasis, trembling with fear. They came to a tall tree with thick foliage, climbed it and hid in its branches. As the black pillar approached, they saw that it was a demon carrying a box on his head, made out of glass. The demon stopped beneath their tree. He put the glass box on the ground, took out a key, unlocked it and helped out a woman with a beautiful, curving figure and a face like a full moon. The demon laid her out beneath the tree, saying, "Let me sleep on your thigh, beautiful bride of mine." He rested his head on her thigh, stretched his legs until they reached the sea, and soon fell into a deep sleep, snoring so loudly that the noise drowned out every other sound. The beautiful woman tried in vain to cover her ears, but as the snoring continued, she looked up to heaven and saw the two Kings hidden above her. She lifted the demon's head off her lap, carefully resting it on her shawl. Then she tiptoed away and gestured to them to come down.

When they realised that she had seen them, the brothers were terrified that the demon would wake and find them talking to her, so Shahrayar, the Great King, answered her in the softest of voices. "In the name of the creator of heaven and Earth, I beg you to let us remain here in the tree, for even seeing him from this distance has filled us with terror."

"But you must come down to me," the woman answered.

Shahrayar pleaded with her. "But this demon is known to be the enemy of mankind. If he wakes and sees us he will certainly kill us."

"Listen, if you don't come down to me I shall wake the demon up," the woman insisted.

So the two brothers climbed down the tree very slowly, desperate not to wake the demon, and stood before her. The woman immediately stretched herself out on the ground, spread her legs and told them, "I am aflame with lust, come on; make love to me, both of you."

Shahrayar said, "We're sorry but we cannot, fear has rendered us flaccid. We can feel nothing at this moment other than our terror of this demon."

But the woman told them, "I am the driest soil in the heat of summer. If you don't quench my thirst now I shall be filled with rage and wake my husband the demon and ask him to kill you. One blow of his little finger and you'll be gone, and then with a single breath he'll blow you both into the sea."

So, horrified and frightened, Shahrayar made love to the beautiful woman first, and then his younger brother followed, his eyes fixed all the while upon the demon. Each time she climaxed the woman looked at the sleeping demon, as if determined to spite him, and take revenge. When they had finished, she got up and said to both Kings, "Give me your rings." She pulled out a small purse from the folds of her dress. "Look how many rings I have in this purse: ninety-eight. Do you know how I got them?"

"No, we do not," was the brothers' answer.

"From the ninety-eight men I slept with. Give me your rings, so that I can add them to my ninety-eight and know that I have slept with one hundred men under the very horns of this filthy demon as he snored happily, assuming that I am his alone! He keeps me trapped beneath the raging sea, believing he can possess me, and keep me apart and unseen from all others. But he is a fool, for he does not know that no one can prevent a woman from fulfilling her desires, even if she is hidden under the roaring sea, jealously guarded by a demon."

When Shahrayar and Shahzaman heard the woman's words, they began to dance for joy. "Oh God, there is no power and no strength save in God the magnificent. How great is the cunning of women!"

The brothers handed her their rings and she placed them in her purse, and jingled it softly, saying, "One hundred rings means that one hundred men have known me."

She resumed her place beneath the tree, lifted the demon's head very gently and placed it back in her lap and gestured to the brothers to leave.

"And now, be on your way or I shall wake him."

The two brothers fled in great haste.

Once they were at a safe distance from the woman and the demon, Shahrayar turned to his brother and said, "Look at this misfortune, by God it is worse than ours! This demon believes he has the woman imprisoned in a glass chest, locked up and kept beneath the sea where she is his alone, and yet she has slept with one hundred men. How lucky we are to have witnessed this. Now we can go home to our kingdoms, but let us be without women. You will see what I shall do."

The Woman and Her Five Lovers

 he other elder sister stood up. "May I tell a story, Oh Commander of the Faithful?"

"Yes, you may," the Caliph replied.

"How grateful am I to God Almighty, and to you, and to the slave Rayhan that I am alive and able to talk once more," she said, and she began her story.

Once there was a woman whose lover was unjustly imprisoned over a dispute with another man. The woman decided to help to get the man released. So she put on her finest clothes, and went to the Wali's house. When the Wali came to the door, she handed him a letter which explained to him that her "brother" (for she could not tell the Wali that the man was her lover) was innocent, the witnesses against him liars, and that he had been wrongly imprisoned. The Wali read the letter carefully and looked at the woman.

"I beseech you to release him, for he is my only next of kin," the woman said.

But the Wali was trying to think of a way to describe the colour of her lips, other than red wine or carnelian or red roses.

"Come into my house now and I will make sure that your brother will be released tomorrow," he said, suddenly unable to control his feelings.

She pleaded with him again: "I have nobody to protect me other than God Almighty, and it is not suitable or right for me to enter the house of a man."

"Well, don't expect me to release your brother unless I have had my way with you."

"I understand very well what you want from me," the woman said. "So come to my house tomorrow and stay with me for the whole day."

She gave him her address and they agreed on a time. Then she left him and went to the Qadi's house.

When the Qadi came to the door, the woman looked at him beseechingly, and said, "My lord, I beg you to help me."

The Qadi fell in love with her beauty right there on the spot.

"Tell me who has wronged you."

"My brother was wrongly imprisoned, after the Wali was given false evidence against him. I am sure, my lord, that you could use your influence to persuade the Wali to release him."

The Qadi, impressed by her elegance and by the eloquent manner in which she spoke, smiled broadly.

"I see that you are indeed desperate for my help, just as I am in great need for you to rest with me in my room. Afterwards, I'll do anything you want me to."

"But you're the judge!" the woman exclaimed. "If you behave like this, how can you punish others for taking advantage of the helpless?"

"Then find another way to free your brother from prison," was the Qadi's answer.

The woman quickly changed her tone, saying sweetly, "Don't you think, my lord, that if you come to my home it would be less conspicuous? Your house is full of slaves and concubines. Of course, I am no expert in such matters, but necessity creates its own rules."

He asked where she lived, and agreed to visit her the next day. She left, cursing him silently, and decided to go to the Vizier. She explained to him the purpose of her visit and the tale of her helpless brother, and as she did so, she shed a few tears, in the hope that the Vizier would pity her and behave gracefully, unlike the previous two. But to her mortification, the Vizier tried to embrace and kiss her.

She pushed him away, and he said, "If you let me have my way with you, I'll guarantee the release of your brother."

The woman said, with ultimate coyness, "Then come to me tomorrow, because I've been on the move most of the day and I am exhausted. And besides, I must first take a bath and burn incense . . ."

The Vizier enquired where she lived, and then tried to snatch a kiss before she left him. The woman now hurried to the King himself, and begged him to help her to free her brother.

"I seek help from the Almighty Creator and from you, Your Majesty," she said.

The King took a liking to her, and indicated that she should go to the third room from the left and wait for him there, saying, "Be assured that the Wali will release your brother when you have finished your business."

"But of course, Your Majesty, whatever the King decides to do with me, and whatever he wants of me could only be my good fortune, but would you honour me and condescend to me by coming to me tomorrow instead? How could I believe my luck, were I to be visited by the King himself?"

"With pleasure," the King answered, and the woman described where her house was, and agreed on a time.

Then she hurried to the carpenter, not quite believing that she had actually conversed with the King himself.

She greeted the carpenter, telling him, "I would like you to make me a large cupboard with four compartments, one on top of the other. Each compartment must have a door which locks. Could you tell me how much the whole thing will cost?"

"Each deck will cost you one dinar, so four dinars in all, but if you let me sleep with you, my respected and chaste lady, then I will charge you nothing," was the carpenter's reply.

"Is that so? Then make me a cupboard with five compartments," said the woman.

She went to leave, but the carpenter stopped her, saying, "Why don't you sit and wait? Then you can take it with you and I'll visit you tomorrow at my leisure."

So the woman sat down and waited while he made the cupboard, and then carried it home on a mule. Once she was home, she placed it in the main sitting room, and tapped it, saying, "Welcome, welcome to my house, my friend!"

Then she hurried to the market and bought four sets of men's gowns—yellow, red, blue and purple—scented candles, food and wine, fruit and sweets.

The next day she woke very early, cleaned the house, spread out carpets and laid more cushions on the couch, washed and perfumed herself from head to toe, dressed in beautiful clothes, lit the candles, spread out the wine and the food and sat waiting.

The Qadi arrived exactly at the agreed time. She welcomed him by kissing the ground before him, and then stretched herself on the couch, saying, "Here I am, my Qadi!"

The man jumped on to the couch, and fondled and kissed her. When he wanted to make love to her, she said, "Why don't you remove your clothes and your turban first and put on this yellow gown, which I made myself for the man who is worthy of it? Look, it even has a hood. Put it on and then come to me. I am all yours!"

The Qadi raced to change his clothes, while the woman pretended to cover her eyes. When he had put on the gown, she got up and took away his clothes. As she stretched out on the couch next to him, they heard a knock at the door.

The woman jumped up, saying, "Oh! It must be my husband!"

"What shall I do, where shall I hide?" said the Qadi nervously.

"Don't you worry, my Qadi, I'll hide you in that cupboard," she said, and she put him in the bottom compartment and locked its door.

Then she opened her front door, and there was the Wali.

She smiled at him, bowed and said, "Feel at home, my master. I am here to serve you. How delighted am I that you will stay most of the day with me. But first, please take off your clothes and put on this red gown with a special hood, which I brought from China, while I light more candles."

She turned away and lit the candles while he changed, then she faced him again, saying, "Oh! This colour suits you so well! Now, why don't you lie down comfortably on the couch and wait for me."

She went and put away his clothes, then joined him on the couch, and began kissing him and fondling him. When he was greatly aroused, she pulled away.

"I shall be yours the whole day, my master, but first I beg you in your infinite kindness to write a note ordering the release of my brother from prison, so that my mind is at rest."

The Wali wrote the note, sealed it and gave it to her, in a great flurry of activity. She thanked him, and began to caress him again, when they heard a sudden knock at the door.

"Who could that be knocking at your door?" the Wali asked.

The woman leapt up in alarm. "Who else other than my husband?"

The Wali became agitated and whispered, "What is to be done?"

The woman led him quickly to the cupboard. "Climb in here until I get rid of him," she murmured.

She put the Wali into the second compartment and locked it, then opened her door to the Vizier.

Once again, she welcomed him by kissing the ground before him, saying, "You honour my house with your visit."

She sat on the couch and he came and sat next to her, and she said in a soft voice, "Why don't you change your clothes into this comfortable gown?" And she handed him the blue gown, with a matching hood.

The Vizier quickly did as she asked.

"Now, try now to forget your duties and your office, my Vizier, and be my lover," said the woman, and she laid herself seductively across the couch.

The Vizier caressed her, and she caressed him, but when he tried finally to sleep with her, she whispered, "Why the hurry! We have all the time in the world on our hands."

No sooner had she uttered these words than there was a knock at the door.

"Who is it knocking?" the Vizier asked.

"It must be my husband," said the woman yet again. "Don't be afraid. Quickly, hide in this cupboard while I send him away. Then we can return to our couch!"

She locked him in the third compartment, and raced to open her door to the King. Seeing him before her she bowed, kissed the ground at his feet and then led him by the hand to the same couch. She made sure that he was sitting comfortably.

"You must know, Your Majesty, that if I were to give you the moon and its stars, the sun and the entire world, it could not equal what you have given me by taking one single step inside my humble house. May I ask your permission to say one further thing?"

The King, delighted to the point of distraction by the woman's beauty, replied, "You may say whatever you want."

"Your Majesty's grand and precious clothes and turban must sit heavily. Why don't you attire yourself in something light and comfortable? Then we shall be able to ensure that nothing will come between us."

The King was now terribly aroused. He tore off his clothes and his turban, which were worth thousands of dinars, and slipped on the cheap purple gown, whereupon the woman began to touch him all over his body. But when the King went to take her, she stopped him, saying, "I promise that if you can be patient, you shall be more than delighted with the surprise I have for you."

She began to unbutton the many tiny buttons on her robe, one by one, when there was a knock on the door.

"Who do you think is at your door?" said the King.

"My husband," said the woman.

"Have him disappear, or I shall force him to do so," the King commanded.

"But Your Majesty, since you are King of all you survey, you should not degrade yourself by dealing with my husband! Allow me to handle this situation in my own way. Perhaps while I do so you might wait in this cupboard? It will be for less than one minute."

And she smiled at him broadly as she led him by the hand and locked him in the fourth compartment. This time the visitor was none other than the carpenter, who knocked incessantly at the door until she threw it open.

"I am not happy at all with the cupboard you've made me!" she hissed.

"What is the problem with it?" asked the carpenter, worried that the woman would not sleep with him if she was angry.

"The compartments are too narrow."

"Narrow?" he exclaimed. "But I am sure that I made them big enough."

"Climb in then and see for yourself if you don't believe me," said the woman.

The moment the carpenter entered the fifth compartment, the woman locked him in and fled her home, taking her most valuable possessions. She rushed to the prison immediately. When she presented the Wali's note to the official, her lover was released and they left the city at once, making for foreign lands.

As for the woman's five would-be lovers, they each kept very quiet, worried that they would be discovered, identified and disgraced. Finally, after three days had passed and the five men's bladders had nearly exploded, the carpenter could hold on no longer, and urinated over the King's head. Almost immediately the King urinated over the Vizier's head and the Vizier over the Wali's head, and the Wali over the Qadi's head.

"Why am I drenched in foul mule urine?" shrieked the Qadi.

The Wali recognised the Qadi's voice at once. "Well, you'd better ask yourself the bigger question, Qadi, for aren't we both in a very bad situation, even without being drenched in urine?"

The Vizier recognised the angry voices of the Qadi and the Wali. He raised his voice, shouting, "May God reward both of you for your actions!"

"And you too, Vizier," said the Qadi.

"That wicked, vile woman tricked and imprisoned all the officers of the state apart from the King," said the Vizier, in great rage.

The King, who had until now remained silent, said, "Hush, hush, gentlemen. Your King was the first to fall into the trap of that goddamned harlot!"

Hearing this, the three men cleared their throats. "At least, Your Majesty, no commoner knows about this."

But a fifth voice piped up. "I am afraid to tell you that I am the carpenter who was asked to make the cupboard you're trapped in for four dinars. When I came to collect payment the woman tricked me and locked me in."

"Carpenter, go ahead and release us," said the King.

"It is impossible for me to do so, Your Majesty. I used the most secure and impenetrable locks."

The five men tried in vain to force open the locks, shaking and rattling and banging their compartments without success.

The next day, the woman's neighbours, who had become suspicious when she had failed to appear for three days, forced the door of the house open and heard all the commotion and moaning coming from the cupboard.

Unable to decide what was happening, they stood about arguing about what they should do, covering their noses against the foul smell.

Finally the Qadi raised his voice. "Listen to me all of you, I am the Qadi. I want you to fetch a carpenter to unlock our compartments."

"But who locked you in, Oh most respected, gracious Qadi?"

"Is this Zein al-Deen?" asked the Qadi.

"Yes, it is I, my Qadi," was the surprised reply.

"Well, stop being nosy, as you always are! Just go and bring a carpenter along with you at once, since we are all hungry and thirsty."

"I'll go and fetch Hasan, the king of carpenters," said Zein al-Deen.

"But I am Hasan the carpenter and I am trapped here," came a voice from inside the cupboard. "Go and fetch my brother Ali."

"But how could any one lock in a carpenter?" the man asked.

"Stop chattering, will you! I command you, man, find us a carpenter immediately," shouted the King.

Everyone recognised the King's voice, and looked at each other in great astonishment. They stood about in silence, pinching their noses at the great stench, until Ali, the carpenter's brother, appeared.

He opened the Qadi's compartment first. And when he came out with his yellow gown and special hood, everyone burst into great and uproarious laughter, which continued and grew as each member of the court was released. And even the captives laughed and teased each other as they came out one by one, especially when the King couldn't find his robe and turban, and had to leave the woman's house as she had dressed him, in his cheap, purple robe.

Budur and Qamar al-Zaman

bu Nuwas took to the floor once again, saying, "We are men and women, and we each blame each other. But can we live apart? I could very easily live without the opposite sex, but most of humankind cannot. Let us find out what happens when we are deliberately denied each other's company."

Once upon a time there was a King named Shahraman, who, after enormous effort and countless prayers and supplication to God, was blessed with a baby boy. The King called his child Qamar al-Zaman, meaning "moon of the age," because as his wife was giving birth, he watched the full moon and made a wish that God would grant him a son, so that one day he might abdicate in favour of him.

When Qamar al-Zaman blossomed and grew to adulthood, the King wished for him to marry and provide him with grandchildren, but Qamar al-Zaman denounced the idea of marriage.

"Be assured, father, that I shall never wed, nor be close to a girl, so long as I live. Hearing tales of their guile and treachery has put me off for life. Let us not forget the poet who said, 'If you aim to please God and seek his love, you'd better stop pleasing Eve, for whenever she enters the arena of love she throws one of her poisonous arrows,'" Qamar al-Zaman told his father.

The King fell into a deep depression, but in his wisdom he left his son alone, showering him instead with love and respect. After another whole year had passed, he raised the subject once more, hoping that his son might have matured.

"Son, will you do what I ask of you?"

Qamar al-Zaman knelt on the floor before the King respectfully, saying, "I was born into this life to obey you, father."

Feeling hopeful, the King said, "I want you to marry while I am still on this Earth, so that I can abdicate and appoint you King."

Qamar al-Zaman answered, "Forgive me, father, for this request is the only one I cannot obey. I remain determined not to marry, for the reasons I've outlined to you."

The King was saddened and disappointed, but because he adored his son, he thought he might wait another year and ask again. But the prince's answer remained the same. In the third year, the King decided to ask his son to marry before the assembled court and his Vizier, in the hope that his son might feel embarrassed and unable to disobey him in the presence of state officials.

So the King summoned his son and said, "I would like to give you an order which you must obey. I want you to marry a royal princess before I die."

Qamar al-Zaman bowed his head for a moment, lifted it, and spoke with all the rebelliousness of juvenile folly: "I'm afraid that you have become forgetful, old man. Haven't you urged me twice before to marry, and haven't I declined? Now, for the third time, I refuse, even if I must die for my decision, and that's final."

Humiliated, the King shouted at his son. "You bastard, how dare you speak to me like that in public!"

He turned to his soldiers. "Take him and lock him up in the deserted tower and leave him there until he learns some manners."

Qamar al-Zaman was seized and imprisoned in the tower. When the guard locked the door, the young man fumed, and yelled, "I curse marriage and all of treacherous womankind until Doomsday. Women are nothing but hovering vultures and I know for sure that if I marry, my wife will lead me astray from the path to prosperity and perfection of virtues."

Later, when the guard lit many candles and offered him some food, the young prince could only manage two mouthfuls. Then he sat and read some *surahs* from the Qur'an before he slept, oblivious to what Fate had in store for him.

It happened that a jinniya named Maimuna, who was the daughter of a very famous King of Jinnis named Dimiryat, lived in the well of the deserted tower. She left the well each night to fly in the sky and watch the angels as they prayed and worshipped God. That night, she emerged from her well, and saw, for the first time in her life of more than two hundred years, a light coming from the tower. Curious, she flew up to the roof and found her way in through a hole in the wall. The guard was sleeping by the door, so she flew through the keyhole and saw a figure in bed, asleep, lit by a candle above his head and a lantern at his feet.

"Blessed is God, the greatest creator," she said as she drew closer and saw in the flickering candlelight the fine beauty of this man, whose lips were like red grapes ready to be squeezed into wine.

Who was he? she wondered. He was locked up like a prisoner, under guard, and yet how many prisoners slept upon a bed of ostrich feathers? Quickly, she entered the dreams of the guard, asking him questions about the sleeping youth, and learned the whole story of Qamar al-Zaman. Angry at the old King's treatment of such a divine creature and feeling great pity for him, she knelt down and kissed him between the eyes and decided that she must visit him each night. She would fly around the tower, keeping watch to ensure that no evil jinni would harm him.

Just then, she heard the beating of wings in the air, and raced towards the sound in great fury, since she owned this part of the sky, and no one else might fly here without her permission. She circled, manoeuvring in the air until she saw the trespasser, a jinni called Dahnash. She swooped down upon him like an eagle, digging her nails into his stomach, and when he realised he was in the grip of Maimuna herself, he pleaded for forgiveness. She demanded that he give his reason for trespassing.

"Love has blinded me, my honourable lady. I have just returned from the islands of China, where I visited a princess each evening, and her dazzling beauty has left me disorientated."

"China?" said Maimuna, incredulously. "What were you doing over there, you liar? Swear by the talisman engraved upon King Solomon's ring that you're telling the truth, because if I discover otherwise, I am going to skin you alive and break your bones."

"I swear by King Solomon and by your father, King Dimiryat, that I fly each night to China in order to catch sight of a princess called Budur, daughter of King Ghayyur the Jealous. She is a rare beauty: her black hair is as the darkest night, her nose as fine as a sword blade, her cheeks like red anemones, her tongue like wine and yet it can speak six languages. Her arms are like two streams, and her breasts two ostrich eggs, her waist as tiny as the neck of a gazelle and her buttocks like sand dunes which get in the way when she stands, and keep her awake when she wishes to sleep. Her thighs are two columns of pearls and her feet . . ."

"And you're going to tell me next that this beauty is in love with you?" Maimuna interrupted him.

"In love with me? She has refused all the suitors her father proposed for her, princes and sons of kings and emperors. She turned down each of them, telling her father that she's not interested in marriage. But each time she refuses a suitor, her fame and notoriety grow, and more and more admirers come forward. The last one was a very special prince, the son of a King named the King of Kings, and he would not take no for an answer. Yet when her father tried to change her mind, by enumerating his good qualities, Princess Budur told him, 'But I wish to be my own mistress, for I hold authority and power over the people. I know that as soon as I marry, my husband will rule over me.' Her father tried repeatedly to get her to see sense until she threatened to plunge her sword into her stomach and push until it came out of her back. When her father heard this threat, he was mortified, and overwhelmed with anxiety. At the same time, he didn't know what to say to the son of the King of Kings, so he locked his daughter away in seclusion."

Dahnash finished his story, repeating that his extreme distress was his excuse for trespassing.

"Are you trying to tell me this is a legitimate excuse for flying through my territory?" Maimuna snapped.

"If you were to see her, my lady, you would forgive me for sure!"

"You can be sure that I will not, because it would seem that this princess of yours is little more than a urinal, when I would expect to hear a description of a sublime creature. And yet there's a strange coincidence here, for when I caught you red-handed,

I was roaming around trying to protect a prince whose story is identical to that of your princess. My youth has been imprisoned by his father in the deserted tower because he refused to marry. And he is as beautiful as that star shining in the sky over there."

"Surely you can use more imagination than to describe someone as a star," said Dahnash.

Maimuna sighed. "My prince's skin is as soft as a baby's; his eyebrows are like two swords and his eyes are darker than a gazelle. His mouth is sweet as honey and his body as strong as the branch of a banyan tree. If you saw him you would drool over him like a dog."

"With respect to you, Maimuna, I could never compare my princess to your prince because no one in the world could ever compare."

"What a liar; what a despicable jinni you are," Maimuna screamed. "There's no one like my prince, the length or width of the universe, and so you are insane to even try to compare your princess to my prince."

Dahnash sensed that he had crossed a line with Maimuna.

"Let's fly together and visit mine, then I'll go to visit yours."

"You foulest creature! If mine is more beautiful than yours, I win, and if yours is lovelier than mine, you win. But be prepared to be the loser." So saying, Maimuna hit Dahnash so hard that he screamed out in pain.

"Take me at once to your princess, so we can compare them or I promise I'll burn you in my fire and throw you in the desert."

Dahnash trembled. "I'll go at once."

"And, I'll come with you," Maimuna said, "because I don't trust you for a moment."

They flew and flew together until they reached a palace perched on top of a mountain. They entered Princess Budur's room, but

Maimuna could only make out the roundness of the princess's face, and her golden nightdress, which shimmered in the dark. Dahnash was overcome with emotion. He took her in his arms, shaking so hard that he nearly lost balance.

"How I wish you would sleep between my eyelids for ever, my beauty," he whispered.

"I understand why you wish the princess could sleep between your eyelids! If she saw you, she would be so frightened she'd try to break free, even in midair."

Then she nudged him out of the way and grabbed the princess around her waist, while Dahnash carried her by the legs, and off they flew, Princess Budur's hair flying out behind her like a dark shooting star.

They reached Qamar al-Zaman's room in the tower and laid Princess Budur down next to him, and the jinniya and the jinni gasped in amazement, for the two bore a striking resemblance to one another.

"Didn't I tell you my princess is more beautiful?" Dahnash said.

But Maimuna knelt down and kissed Qamar al-Zaman between the eyes, and said to Dahnash, "I'm going to forgive you, for it seems that you are shortsighted and your heart has shrunk. And I'll forgive you if the beauty of your princess inspires you with a description better than my description of my prince, which is this: the mole on his cheek is the place where musk is created."

"Listen to this: one glance from her would be my food for ever," Dahnash replied as he kissed Princess Budur's hand.

"Food? You describe her as food, you greedy, starved jinni? But let us not waste more time with words. We need to decide who is more beautiful."

"I will not change my mind, my princess is more beautiful," Dahnash said.

"No, my prince is more beautiful," was Maimuna's reply.

"Mine is prettiness itself and I will never deviate from the truth, even if you knock the breath out of me. Since I have great respect for you, I am obliged to be totally honest."

"We should wake each of them in turn. Whoever burns with love for the other must be less beautiful," Maimuna suggested.

"I shall become a flea and bite the prince and wake him, and send the princess into a deep sleep," Dahnash said and he sank his teeth into the prince's neck.

Qamar al-Zaman awoke and scratched his neck where Dahnash had bitten him. When he saw Budur fast asleep next to him, he was taken by surprise but couldn't help pulling back the covers. He lifted up her shirt, pulled down her drawers and gasped.

"What a beauty!" he breathed heavily and went to wake her up.

As he lowered his head to kiss her, Dahnash whispered to Maimuna, "Though I'm thrilled that he burns for my princess, your youth is a thug with no scruples. If you will allow it, I shall stop him from kissing her."

But Maimuna hushed the jinni, furious that she was going to lose the bet. Then Qamar al-Zaman changed his mind, and turned his head away from Budur. Maimuna burned with pride as Qamar al-Zaman pulled down Budur's shirt, pulled up her drawers and shook her gently.

"Wake up, my darling. Stop playing games with me. I know full well that my father, the King, had you climb into my bed and sleep, so I would fall in love and worship you, and wed you and have children. I have resisted the idea of marriage for three years, so let us not dally: get up, my sweet and precious beauty. Let us marry as soon as day breaks, if I can bear to wait." He went again to kiss her, but then withdrew, saying to himself, "Be patient,

Qamar al-Zaman. God forgive me for what I was intending to do."

He stroked the girl's long, dark hair. "Did my father ask you to pretend to sleep, so you could report to him what I had done to you? I bet he's testing me! Perhaps he is hiding somewhere and observing my every move, so that he might delight in winning the battle, after I insulted him before his men and council. Well, now I am head over heels in love with you."

He touched her face with his hand, and when she still didn't open her eyes, he said, "I love your strength of will as much as I love your beauty."

He brought her hand to his cheek and saw a ring on her finger, which he took off and examined carefully.

"A seal ring? Who are you, my princess? I shall take it as a keepsake to remember you by, a token of our love."

He put the ring on his little finger and closed his eyes, murmuring, "Better to sleep, then I shall not waiver in the face of temptation and desire."

Maimuna clapped her hands joyfully.

"Did you see how the great honour of my prince goes hand in hand with his beauty?"

"Yes, I saw," Dahnash replied.

"Now it is my turn to become a flea and wake your princess."

Maimuna flew into Budur's clothes and bit her on her thigh and navel. The girl opened her eyes and sat up in bed. Seeing the young man sleeping next to her, breathing heavily, she gasped.

"Who are you, the most gracious of God's creations? Who brought you to me? *Houris* would hesitate to think their eyes so splendid and extraordinary if they saw how white the whites of your eyes, how black their darkness. I can't believe how my heart is throbbing with love for you, when I have shied away from men and marriage! If the prince of the King of Kings who sought my hand again and again was you, I would have agreed at once!"

Qamar al-Zaman remained asleep. Budur shook him gently, saying, "Open your eyes, my master and light of my eyes, for you might like what you see."

But Maimuna had put him in a deep slumber and Budur's efforts were in vain. "Wake up and embrace the narcissus, and play with me until the break of day, till midday and evening. Get up, my knight, taste my fruit which ripened, ready, as soon as I set eyes on you," she pleaded.

But Qamar al-Zaman remained motionless. "I can't believe that you're actually asleep," Budur said. "Could it be that your charm and beauty has filled you with enormous pride and vanity? Or are you carrying out the wishes of my father, playing hard to get in order to teach me to listen to him and obey him? But aren't you happy that I resisted the charms of others and waited for you? Now here I am, please take me into your arms!"

When he still didn't stir, Budur embraced him, spotted her ring and cheered, planting a loud kiss on every finger.

"I'm in ecstasy, or perhaps I'm not," she said, "to realise that you came to me while I was fast asleep. Worried that I would refuse you, you decided not to wake me, but asked for my hand silently. Be assured, I accept you as my husband." She kissed him on the lips, took his own ring and put it on her finger.

Then she lifted the covers and ran her hand over his chest, saying, "Your chest is my home now, and your chest hair the trees which shade me." Then she moved her hand to his waist, his upper thighs and when she reached his you-know-what . . .

Abu Nuwas broke off from the story and lowered his voice as if revealing a secret. "As some of you know, a woman's lust is stronger than that of a man. Poor souls! When they become horny they'll seek to satisfy themselves in any way, with anybody, with anything."

Abu Nuwas giggled. "But let me take you back to lusty Budur," he said.

When her hand reached his you-know-what, Budur began to tremble. She felt ashamed and stopped touching Qamar al-Zaman, then she too fell asleep, holding him in her arms.

Maimuna cried out with happiness. "Oh how I love victory! Did you see what your princess has done to my prince? Are you now willing to admit he is more beautiful and graceful?"

"Yes, yes," Dahnash mumbled.

But Maimuna said, "I can't hear you! Sorry, what did you just whisper?"

"Yes, yes, you've won, OK?" Dahnash told her.

"Then hurry up and return the defeated princess to her country, because I'm so elated by my victory I can't fly, I must dance instead!"

So Dahnash carried the sleeping princess back to China and Maimuna spent the rest of the night dancing wildly, and singing to herself, "Yes, yes I won the bet, I won and I always come out on top."

When Qamar al-Zaman woke in the morning, turned to his right and then to his left and couldn't see the girl, he jumped up from the bed, banging at the door like a madman.

When the guard opened up, he asked, "Who came in here and took the girl away?"

"A girl? What girl are you talking about, my master? I can assure you that nobody entered your room last night, not even a fly."

Qamar al-Zaman shouted out in fury: "I'm going to ask you once more about the girl who slept next to me in my bed. Tell me where she has gone!"

"I never left your door, my master. I lean on your door when I doze during the night, in case you wake and want something."

"Confess that you sneaked her in and then away again, on the orders of my father, the King," Qamar al-Zaman shouted, in great agitation.

The guard repeated that no one had entered the room, and Qamar al-Zaman lost his mind completely and began to punch and kick the guard. Terrified that he'd lost the girl for ever, he dragged the guard over to the decrepit well, tied him to the well-rope and lowered him to the water, dipping him in repeatedly and demanding that the man confess. The guard shrieked in terror, calling for help. Eventually he cried out, "Yes, yes, master, I will tell you the truth."

The prince lifted him out, shivering and dripping, teeth clenched, unable to speak. He asked if he could go and change his clothes before he told Qamar al-Zaman the whole story.

"If I hadn't threatened you with death, you'd still be lying to me," Qamar al-Zaman said, kicking the guard and cursing him.

The poor guard hurried to the palace, not quite believing he'd managed to escape. Standing in the presence of the King he said, "Your Majesty, Prince Qamar al-Zaman has lost his mind completely."

The guard appeared to have lost his wits. He was sobbing, with his hair stuck to his head, and his face black and blue from the beating.

"Look what he's done to me, Your Majesty," he continued. "He woke up this morning asking about a girl and claiming that he'd found her in his bed that night, and that she vanished in the morning, and then he attacked me and nearly killed me. He demanded that I tell him who had sneaked her out, and no matter how many times I assured him that no one came in or out of the locked room, all my efforts to convince him scattered in the wind."

When the King heard what the guard said, he hurried to his son, followed by his Vizier and the guard. He entered Qamar al-Zaman's room and his son, who was reciting the Qur'an, stood at once, bowed his head and placed his arms behind his back in an expression of humility and respect.

"I have sinned against you, my father," he wept, "and now here I am before you, repenting and seeking your forgiveness."

The King embraced his son, kissed him on both cheeks. Taking his hands, he sat with him on the couch and asked, "Son, what day is it today?"

"Today is Thursday and tomorrow is Friday and after tomorrow is Saturday." Qamar al-Zaman went on and counted the seven days of the week and the twelve months of the year.

The King spat at the guard. "How dare you, dog, accuse my son of madness? No one here is insane except you!"

Then the King turned back to his son. "Tell me, did you really ask the guard about a girl who shared your bed yesterday evening and then disappeared?"

Qamar al-Zaman laughed. "Father, let us not dwell on this any more. Yes, you were right to ask that I marry and provide you with a grandson. I was arrogant and stubborn to refuse, and now I am willing to marry the girl who shared my bed until dawn broke. I am certain that you sent her to me, so that I would desire her and change my mind."

The King shook his head. "I swear by Almighty God that I have no idea about this girl you're obsessed with. Listen to me, son. Could it be that being here on your own, banished, made you hallucinate, or could it be that you ate a heavy meal, whose ingredients confused you and made you dream dreams which you took to be real? God cursed marriage, and who shall force it upon you! Oh, how eaten by guilt am I for what I have done! Come on, my son; let us go back to the palace and turn over this black, ill-omened page."

Qamar al-Zaman bottled up his fury and tried to remain calm.

"May I ask you a question, father?"

"Go on, son, ask me one hundred questions."

"Have you heard of any soldier who dreamed that he fought in a furious battle and, when he awoke, found a sword in his hand dripping with blood?"

"No by God, my son, this has never happened," the King answered quickly.

"Then I shall tell you what came to pass last night. I woke to find a girl as pretty as a rose fast asleep next to me. I embraced her, and slipped her ring from her finger and put it on my own. I won't conceal from you the fact that I nearly kissed her on her lips, but drew back, not because of my virtue and good breeding, but out of shame, as I assumed that you were hiding somewhere, watching what I would do to her. And then I awoke this morning and she was gone. So I questioned the guard, and my frustration grew as he denied everything."

He took the girl's ring from his little finger and showed it to his father, who studied it carefully before he spoke.

"I believe every word you've said, my son. Your story is strange, and you must believe me when I say that I do not know the girl; nor where she went. All I want is for you to be patient. I am so thrilled that your mind is sound and your logic is more acute than ever."

"Please, father, help me look for the girl, the owner of this ring, or death will carry me away. I am devastated and filled with great grief and turmoil."

He wept and moaned, moaned and wept, and when his father asked him to return with him to the palace, Qamar al-Zaman refused.

"I should remain here, in case the girl comes back tonight."

His father left, but not before he had assured his son that he would help him find the girl.

That night, Qamar al-Zaman waited in vain for the girl to appear, refusing to eat or drink. In the stillness of the night, he cried out from his window:

> "Return, my own true love,
> Enchantress, immortal dove,
> My eyes are useless unless I glimpse you,
> My lips dried leaves without tasting your dew."

These agonised words of Qamar al-Zaman reached Maimuna, who had been down in the well when Qamar al-Zaman had lowered the guard into the water. She had been unable to leave the well and help her prince until darkness fell. Now, she set out and hunted for Dahnash, to no avail, finally sending one hundred jinni fairies to find him, without success. Then, to her great distress, Qamar al-Zaman's cries reached her again:

> "Come back to me before my last breath, last sigh,
> Last effort to murmur your name,
> Then my faint breath can live,
> Captured in your soul's flame."

Maimuna was sure that Dahnash must be in China visiting his Princess Budur, so she set out after him, flying higher and higher so she would arrive in China at great speed. But when she reached the princess, she found to her horror that the once beautiful girl was now dishevelled, with veins bulging on her face and neck. She stood, screaming and yelling, her sword drawn as she threatened the slaves, eunuchs and ministers of her father's court.

"Where is my man? My beautiful knight, who slept in my arms last night until dawn?"

"We have all advised you, Princess Budur, not to engage in such filthy talk. For the tenth time, I tell you that there was no man in your room!" her duenna told her.

But the princess continued to wail. "Where is the young man with black eyes like a gazelle, whose body was so lean and warm in my bed last night?"

"Stop this nonsense before your father hears you; he'll be livid and go on the rampage," the duenna told her. "Please, stop playing this dangerous game!"

But Budur continued to weep and tremble with emotion. "Bring me the young man whose lips were like honey, for I can still taste the sweetness in my mouth," she yelled.

"You've gone mad, my beloved princess, I think that an evil spirit has invaded and corrupted you with a great desire to fornicate!"

Budur rushed at the duenna with her sword in hand, but then she noticed Qamar al-Zaman's ring around her finger. "Can you tell me who this ring belongs to?" she shrieked.

She struck the duenna with her sword, killing her. Everyone screamed in horror, fearing for their lives. The entire court fled to King Ghayyur to tell him his daughter had lost her wits. The King hurried to his daughter.

Upon seeing her father, Budur asked, "Dear father, what have you done with the young man you sent to me? He slept in my arms all night long and his breath was like a summer breeze on my neck. You sent him so he might change my mind about marriage! Well, here I am, father, fit and of sound mind and ready to marry him."

"Stop this nonsense at once! Or people will think you're mad," Budur's father shouted.

Budur was astounded. Even her father doubted her. She spread her hand before him and said, "I am not mad! Those who don't believe me are the ones who are insane. Look at my ring, father. To whom does it belong, and how does it come to be on my finger, replacing my own? None other than the man you had brought into my room last night!"

Her father answered her with a broken heart. "Perhaps this is your ring and you are somehow mistaken? I am going to get you the best doctors and astrologists so they might cure you."

Budur shrieked and yelled and tore her robe from top to bottom as she hunted for the youth under the couches and carpets. "Where have you hidden him?" she repeated, over and again.

The King gave orders for his daughter to be restrained, for her sword to be removed, and for an iron chain to be placed around her feet. Budur fought and kicked the slaves, who restrained her savagely, until finally she surrendered. When everyone left her alone, Budur sang:

> "You say I've coloured your hands with red henna,
> It is not true,
> Yet my tears are red as they sprinkle my cheeks
> When I wipe them they colour my hands
> If you think me mad, summon he who made me insane."

And Maimuna wept, and reproached herself for committing this horrible crime. She knew that she had acted out of vanity and arrogance, desiring only to prove to Dahnash that her prince was more beautiful than his princess. In doing so, she caused these beautiful young creatures nothing but woe and excruciating pain and sorrow, and their despair had driven them both insane.

Zumurrud and Nur al-Din

The flogged sister asked the mistress of the house if she wished to tell the story of Zumurrud and Nur al-Din, but the mistress of the house tapped her sister on the shoulder with love and sympathy, saying, "No, but you must tell it."

So the flogged sister rose and addressed the Caliph. "When I came back home devastated, my sister tended to me, encouraging me to learn to fend for myself, take my life in my hands and not rely upon men. She told me the story of Zumurrud and Nur al-Din, which I should like to tell now, with your permission, Oh Commander of the Faithful."

"I am eager to hear it, my lady," said the Caliph.

And so the flogged sister began.

Once there was a young man called Nur al-Din, son of a prominent merchant from Cairo, who never stepped out of the house of his father's shop without his father's permission. One evening, a group of merchants' sons invited him to a picnic in a garden. Nur al-Din asked his father if he might go, and his father gave him his blessing and some money.

When the merchants' sons entered the garden through a sky-blue gate, just like the portals of Paradise, they gasped in wonder at trees laden with fruit: grapes, peaches, apples, figs, and trees of almonds. One of the young men said:

> "Look, my friends
> At those luscious red grapes
> Hanging above your head,
> They're the ruby nipples of a nubile maiden,
> Now gaze on the succulent pomegranates:
> Round breasts aglow and exquisitely laden."

As if by way of answer, another boy said:

> "Dearest friends, behold the dappled apples,
> Reflecting the soft cheeks of youth:
> One aflame with brazen lust
> The other paled by sweetest trust?"

A third boy took up the theme:

> "A double almond asleep in its shell
> Where two hearts locked eternally dwell."

A fourth boy said:

> "My favourite are the figs.
> So unlike their fellow fruits
> Seed-studded and quivering
> No sharing and no disputes!"

Then they removed their turbans and coats, while slaves came in with wonderful food, including many kinds of bird: ones that flew, walked, swam—pigeons, quails and geese. The boys ate amidst the aroma of jasmine and roses, henna and myrtle, and when they were satisfied the gardener appeared, carrying a basket filled with roses.

"Whoever can speak the most delicate lines of poetry on the subject of roses shall win the basket."

All the young men took a turn, except Nur al-Din, who hung back and remained silent. The gardener insisted that the young man attempt a line or two, and so Nur al-Din said:

> "Miraculous and strange, my friends,
> That what was watered with silver
> Is now blossoming in pure gold."

The gardener chose these beautiful lines and everyone clapped as he handed Nur al-Din the basket of roses and then poured wine. Nur al-Din declined, insisting he had never touched so much as a drop before, and he never would.

"Why have you made this decision?" asked the gardener.

"Because to drink wine is sinful!" said Nur al-Din.

"But God is generous and forgiving," the gardener insisted. "There are only two sins which He will not tolerate: to worship false Gods and to harm people."

At these words, Nur al-Din accepted his first drink, sipped it and found it bitter. He set down his cup.

"Don't most medicines taste bitter?" said the gardener. "Besides, wine purifies the blood, cures wind, aids with digestion of even the heaviest food, and above all encourages you to copulate!"

Everyone laughed, including Nur al-Din, who finished his first cup, then drank a second and a third. He was on his fourth when the gardener brought in a beautiful girl, dark-eyed, with hair so long that it was like a cape trailing behind her. She was holding a satin bag, from which she took thirty-two pieces of wood. She fitted them together into an Indian lute and started to play and sing, her voice pure and clear, like a bulbul:

"Surely you know that pleasure soon evaporates, into thin air?
Then all we are left with are stories."

Nur al-Din was overwhelmed by her beauty and her voice, but at dawn he stood up to leave, worried that he was very late getting back home. The girl saw him and quickly sang:

"Surely you're not thinking of fleeing, my fine lover?
Enjoy your good fortune, stay and kiss me until daybreak."

Nur al-Din changed his mind and stayed with the girl until nearly midday. They kissed each other over and over, on the mouth and eyes and cheeks. When he finally stood up, she asked him where he was going.

"To my parents," he answered.

She laughed. "Are you a boy or a man?"

When he arrived home, his mother said angrily, "We've been worried about you. Your father blames himself for giving you permission to go out with your friends."

She leaned forward and smelled the wine on his breath.

"Have you started drinking wine and disobeying the Almighty?"

But Nur al-Din didn't answer. He went to his room and fell asleep.

His father, who had lain awake the whole night, heard that his son was back.

"Why was our son out all night?" he asked.

His wife lied, telling her husband that the air in the garden, and all the rich and heavy fragrance of the flowers, had made Nur al-Din fall asleep.

But the father went into his son's room and when he smelled the stench of wine, he shouted, "Damn you, Nur al-Din, have you forgotten what your name means, the light of religion? Yet it seems that you have become such a stupid imbecile that you will drink wine."

Nur al-Din was still drunk. He reared up and struck his father with all his might. His fist landed on his father's right eye, so that it dislodged and hung on his cheek. His father blacked out in pain and horror.

Nur al-Din's mother wept as she sprinkled rose water on her husband, not stopping until he came round. He immediately swore that he would cut off his son's right hand next morning. His wife tried to placate him, but he insisted he would punish his son in the most awful way imaginable. Eventually she convinced him to go and sleep and then she stayed by Nur al-Din's side. Once he had sobered up, she gave him a thousand dinars and told him he must flee. Nur al-Din asked her why, and when she told him everything, he was unable to believe what he had done while drunk. But his mother urged him to leave.

"Run, before your father wakes up and cuts off your right hand as he promised to do. But try to send me your news in secret."

They embraced, weeping.

Nur al-Din walked to the river and came upon a ship at anchor, with passengers boarding it. He asked the crew where they were sailing, and when they told him Alexandria, he immediately joined them. As the ship left Cairo, Nur al-Din was in floods of tears.

But when he reached Alexandria, with its walls that were closed each night, and beautiful parks and buildings within, he felt safe. He found himself a room at the apothecary's shop and the next morning he visited the market and bought goods with which to trade. As he wandered the streets he caught sight of a girl climbing off the back of a mule.

Her face was veiled, but he glimpsed her bewitching eyes. When she walked, her curving figure and slender build made all the men in the market gather around her. The man accompanying her seemed not to mind the admiring stares of the men; instead, he brought a chair for the girl to sit on, and Nur al-Din realised that the girl was a slave being auctioned.

The auctioneer lifted the veil from the girl's face, and everyone gasped at her beauty.

"Men of wealth, men of power, merchants: who will bid, starting from five hundred dinars, for this mistress, who is as beautiful as the moon and its stars, or a glittering diamond!" cried the auctioneer.

Frenzied bidding between the men began. The highest bid, of nine hundred and fifty dinars, was from an old man. The auctioneer addressed him.

"I must seek her consent, for during our journey here I fell ill and this girl looked after me as if I was her own father, so I promised not to sell her to anyone without her permission."

But the girl was not impressed. "What? Sell someone like me to a decrepit old man who is barely able to stand? His penis will most assuredly be as soft as a piece of dough!"

Everyone laughed, but the old man was furious, and shouted at the auctioneer.

"Refrain from insulting people, will you!" the auctioneer told the girl.

Another old man increased his bid to one thousand dinars, but the girl told the auctioneer, "What is wrong with you, parading me from one old man to the next? This man is concealing something about himself; I sense that he is a fake."

"You have forgotten your manners," shouted the auctioneer. "And how can you insult this man by calling him a fraudster when you haven't exchanged so much as a single word with him!"

"It is easy to detect a crumbling wall, even one painted with the best paint. This old man has dyed his hair and his beard, which to me is the foulest of lies, a deceit begun in the heart that exudes out to the hair."

"And what if I have got white hair anyway, isn't it a sign of dignity and maturity?" asked the old man.

"White hair? Why should I stuff my mouth with cotton while I am still alive?" was the slave girl's answer.

The old man was enraged. "This slave girl you've brought to the market does nothing but hurl abuse. Take her away or I'll tell the Wali to ban you from selling slaves," he told the auctioneer.

"Do you realise what you've done to me? You've ruined me," said the auctioneer, turning on the girl. "Let us leave before someone attacks me."

But a young man, who was tiny, stopped them and asked if he might buy the girl for any price she named.

"I am no old man, as you all see. I am her age," he said.

"I'd be willing to be your slave if I owned a chicken farm and you helped me to gather the eggs, since if you dropped an egg it wouldn't break, because your hands are practically touching the floor."

The auctioneer was furious. He grabbed the slave girl by the hand.

"Enough! We have lost the chance to make money for us both, and so I will return you to Persia, to the man from whom you ran away."

But the slave girl, whose name was Zumurrud, was terrified at this idea. She pleaded with the auctioneer to give her another chance. She looked frantically around and spotted Nur al-Din, tall and beautiful, with his radiant forehead and teeth like pearls.

She freed herself from the auctioneer's grasp. "Look, why don't you ask that man to bid for me?"

"If he wanted to buy a slave he would have bid for you already, even if it was a small amount."

Zumurrud removed a huge sapphire ring from her finger and gave it to the auctioneer.

"If this young man buys me, then I'll give you this ring in return for the trouble I caused." The auctioneer took her immediately to Nur al-Din, and the slave girl addressed him directly.

"Am I not beautiful? Sir, in God's name you must tell me if I am not!"

"You're beauty itself, no one is lovelier than you; you're the *houri* God promised his believers in the afterlife."

"Then why didn't you bid for me? I would have been happy if you'd bid even one dinar."

"Were I at home I would have won you with all the wealth I own," was his answer.

"Sir, come closer and inspect me. I might be a fake."

Nur al-Din laughed and moved closer. She quickly stretched out her hand and gave him one thousand dinars.

"Come on, sir, bid for me," she said, aware of Nur al-Din's embarrassment.

"One thousand dinars for this lovely slave, unless she finds fault with me."

"Give me your answer, but remember no insults this time," said the auctioneer.

"Only the moon and gazelles match the beauty of my buyer," was Zumurrud's answer.

In the blink of an eye, the auctioneer had fetched the Qadi and notaries and Zumurrud became Nur al-Din's slave. They were both eager for night to fall so that they could be together. They hurried to Nur al-Din's room. Zumurrud couldn't believe that he had no furniture and so he told her his story, and then he asked how she had come to be a slave.

"The past is nothing to me but a soap bubble," was all she would say. "Now, go and buy me some lamb and rice."

He raced out and when he returned, she prepared the most delicious meal. When they had eaten, Zumurrud lay down beside Nur al-Din, and they kissed and then to their surprise they took each other's virginity, and they slept holding each other, like two bees hungry for the sweet nectar.

The next morning Nur al-Din told Zumurrud that he had not even one dirham in his pocket and that he would have to trade wares so that they could survive. In response, the slave girl removed some money hidden in her bosom, saying, "Go and buy twenty dirhams' worth of silk threads in five different colours."

Nur al-Din did as she asked. After they had eaten, she settled down next to him, and he closed his eyes and caressed her gently, saying, "Am I touching the silk I bought you? No, I don't think so, for what I touch is even softer."

Nur al-Din went off to the market to trade and the slave girl sat making a sash with the silk, not moving until she had finished it. Next morning, she told him to take the sash to the Persian market and ask the auctioneer to put it up for sale.

"Don't accept less than twenty dinars for it," she told him.

Nur al-Din hesitated, unable to believe that something which cost twenty dirhams to make could be sold for twenty dinars.

"You've no idea how valuable this sash is," Zumurrud told him.

And she was right, for the sash sold for twenty dinars.

Nur al-Din returned excitedly and asked Zumurrud to teach him how to make sashes.

"To hell with trading, this is more profitable," he said.

And for a whole year, Zumurrud would work on the sashes and Nur al-Din would sell them, and they made good money and moved to a small house of their own.

One morning Zumurrud told Nur al-Din to buy her more thread than usual, because she wanted to make him a mantle to drape on his shoulders, and the very next day Nur al-Din walked to the market draped in the mantle, accepting the compliments of the other traders, and proud that his lover had made it for him.

But a few days later he went to say "see you later" to Zumurrud one morning and found her weeping.

"What is wrong?" he asked her.

But Zumurrud only cried harder. "The pain of parting from you has smote me."

Nur al-Din could not understand why Zumurrud was lamenting their beautiful days together, as though they were coming to an end.

"Why would you leave, when you're now dearer to me than my very self?"

"Do you not know that clouds rise in the bluest of skies whilst pearls found in the depths of the sea are corpses rocked by waves? I have learned that over time most people reveal themselves to be rotten at heart."

Nur al-Din begged her to explain her distress.

"I fled Persia because, just as you witnessed the day you bought me, I was unable to resist insulting men who were deserving of it. One such man was so enraged that he swore he would hunt me down, even if I hid in one half of a walnut shell, and force himself on me and become my master. But I had a glimpse of him yesterday when I was about to step out of the hammam. Now listen to me carefully, my master and my love: you must be on your guard against that devil of a man. He drags his left leg and has a very thick beard like a ram. I am sure he came here to find me!"

"I shall kill him when I see him," said Nur al-Din, filled with fear and anxiety.

"No, don't kill him, but don't speak to him or trade with him, even if he begs you to. Don't even exchange greetings with him."

The very next day, while Nur al-Din was enjoying the sun in the market, the Persian whom Zumurrud warned him about took him by surprise.

"Where did you get this mantle from?" he asked.

"My mother made it for me," Nur al-Din said brusquely.

The Persian offered to buy it, but Nur al-Din refused, even when the Persian raised his price until it reached six hundred dinars, saying, "I shall not sell it to you or to anyone else, for my mother made it with her own hands—and this is final!"

But the Persian kept offering more money until he reached one thousand dinars. Finally an old merchant intervened, urging Nur al-Din to accept the offer, since the mantle was worth no more than one hundred dinars. He kept on trying to persuade Nur al-Din, until he was embarrassed and gave in, took the money, and handed his mantle to the Persian. As he prepared to go back to Zumurrud and tell her what had happened, the Persian invited everyone to dine on a roasted sheep, wine and fruit in a nearby tavern. Nur al-Din declined the invitation, but once again the other merchants insisted he accompany them, swearing to divorce their wives if he didn't, until Nur al-Din relented and went with them.

The Persian waited for Nur al-Din to drink a few glasses of wine and then asked the young man to sell him the slave he had bought the previous year for one thousand dinars, saying he was willing to buy her for five thousand dinars.

"I won't sell her even for all the treasure of the world," Nur al-Din said. But the cunning Persian kept tempting him with greater sums of money, pouring more wine all the while, until he had reached ten thousand dinars.

By now Nur al-Din was very drunk. "Yes, I shall sell her to you for ten thousand dinars, just show me the money," he told the Persian.

The next morning the Persian produced ten thousand dinars. But Nur al-Din was now sober and composed.

"Damn you, Persian liar!" he said. "I sold you nothing! Besides, I live with my mother, and I have no slaves at home!"

But the Persian accused Nur al-Din of lying, asking all the merchants to be his witnesses, and they agreed to testify that Nur al-Din had sold his slave to the Persian. They gathered around him, cajoling him and insisting he agree to this sale, reminding him that he could take the ten thousand dinars and buy another slave girl even more beautiful than his, or instead marry one of their daughters, until finally he accepted and took the money. The Qadi was summoned, and Nur al-Din signed the papers confirming that Zumurrud was now the Persian's slave.

Nur al-Din sat with his head in his hands, thinking of poor Zumurrud. Meanwhile, when he had failed to return home, the slave girl had begun to weep so bitterly and fiercely that her neighbour had come to see what was wrong.

"My master has not returned home, and now I am terrified that he has been tricked into selling me."

"But when he sees the sun in you, how can he live without its rays?" the neighbour asked, trying to comfort her.

Zumurrud looked out the window and saw Nur al-Din coming home, with the Persian and a group of merchants trailing behind him.

"Oh broken heart, woe is me! I taste bitterness as though the hour of parting has already come."

When Nur al-Din came in trembling, Zumurrud said, "Oh! My master, your face shows nothing but sorrow! You've sold me!" and began to strike her face.

"I am like a fool who has lost a limb, but surely God who united us once before must grant us reunion?"

She held him in her arms, pressing him to her and kissing him between his eyes.

"But I warned you, my love, didn't I?" and then she kissed him again between his eyes and said, "I don't know how I can live with no heart, because I am leaving it with you."

"Damn you, keep away from me," she said to the Persian as he approached.

"Your master has wronged you, not I! He sold you of his own free will, while I paid handsomely for you because I loved you."

Nur al-Din banged his head on the wall, while the Persian with the aid of the merchants carried the weeping and lamenting Zumurrud away.

"Take my bones with you as you go and give them a burial," Nur al-Din cried out, and then raced after Zumurrud, following her until he watched as she was forced to board a ship bound for Persia. He decided that he would follow her to Persia on the next boat, since he knew where the Persian lived.

Nur al-Din never went to Persia, for Zumurrud managed to escape before the ship sailed, aided by one of the crew whom she bribed with a valuable ruby ring. Afraid that the Persian might leave the ship and hunt for her, she hid in the hammam and sent a eunuch with a message to Nur al-Din, telling him to come at midnight and whistle. Then she would come down to him and they would flee immediately for a foreign land.

Nur al-Din was deliriously happy. He decided that when he was reunited with Zumurrud he would leave Alexandria and return to Cairo, make peace with his father, seek his blessing and marry Zumurrud. Unable to wait a moment longer, he hurried to the hammam and tried to sleep on a bench outside, counting the seconds until he would embrace his love.

But it happened that a thief who was planning to rob a house next to the hammam was below in the alleyway when Zumurrud peeped out the window to check the street. She thought he was Nur al-Din come earlier than midnight and raced down with a saddle bag to meet him. But the thief, who was trained to be quick as a magician, grabbed her, flung her on his mule and fled. Nur al-Din tried in vain to save her. He jumped in the air, yelled and then ran after them but it was too late.

Blaming his ill luck, Nur al-Din went back to the market, not knowing what to do. He sat down, planning to cry until the morning, but saw the old merchant who had convinced Nur al-Din to sell Zumurrud.

"Look what has happened to me! My heart is broken for ever. Even the ten thousand dinars which all of you made me take in exchange for my lovely slave girl, my sweetheart, mean nothing to me!"

The merchant felt so sorry for the young man that he apologised, offering Nur al-Din his daughter's hand.

"Don't you love your daughter? If you do, why do you want her to suffer life with an unlucky man?"

And he described to the merchant how he lost his slave for the second time.

Hearing this, the merchant, who was old and wise, said, "But God loves you, for she rode on a mule. Follow the track of the mule, my son, and then you will know where your slave was taken."

Nur al-Din thanked the merchant and decided to trace the mule, hoping to find Zumurrud and be reunited with her for ever.

Before Zumurrud realised that the man she had escaped with was a horrible thief, she said to him, "At last, my love, we're together and I am happy you thought of getting us a mule."

"Whore!" replied the thief. "I am not so soft that I would be the lover of any woman. I am a member of a gang, and soon the forty of us will be banging away at your womb by way of welcoming you to our meeting tomorrow morning."

Zumurrud struck her face, weeping. "Why do I escape from one trap, only to fall into another?"

Then she fell silent, for she was trying to come up with a plan to save herself. Eventually they reached a cave outside the city, which the horrible thief entered, dragging Zumurrud with him. To her relief, she discovered that his mother was inside the cave. She was less than happy to see her son, particularly when he left again straightaway, instructing her to watch over the girl until he returned in the morning with his company of thieves.

Zumurrud lay awake all night, and when dawn broke she woke the thief's mother, saying, "Aunt, you were scratching your head all night long, do you want me to delouse you?"

"Yes, my daughter. I haven't had a bath for an eternity as these pigs of men, chief among them my son, uproot me constantly from one place to another."

The old woman took Zumurrud out of the cave via a secret passage and Zumurrud deloused her, killing more than one hundred lice. She left the old woman happily asleep in the sunshine, went back to the cave, dressed in men's clothes, wrapped her head in a turban and strapped a sword at her waist. Next she helped herself to some of the gold she found hidden in the cave, took her saddle bag, mounted one of the two horses in the cave and fled.

She travelled on her horse, eating what she could scrounge and drinking from springs for ten days until she reached the city. As she entered the city gates she saw a huge gathering of officials and emirs. As she approached they bowed and kissed the ground before her, and when she dismounted, one Vizier addressed her.

"God send you all the victory and prosperity, our magnificent sultan! May your arrival, King of the Age, bring us great blessings and fortune."

Zumurrud glanced around her, puzzled.

"Your Majesty, God has made you our King!" said the chamberlain. "You must know that we follow a custom in our city. Whenever our King dies we wait for three days and then we stand by the city gates. The first man who arrives in the direction from which you came is appointed our King. Praise God, who has sent us a handsome young fellow this time. But were you an older or lesser man, you would still be our King."

Zumurrud tried to speak in a deep manly voice. "I am no common man, I was born to a noble family but I fell out with my father, and so I left, and my lucky fate brought me and my gold to you."

Everyone called for blessings on the King. "How fortunate that we have found you, Your Majesty," said one of the emirs.

"And how wonderful and fortunate that I have found you and become your King," Zumurrud replied.

Then she entered the city in a grand procession, escorted by officials, who led her to the palace and sat her on the throne. When night fell she dismissed all of her slaves and eunuchs, so that they would not see her without her turban and men's clothes.

She prayed, whispering, "Thank you, God, for making me a King. I plead with you to reunite me with my master one day."

Zumurrud proved to herself and her people that she was the greatest of Kings. She opened the coffers and gave money to the needy, and everyone obeyed her and loved her for her justice and virtue. When it was rumoured that the King had no wife and never visited the concubines, Zumurrud said, "The King is saving himself to marry and have children, but only when he has fulfilled all of his many duties."

Zumurrud erected a big arena in the heart of the city, where tables were set out, laden with food of all kinds, free for the people to come and eat on the first day of each week. She issued a decree that anyone who didn't come to eat from the free dishes would be hanged, and anyone who helped themselves to the plate of rice pudding in the centre of each table would also be hanged. And the first day every single person, young or old, came and ate at the King's tables, while the King sat watching, remaining there all day, until every one of her subjects had eaten their fill and left, having prayed that she would be granted a long life.

Zumurrud went back to her palace that night and prayed that God would send her Nur al-Din, weeping with longing for him. She continued to attend the lunches in the big arena each week, and her subjects assumed that the King was wonderfully generous in wishing to feed the people. But in truth, Zumurrud was trying to see any foreigner who came to her city, wishing that a miracle would bring her master to her tables.

Her plan at last succeeded, but, alas, instead of finding her master she found the robber, from whom she had fled, taking his horse and gold. He entered the arena, snatched the plate of rice pudding from the middle of the table, and asked for more sugar.

Zumurrud asked the soldier to bring forward the man who didn't obey the rules.

"I am going to ask you your name and your occupation and what brings you to our city, and I expect you to be truthful in every word you utter. Be certain that if you don't, you'll be hanged."

The thief said that his name was Ahmed and that he was a doctor, and, "I came here to help the sick and the needy."

"Bring me the divination table and the brass pen," Zumurrud said to her chamberlain.

Once they were in front of her, she shook the sand and threw it over the table, then drew a man carrying goods on his back next to forty dots.

"Aren't you a robber who belongs to a gang of forty thieves outside Alexandria? Let me tell you what you do in life! You rob people of their goods, money and animals, then, having deprived them of what they once owned, you terrorise and kill them. Is that true, you wretch, or not?"

She didn't add that he was here to look for her, and for the gold she had snatched from the cave.

The robber hesitated for a moment, but then seeing how angry the King was, he said, "It is true, my King."

"Take him and cut off his head, for fate has brought him here so that we may stop his atrocious behaviour."

All of the King's subjects, from emirs, ministers, down to the common people, murmured, "Our King is the master of geomancy, glory to God who granted him this magical gift."

And nobody dared to eat from the rice pudding plate, until a week later, when a man rushed in, taking the best seat at the table, eating and eating and then stretching his hand out for the rice pudding. When the soldier brought him to Zumurrud, she asked his name, occupation and why he had come.

"My name is Grain and I do nothing but fill my stomach with food. I come from beyond the mountains. As I am very greedy, and snatch food even from my children, my wife suggested I travel to the place where a generous and good King feeds his people and visitors to the city."

Zumurrud pretended to consult the sands and those gathered expected to hear her pronounce a sentence of death, but she surprised them by instead saying, "You're an honest man, eat whatever you wish and take some food back with you to your family."

Months passed and Zumurrud despaired of ever seeing Nur al-Din again.

The third foreigner to the city was none other than the Persian, who grabbed at plates, and when he reached for the rice pudding, the man next to him said, "Don't touch it, brother, or you'll be hanged."

"I know that you're scaring me so you can eat it yourself," said the Persian, helping himself.

Zumurrud ordered a soldier to seize the Persian, and when he was brought before her, she said, "Man, answer only the truth or I'll cut off your head. What is your name, occupation and the reason for visiting our city?"

"My name is Uthman, and I am a gardener. I was told that here I might find the dardar tree and with it cure my poor dying mother."

"What a wonderful son! But let us see if you're telling the truth!" said Zumurrud.

She shook the sand and threw it over the table, and pretended to draw things.

"Dog, how dare you disobey kings and lie to them! You're known by the name of the Persian, and you seize women, force yourself on them, and rape them, putting them to the worst of despair and pain! You heartless, foul creature. Then, when they escape your tyranny, you seek every despicable, horrifying trick to snatch them back. Is that not the truth?"

"Yes, it is true. You know everything, in the way of the prophets, Your Majesty. But since I am only passing through this city, forgive me and I promise to be good from now on!"

"I don't think that you know the real meaning of the word 'promise,'" Zumurrud said. Then she turned to her soldiers. "Cut off his head, so that we may teach criminals to follow the right path," she said, and the Persian was taken immediately to his death.

Zumurrud earned even greater respect and love from her people, drawing secret criticism only over the fact that she remained unmarried. Her advisers hinted more than once about her celibacy.

One day an old prince visited Zumurrud.

"Our precious King, since the customs of our city dictate that the King should marry, and since you promised your court that you would some day, let me suggest that you marry my daughter. She is beautiful, has high scruples like you, she's God-fearing."

Zumurrud's forehead broke out in sweat, as she thought to herself, "For how much longer can I delay my marriage, and yet how can I marry while I am a woman!"

"Yes, I am willing to marry your daughter," she said, thinking to herself, "I may be disgraced but I have no other choice if I am to remain King."

There was great celebration throughout the city, and decorations were put on every tree and everyone came to congratulate the King and pay their respects.

"Now our King is complete, let us pray that his reign might continue for ever," they said to one another.

After the wedding ceremony was over, the bride was brought to the King's chamber and the doors were closed and curtains were drawn, and flowers of every kind were laid on the prepared bed.

Zumurrud sat beside her bride, whose name was Hayat, held her and kissed her on the mouth. Then she pretended to be allergic to the flowers, she had a coughing fit and didn't stop coughing even when Hayat removed the flowers. The bride waited and waited for the King to approach her, but when he failed to do so she fell asleep.

The next day, the prince and his wife came to see their daughter and she told them everything. They both asked her to be patient. The next night Zumurrud sat with Hayat, patted her on her shoulders, sighed as the tears fell from her eyes, kissed her between her eyes, sighed again and got up and performed her ablutions and began to pray, and each time Hayat thought that the King had finished, Zumurrud prayed some more, on and on until once more Hayat fell asleep.

The next day when her parents came to visit her she said, "My husband the King is a jewel, he is pious and kind and intelligent but for some reason he keeps praying and sighing and weeping in silence."

"Be patient," her father counselled. "Wait and see what happens tonight, but if he continues with this behaviour then I'll have a word with him."

When Zumurrud entered the chamber that night, she found that Hayat had lit many candles around the room. She sighed, kissed Hayat on the head and wept, and then as she stood up to pray Hayat grabbed the bottom of Zumurrud's robe, saying, "Master, this is our third night together and you have left me all alone. Is it because you're so handsome and conceited that you don't need anyone? What do I tell my parents tomorrow?"

"But, my darling, what are you telling me?" Zumurrud asked.

"What I am saying, my King, is that I want you to come and lie with me. Take my virginity; let us be bride and bridegroom, man and a woman, husband and wife."

Zumurrud's eyes filled with tears again as she thought, "I have nowhere to go from here, and this city is the ideal place for Nur al-Din to find me. But at the same time I can't avoid my responsibilities any longer, or my bride's father will tell all the emirs and viziers and they'll discover that the King is not complete."

Then she said to Hayat, "I am entrusting my affairs to God and to you. I must tell you the truth. I have behaved in this way because I am not able to deflower you, for I am not a man. I will tell you my story."

Zumurrud told her everything and Hayat couldn't but feel sympathy towards her, though she was utterly astonished. She promised to keep her secret, saying, as she pointed to her heart, "I shall keep your secret inside a locked room, my woman King."

They embraced and kissed on the mouth, cuddled each other in bed and slept happily. Early in the morning Hayat managed to lure a pigeon which had landed on her windowsill. She cut the bird's throat and smeared blood over her nightgown and drawers and shrieked as loud as she could.

Waiting outside, Hayat's mother ululated happily and so did the woman's slaves. The King had finally deflowered his bride and the marriage was complete. The two women carried on blissfully fooling everyone around them, and Zumurrud's secret remained secure.

One day, a young man came in late and took the only empty place in the arena, opposite the rice pudding plate. Zumurrud's heart throbbed and fluttered as she looked at him, studying him carefully until she was sure that he was her master and lover. She nearly cried out in joy, but kept her emotions concealed until the hungry Nur al-Din reached for the rice pudding plate.

His neighbour tried to tell him not to eat it or he would regret it, but Nur al-Din started to devour it. Zumurrud thought he looked so pale and thin that she waited for him to finish eating the rice before she sent a eunuch, who asked the stranger very gently to come and speak to the King. Nur al-Din kissed the ground before Zumurrud, who spoke to him respectfully and then asked him three questions, telling him to be truthful or he would be hanged.

"My name, oh King, is Nur al-Din, I come from a merchant family in Cairo, and I've been looking for a slave girl whom I lost because of my weakness and greed and I will keep looking until I die because she is dearer to me than my eyes. I lost her, but still she holds my soul."

Nur al-Din wept and then fainted. Zumurrud tried to compose herself and not to revive him with a kiss. She ordered rose water to be sprinkled on his face, and when he recovered he pretended as always to divine the truth.

"You've told the truth and let us hope that God will unite you with your slave soon," she said.

She ordered her chamberlain to take him to the baths and bring him back to the palace. She told Hayat about Nur al-Din, and Hayat rejoiced with her and joked, saying that she wouldn't let them spend the night together.

While she was waiting, Zumurrud made herself beautiful, combing her hair, but then wrapped her hair in a turban. She lit candles throughout the room, and sent for Nur al-Din.

The King's advisers grew suspicious, and the rumour that the King had fallen in love with the merchant boy was on every lip in the palace.

"Oh! poor, poor Queen Hayat, who is so innocent and knows nothing of what is going on," they whispered.

In reality, of course, Hayat was in an adjoining room. When Nur al-Din was brought in, he bowed and kissed the ground before Zumurrud and she said, "Eat some of the chicken and drink some wine and when you're done come and sit here."

"To hear is to obey," he said.

When he had eaten his fill, he came to the couch and remained standing until she ordered him to massage her feet. He obeyed, thinking how soft they were, softer than silk.

"Go higher," she said, and he massaged her legs, thinking to himself, "Do Kings in this country pluck the hair from their legs? This King's legs are as soft as velvet."

"Go higher, higher," she ordered him.

But Nur al-Din said, "Forgive me, my lord, but I can't go higher than your knees."

"If you disobey me then this night will be unlucky for you! If you do as I ask, I'll appoint you as one of my emirs."

"What do you want me to do, Your Majesty?" Nur al-Din asked.

"Take off your trousers and lie on your face."

"Let me, Your Majesty, leave your city in peace, for what you're asking me to do is something I have never done and will never do. If you force me, my God will be my witness and I shall take my case against you on the day of judgement."

"Take off your trousers and lie on your stomach or I will cut off your head."

Nur al-Din started to cry and weep as he took off his trousers. He lay on his face and Zumurrud sat on his back. He felt the softest and lightest body, like the wings of a butterfly.

When she didn't move Nur al-Din said to himself, "Praise to God, the King can't get an erection."

But his happiness died as Zumurrud said, "Nur al-Din, I will never get an erection if my penis is not stroked. Hurry, stroke it until it rises and if you decline I'll kill you."

She arched her back and Nur al-Din placed his hand on her vagina.

"What an extraordinary, unusual thing. This King has a vagina."

Nur al-Din's lust was suddenly aflame, and when Zumurrud saw that his penis had grown to its fullest, just as she remembered it, she laughed.

"Master Nur al-Din, don't you recognise me?" she asked.

"But who are you, King?"

"I am Zumurrud, your slave girl!"

He pounced on her, kissing her and embracing her, and then the two of them turned the couch into a volcano that erupted with desire and ecstasy, love and yearning, as they rose and fell and cried out in pleasure, so loudly that all the eunuchs heard them and they hurried to peek through the keyhole, one after another.

In the morning Zumurrud introduced Hayat to Nur al-Din. Zumurrud told her that she was leaving, and Hayat asked Nur al-Din if he had a brother as handsome as he was.

"A cousin, who is like my brother. He will fall in love with you and marry you at once."

Zumurrud the King sent for the whole army, emirs and state officials. When they were all standing before him, he said, pointing at Nur al-Din, "I am going with my wife to this man's land. Find someone to rule on my behalf until we return."

Then the three of them returned to Cairo, bearing many treasures and gifts, but above all filled with the joy and bliss of having found each other. They continued to enjoy each other's company until they were overtaken by death, the destroyer of delights.

The Fourth Voyage
of Sindbad the Sailor

t was observed that the porter was cheering after each story was told, whether it was in favour of women or against them. And when the flogged sister had finished telling the story of Zumurrud and Nur al-Din, the porter stood up.

"Can I tell a story, Oh Commander of the Faithful?"

"It had better be as good as the others," said the Caliph. The porter bowed.

"I assure you, Commander of the Faithful, that my story is far better than every single story you've heard so far."

The Caliph smiled and the porter began. "They say marriage is nothing but a graveyard of love, but my Caliph, Vizier, gentlemen and ladies, I don't believe in this saying, and I yearn to be a husband and a father. But since you are all here disputing the relative superiority of men and women, and telling stories to prove your point, I thought that I'd pretend to be greatly involved in this battle. In reality, I just want to be able to tell a story like everyone else, and let me stress again that I believe in marriage, and that my love for the mistress of the house . . ."

But the Caliph interrupted him. "Tell us the story."

"I am known as the porter to all of you, but my name is Sind-bad," the porter began, and then he paused for a second as everyone in the room fell silent and listened intently.

I set out as usual one day, which wasn't just like any other day because it was extremely hot and humid, making me completely lethargic. I toiled with the heavy load on my head, feeling as if I was carrying the city itself with all of its markets, homes, furniture and mules. As I passed by the grand gate of a merchant's house, I noticed that the ground before it was sprinkled with water, and when I saw a bench to one side of the gate, I found myself taking my load off my head and sitting down to enjoy the breeze wafting down from the high trees around the house and drying the heavy sweat on my brow. I sat there, listening to the songs of bulbuls and turtle doves, smelling the appetising aroma of food, which I imagined was being prepared by cooks and slaves, and soon I found myself singing:

"Pity me, a poor mule
Parched by the midday sun,
The salt of sweat on my tongue,
I assess the distance from my lowly bench
To this magnificent home.
Oh, how I envy those living there,
The comfort and contentment they share.
My life's one of hardship day after day.
We were both conceived from a drop of sperm,
Yet our lives so disparate, as I had to learn,
How I yearn to be in his place,
Though he, I know, doesn't see my face."

When I had finished my song, I shut my eyes and dozed off for a few moments, enjoying a momentary state of bliss before returning to my life of hardship. I awoke to find a very well-dressed young slave standing over me.

He took my hand, saying, "My master invites you in, for he would like to have a word with you."

My first reaction was naturally to refuse, because I knew how ill at ease I would feel inside this piece of Paradise. But I left my load with the gatekeeper and allowed myself to be led inside. There I saw dignified, important men sitting at an amazing banquet table laden with food and wine, while in the background slave girls played the most beautiful music. I was at a loss, for my eyes, ears and nose were totally overwhelmed by what I saw, heard and smelled. But then I gathered myself and remembered my manners, bowing my head to the man at the head of the table, whom I assumed was the master of the house—or rather palace, for it was fit for a sultan or a prince.

He indicated an empty space next to him, and I took my seat and thanked him for his invitation. He smiled and welcomed me, asking me about my name and occupation. So I told him that my name was Sindbad and I was a porter who carried people's goods on my head for a fee.

"You and I have the same name, porter. I am Sindbad the sailor and I heard you singing as I was feeding my gazelles in the garden."

I apologised for my song, which revealed poor breeding and jealous envy, but he simply smiled once more.

"On the contrary, my friend! I enjoyed it very much. Now, why don't you help yourself and eat something."

And I found myself eating as never before, the food was so delicious . . .

*   *   *

The porter paused, eyeing the mistress of the house. "Not as delicious as your food, my three generous, respected ladies," he said, and then continued with his tale.

When I had finished eating, Sindbad the sailor leaned towards me and told me how my songs had transported him back to the poverty of his youth, when he had despaired at his family's plight, and his mother would say, "A dog alive is better than a dead lion."

He described to me how he and his mother would gather wool left on rocks and stones by the river by wool washers, which his mother would weave into prayer rugs. When he had ten carpets in his hand he boarded a ship and sailed away to trade with other merchants.

For, let me tell you, my Caliph, my Vizier, my poet, my three dervishes and my respected ladies: Sindbad described to me in great detail the seven journeys he undertook. So mesmerised was I that I would have stayed in my seat, listening to him for as long as seven years rather than seven days, which is how long I in fact remained. Each day he would tell me the story of one journey, each more amazing than the previous one. It is impossible to describe how extraordinary these stories were: at times I was so terrified that I nearly shat myself, as Sindbad encountered strange creatures, animals and horrible people alike; then I would find myself on the verge of tears as he outlined his despair, the great labour and hardship he'd undertaken; then my eyes would shine as he described his great good luck in trading wares. I would sigh with happiness and contentment as he described each return to Baghdad, back to his home to be secure among family and friends, swearing never to set foot on a ship again. But then, time and time again, he would answer the call of the sea, exhilarated once more at the prospect of travel, of new encounters with merchants, other races of people and different parts of the world, allowing himself to forget that on his previous voyage he had been nearly eaten alive by the angel of death, before being spat out into life once more.

Abu Nuwas interrupted the porter. "Let us hope, Sindbad the porter, that you don't force us to listen to your story for seven hours!"

The porter smiled.

To tell you the truth, I have forgotten much of the detail, but not how he was nearly eaten by a whale. He and all the other passengers of a ship had rowed ashore to a beautiful wooded island strewn with beautiful shells. They decided to light a fire and to roast a whole lamb. But as soon as they gathered wood and lit it, the island began to shake and roar and the captain shouted out in terror that this was no island, but rather a lazy whale which had stayed still for so long that moss and trees had grown over its skin. Scorched by the fire, the whale went on a rampage, flipping his tail and creating a huge wave which destroyed the ship and washed the passengers off his back, whereupon some were swallowed and others crushed. In the blink of an eye, Sindbad found himself in the middle of the churning sea. He managed to climb upon a floating wooden beam and lash himself to it, pushing his two arms and kicking his two legs, until, exhausted, he drifted on through the currents until he came close to land, and was spotted by farmers who had climbed high into trees to collect black peppers. They used their small wooden felucca to rescue him, giving him food and shelter. He told them about the whale they had mistaken for an island and the farmers were amazed, and presented him to their King, who welcomed him and enjoyed listening to his adventures.

Sindbad asked how often ships visited this city, bound for Baghdad, but no one seemed able to give him a clear answer, and he sensed that although the city was by the sea, the inhabitants were in some way isolated. Then, to pass the days while he waited for a ship, he taught them how to trade their goods with one another.

He also noted that everyone, old and young, high and low—even the King—rode very good horses, bareback. It occurred to Sindbad that he might introduce the people to saddles, and when he was invited to dine with the King, he remarked that a saddle made riding more comfortable and allowed the rider to exert greater control over his steed. The King was perplexed and asked what was this thing called a saddle?

So Sindbad asked the King's permission to make him a saddle and the King graciously acquiesced.

Sindbad acquired the best possible wood, found a carpenter and sat with him, showing him how to fashion a saddle. Next he took wool and made it into felt to place over the wooden frame and then covered the saddle with leather and attached the stirrups and reins. When the saddle was finished Sindbad went to the palace. He chose the best of the King's horses, a stallion, saddled it and then presented it to the King.

The King mounted the horse and was filled with admiration and delight. He called for his Vizier, who tried it, and then all the state officials tried it after him, and everyone was greatly impressed and adopted this invention. In no time Sindbad and the carpenter began to manufacture saddles for all the people of the city, making a great deal of money and a name for himself.

Soon, the King decided that Sindbad should marry, and found him a bride from the best family in his kingdom. Sindbad tried to explain to the King that he wished to return to Baghdad when the first ship appeared. But the King insisted that Sindbad marry, saying that he shouldn't be living without a woman, and that he had found him the best bride. Sindbad was embarrassed, but he remained silent and obeyed the King, and found himself fortunate enough to be married to a beautiful, rich and distinguished lady. He told himself that as soon as a boat arrived he would leave for Baghdad, taking his wife along with him. Over the days and months, Sindbad fell deeply in love with his wife and they both lived comfortably on what the King and her family provided for them.

But fate didn't allow Sindbad to continue in this state of bliss. His wife fell ill and died. He wept and mourned her, and wept again at her beauty as professional washers washed her body. To his surprise they dressed her in her wedding dress, which was studded with glittering diamonds, and they put on her every item of jewellery she owned before they placed her in a coffin.

The people of the city rushed to console Sindbad, even the King, who was so overcome with emotion that he wept as he embraced Sindbad strongly.

"We shall meet in heaven, farewell, my good friend," he said.

Meet in heaven? Sindbad didn't understand what the King meant. Did he wish for him to leave his country?

The coffin of his wife was borne out of the city, with the cortège following, while the King took Sindbad in his carriage, pulled by four horses. When they reached a mountain overlooking the sea, a number of men lifted a huge stone on its side, opened the coffin and to Sindbad's horror they threw his wife's body in the hole left by the stone. Then they came towards Sindbad, who was standing weeping for his wife with the King's hand on his shoulder. One of the men went to tie a rope around Sindbad's waist.

"And for what reason are you doing that?" Sindbad asked, perplexed.

Another man came forward, holding a large jug of drinking water and seven loaves of bread.

"Didn't you know? You won't be separated from your dead wife, because you'll be buried alive with her in the same grave."

Poor fellow! Sindbad felt as though his heart had been wrenched from his chest.

He pleaded with the King. "Surely what I have heard cannot be true, Your Majesty?"

But the King squeezed Sindbad's shoulder, saying, "It is true unfortunately."

At these words Sindbad was astonished and terrified, more so even than when he'd faced being swallowed alive by a whale.

"King of the Age, since I am a foreigner and the customs of my people are different from yours, will you save me, as your people have done once already, so that I might return to my country and be with my family and relatives?"

"This tradition has been handed down from our ancestors for thousands of years, so that neither partner could enjoy life after the death of the other. I am afraid that these customs are sacred and they cannot be broken, even for the King."

Then he embraced our poor man and left. Sindbad told me that his gall bladder almost shattered like a broken mirror at these words. He was seized as he tried to run after the King, screaming, "But I am a foreigner, I have nothing to do with your customs."

He was knocked to the ground and tied to a rope, fighting and kicking all the while. The men attached the jug of water and the seven loaves of bread to his waist and lowered him down into the hole, which opened out into an enormous cave beneath the mountain. He screamed as they replaced the huge stone over the opening and the cave was plunged into total darkness.

Sindbad released himself from the rope and picked his way among the bones and corpses in the darkness of the cave, promising himself that he would not die this terrible death. He didn't touch the bread or the water until he became famished and violently thirsty.

Making his way through the pitch-black darkness, broken only by the glittering of precious stones and diamonds adorning the bodies of dead wives, Sindbad searched for a way to escape, but to his horror and despair he found nothing but bones and rotten flesh and glittering jewellery in the foul, stinking grave.

Soon, his provisions were down to a few mouthfuls of bread and a few sips of water. He lay down and closed his eyes, imagining himself dying on top of a mountain or drowning at sea. Suddenly he heard a tremendous sound and the cave was flooded with light. He saw the corpse of a man being thrown down, and then a woman was lowered down just as he had been. As soon as the big stone was replaced over the opening, Sindbad pounced on the woman and struck her head with a stone, killing her.

Then he knelt and asked for God's forgiveness, explaining to the Almighty that he had committed this bad deed because he needed to be with his family, whereas this widow's family had sent her to her death willingly if not gladly. He took the dead woman's water and the seven loaves of bread.

After this, he found himself killing many more women and men who were buried alive with their dead partners, surviving he did not know for how long, since he had lost all sense of the days and nights.

There came a time when he despaired of ever escaping this hell, and he prayed once more to God, asking the Almighty to do with him whatever he wished. But as he murmured these words, he heard a faint noise coming from one corner of the cave. Sindbad grabbed the jawbone of a dead man and followed the sound until he saw a tiny ray of light. He hurried towards it and found a small opening in the wall, beyond which was a tunnel dug by wild beasts, so that they could sneak in, eat human flesh and escape.

Sindbad wept silently and thanked God for letting him hear that noise. He squeezed himself into the tunnel, using the jawbone to clear his path, until he heard the sea and came out by the shore. He cheered and jumped into the air. Life was beautiful once more! But then he reflected that so too were wealth and prosperity. He rushed back into the cave, collected the jewels of the dead women, put them in a bundle and dressed in several layers of the clothing of the dead men. Then he made his escape through the tunnel once more.

He waited patiently and happily by the sea for days and then weeks, drinking from the salty water and eating what little he found in the sea, seaweed and tiny fish, until one morning he saw a passing ship.

Sindbad cried for joy, and tied a white robe on a stick and ran along the shore with it. Eventually one of the crew spotted him, and the captain sent one of his crew out with a small boat.

When he was taken aboard the ship, the astonished captain told him that he had been sailing for forty years, and that this was the first time he'd ever seen a human being alive on the shores below that mountain.

Sindbad said simply that he was a merchant whose ship had gone down in a storm, and that he'd lashed himself to a plank with some of his belongings, and after a great struggle he had finally reached the shore. He was careful not to reveal what had really happened, lest one of the crew was from that city.

Then he offered the captain and crew some of the jewels in return for their help, for they had rescued him from that terrifying, deadly mountain. But the honourable captain refused to take anything, saying that he and his crew would save any man from the sea, and give them food, water, shelter and clothes. They would even, he told Sindbad, give them a present before they disembarked their ship. These were acts of generosity which reflected the most generous actions of God.

When the ship finally reached Basra, the captain gave Sindbad a seashell, explaining that if he held it to his ear he would hear the roar of the waves and the crashing of the sea.

The porter paused.

"Sindbad put the shell to my ear and, oh, what joy! I heard even the mermaids singing to each other," he said, and then fell silent in reverie.

"And now tell us, porter," said Abu Nuwas. "Sorry, I meant to say Sindbad the porter. Do you still visit Sindbad the sailor?"

"Yes, I do, often. But let me assure all of you that next time I visit, I shall be able to say to him, for the very first time, 'Sindbad the sailor, give me a break! Let Sindbad the porter recount to you his own adventures, which began in the market itself, when a beautiful lady asked me to carry her purchases.'

"And I shall not stop until I have explained to him that in just one night I visited Basra, China, India and Persia—all without a ship!"

The Resolution of the Porter
and the Three Ladies

"orter, you're such a good storyteller!" said Haroun al-Rashid, when the porter had returned to his seat. "And now your Caliph will surprise you with another story."

Once, as I was taking a stroll in my garden early in the morning, I overheard a Bedouin yelling at my guards, insisting that he needed to see me immediately. The guards were explaining to him that it was still early and that he should come back at a certain hour. I found myself hurrying to my audience chamber and ordering the guards to bring the man in. Why? Because of the urgency in the man's voice, and the agonised way that he sighed as he spoke.

As I had foreseen, the man, who was brought in barefoot, said, beseechingly, "Prince of the Faithful! Please, grant me justice against an oppressor, who robbed me of Su'ad."

I asked him who was Su'ad and who had taken her.

"Su'ad is my heart, she is my wife, and the robber is none other than your Governor, Hisham bin Marwan."

Then, as though the words were being wrenched out of him, he described "the burning coal which shoots sparks in my heart." Yes, this was how the Bedouin expressed his pain. He described how his father-in-law had taken his daughter away when the famous drought killed all of the Bedouin's beasts, camels and horses, leaving them starving. The Bedouin had gone to the Governor and pleaded with him to interfere on his behalf and force his father-in-law to return his wife. The Governor sent for his father-in-law and asked him why he had removed his daughter. But the father-in-law insisted that he had never set his eyes on this Bedouin before.

So the man pleaded with the Governor to summon his wife so she could refute what her father had said. But when Su'ad entered the court, the Governor was so overwhelmed by her beauty that he dismissed the Bedouin's case, and sent him to prison.

A few days later he was brought before the Governor, who sneered at him like an angry tiger and ordered him to divorce his wife. When the Bedouin challenged the Governor, saying that he would never divorce his wife, the Governor ordered his servants to torture him until he couldn't take it any more. Eventually he agreed to divorce his wife. He was locked up again until the compulsory period during which a woman must wait before remarrying was over. Then the Governor married her, after giving her father a dowry of thousands of dinars.

When I heard this story I was enraged. I wrote to Hisham bin Marwan, telling him that he had abused his position with his wicked and wrongful behaviour. I ordered him to divorce the woman immediately, which he did as soon as my messenger reached him, but he sent a letter back begging my forgiveness. He sought to explain how he had fallen in love when he was confronted by a beauty which had no match among Almighty God's creations.

I found myself so curious to see this beauty from the desert that I asked her to be brought to me. Soon the sun itself shed its light on my audience chamber and on my heart and remained there, for the Bedouin woman was indeed a truly rare beauty.

I gasped when I saw her, and said to her husband, "Bedouin, I will give you three times the number of beasts and camels you lost, one thousand dinars for every month since your wife departed, and on top of that a yearly allowance for your needs. All of this will be in consolation for the loss of your wife."

And you should have heard the groan of the man. It was so terribly agonised that I assumed he was on the verge of dropping dead.

But instead he said, "I asked your help against the Governor. Now from whom can I seek redress for my unjust treatment?"

I felt deep shame at that moment, but the twinkle in that woman's eyes made my heart flutter more and more.

"Prince of the Faithful," the Bedouin continued, "were you to give me everything you own—even the caliphate itself—still I would want only Su'ad. For she is my food, and my drink."

The woman looked at me boldly and gave me a faint and coy smile, and I found myself saying to the Bedouin, "Well, Su'ad must choose between you, Hisham bin Marwan or the Caliph. And I shall help her to do what her heart desires, do you agree?"

"Su'ad, who is dearer to you?" I asked her, when the Bedouin had sadly nodded his head in assent. "The gracious and noble Commander of the Faithful and all of his palaces? The unjust Governor Hisham bin Marwan? Or this impoverished Bedouin to whom you were married?"

Su'ad replied passionately:

"Neither silver, gold, nor marble palaces tempt me
All I yearn for is my wretched hungry man
He who once owned camels and horses
Until Fate herself betrayed him
My bliss is here with him
Reliving our golden years,
I'll remain thus
Until the wheel of fortune turns."

I still remember how stunned I was at her fidelity and integrity. And so I handed her over to the Bedouin, who took her and left.

Abu Nuwas couldn't help but exclaim, "What a story, Oh Commander of the Faithful. What a woman is this Su'ad!"

The rest of the audience fell silent, but their eyes reflected what they thought. The Caliph's eyes were lowered; Jaafar's eyes were fixed on his master; Abu Nuwas's eyes flicked anxiously like a sparrow from face to face. Meanwhile, the Indian sat with eyes downcast, hoping to avoid being forced into marriage, but at the same time anxious not to give offence. The porter's heart leaped in hope and sat behind his eyes, which pleaded silently with the mistress of the house and those around her to tell him what would be next.

But then a rooster crowed and the first faint light of dawn filtered into the room.

The shopper stood, saying, "May I tell you a story?"

The Caliph smiled at her. "Of course. Tell me a story or two."

And now it was time for the shopper to begin.

It happened that the rooster you have just heard crow had an ancestor years ago in the faraway lands of India and Indochina at the time of King Shahrayar and the brave and brilliant Shahrazad.

Shahrazad chose to marry King Shahrayar, knowing that she would be killed the following day like hundreds of virgins before her, daughters of princes, merchants and army officers. The King would deflower one girl each night and then kill her in the morning, wreaking his revenge on womankind after he had seen his wife taking part in an orgy with her slaves.

Amidst the growing, silent anger of his people, who muttered in hushed revolt and raised prayers to God, begging him to strike King Shahrayar down with a fatal disease, the King continued his campaign of bloodshed.

Shahrazad, who was none other than the daughter of the King's Vizier, whose task it was to select a girl for the King each night, decided that she alone could bring an end to this bloodbath. Much to her father's horror and mortification, she volunteered to be the King's next bride. But she had a plan: she would tell a story each night, bringing it to a dramatic climax at dawn. Then the King would burn with curiosity to hear the conclusion and would decree that she could live until the following night. Shahrazad's peaceful, eloquent plan worked. She began with one single story: that of the fisherman and the jinni. And from there, the stories accumulated into heaps of stories, like a dry stone of a date growing into a palm tree, with hundreds of dates covering its branches. Soon Shahrazad's words took over, becoming her shield against the sword hanging over her like an augury of dawn. The King was hypnotised by her stories and his violent, murderous soul was quelled, tamed. Until one day . . .

Acknowledgements

My gratitude to Tim Supple, who took me by the hand and showed me what I knew.

My thanks to Margaret Stead, who helped me to let these stories shine in the English language, and to Amal Ghandour, Ten Gorten and Susan Willock who tenderly polished the poems.

ABOUT THE AUTHOR

Hanan al-Shaykh is one of the contemporary Arab world's most acclaimed writers. She was born in Lebanon and brought up in Beirut, before going to Cairo to receive her education. She was a successful journalist in Beirut, then later lived in the Arabian Gulf before moving to London. She is the author of the collection *I Sweep the Sun off Rooftops* and her novels include *The Story of Zahra*, *Women of Sand and Myrrh*, *Beirut Blues*, and *Only in London*, shortlisted for the *Independent* Foreign Fiction Prize. Most recently she published the acclaimed memoir of her mother's life, *The Locust and the Bird*. She has written two plays, *Dark Afternoon Tea* and *Paper Husband*, and collaborated with Tim Supple on a theatrical adaptation of *One Thousand and One Nights*. Hanan al-Shaykh lives in London.

A NOTE ON THE TYPE

This book was set in a modern adaptation of a type designed by the first William Caslon (1692–1766). The Caslon face, an artistic, easily read type, has enjoyed over two centuries of popularity in the English-speaking world. This version, designed by Carol Twombley for the Adobe Corporation and released in 1990, ensures by its even balance and honest letterforms the continuing use of Caslon well into the twenty first century.

Typeset by Scribe, Philadelphia, Pennsylvania
Printed and bound by RR Donnelley, Harrisonburg, Virginia